THE THREE DAUGHTERS
OF MADAME LIANG

BY PEARL S. BUCK

THE
THREE DAUGHTERS
OF MADAME LIANG

A NOVEL BY

Pearl S. Buck

THE JOHN DAY COMPANY
NEW YORK

The Way that can be mapped is not the Eternal Way.
The Name that can be named is not the Eternal Name.

—opening words of the TAO TÊ CHING

THE THREE DAUGHTERS
OF MADAME LIANG

It was past midnight. Madame Liang put down her brush pen and closed her account book. Her house was quiet. Downstairs in the restaurant guests were gone save for the few who, reluctant, would not leave until the lights flickered and went out. She rose from the carved blackwood chair, which matched the huge Chinese desk once belonging to her father in the distant province of her childhood home, and went to the window. The red satin curtains, floor length, were drawn across the glass and she did not pull them back. Secure in her favored position as owner of the most fashionable restaurant in modern Shanghai, it would not have been safe for her, nevertheless, to be outlined against the light behind a window. One never knew where the enemy hid. There were too many men and women who were jealous of the famous Madame Liang, who managed, no one knew how, to keep open a restaurant whose daily menu carried the finest gourmet foods. Among her patrons were the highest officials, the most successful merchants, the top officers of the army. All were her

11

friends, or at least her customers. Serene, seemingly unperturbed by political disturbances, she came and went as she wished. Inevitably there were those who hated her because they envied her. Therefore she slipped behind the curtain and in its shadow she slid open the window.

The air was mild with coming summer and a scent of jasmine floated upward from the gardens. Her house had once belonged to a wealthy American businessman and his family, who were her friends. When his import-export business was confiscated and closed and he was compelled to take his family back to the United States, she had bought the house and the gardens in what had been the British Concession. Many Americans had lived in the British and French concessions here in Shanghai, for they had never had land concessions of their own. In pre-Communist days Madame Liang had made friends among the Americans, and because she found them likable she had sent her three daughters to America to be educated. Now of course there were no Americans left in China, and a whole generation of young Chinese was growing up without ever having seen an American face or heard an American voice. They heard only words of hate against a people who in her opinion had been the least hateful among the Western peoples. Americans alone among white men had seized no land from the Chinese and had imposed no cruelties.

She sighed, remembering the gay and impulsive family who had once lived in this house. Mr. and Mrs. Brandon and their five children. How well they had loved China—so well indeed that they had furnished their house in Chinese furniture and had hung Chinese scrolls and paintings upon the walls! Suddenly they had been compelled to leave and she had hurried here secretly to say good-bye. Mrs. Brandon had sobbed on her shoulder.

"O Madame Liang, will they ever let us come back?"

She had put her arms about the American woman, but she had made no answer. How could she say, "You will never come back"? And so she had said nothing, and the years had slipped past, each more difficult than the last. But she had sent her daughters to the Brandons, and sometimes—

Her thoughts were interrupted by Chou Ma, her old and faithful woman servant.

"Lady, why will you stand by the window? The curtains cannot hide you. No, they do not! Lady, I myself went into the street last night and I saw with my own eyes your shape, your shadow!"

"At least no one knows the shape and shadow are mine," Madame Liang replied.

She came out from behind the curtain nevertheless, and she allowed herself to be undressed by Chou Ma's accustomed hands, in preparation for her bath.

"Everyone knows you," Chou Ma retorted, "and who has a shape like yours? Certainly they know it is not my shape, and who else is here on this floor except us? They know everything, these accursed new people!"

"You may not call them accursed," Madame Liang warned. "Remember, they are my customers. I have no others now."

"We live among lions and tigers," Chou Ma agreed, her voice mournful.

"Take heed how you speak," Madame Liang commanded. In silence, therefore, Chou Ma removed the last silken garment from the slim, cream-pale body of her mistress, admiring in silence the fine-boned frame, the small round breasts, the exquisite delicacy of the nape.

"Bath is drawn," she announced. "I prepare your bed while you wash, then I brush your hair."

Madame Liang walked across the room into the bathroom. She was one of the few, the very few, who still had the comforts of the past. For this she must be grateful to her husband, Liang Cheng, whom she had left years ago. He had been a friend and follower of Sun Yat-sen, the archrevolutionist, and in the eyes of these new people now in power she was still respected as his wife—as in fact she was, since she had never troubled herself to get a legal divorce. Yet she had her own success also to thank for her present safety. The new rulers were Chinese and therefore were gourmets. In these harsh times it was not easy to find the traditional delicacies, the tender-fleshed river fish, the specially fed Peking duck, the Chinkiang ham, the millet soup of the north and the steamed breads stuffed with spiced pork or with dark sugar. Fortunately, her chef had stayed with her through wars and governments.

The tub, a deep round porcelain jar as large as a small pool, a Soochow tub, was brimming with hot water. She stepped into it, and seating herself Buddha-wise, she sank shoulder-deep into the pleasant warmth. She was grateful to the American engineers and plumbers who had built into the thick walls of this house the conveyance of water and heat, and she had no sense of guilt in enjoyments. While she listened in docile silence to loud and endless talk of self-sacrifice and equality, she preferred to believe privately, as her Confucian parents had taught her, that life was meant to be

14

enjoyed, although within the limits of the five human relationships, and that equality was only the dream of inferior
persons. There were stupid people and people not so stupid
and a few who were not stupid at all. No government could
change this eternal truth.

"Lady!" Chou Ma called. "I hear footsteps!"

Madame Liang turned her head to listen. "I hear nothing," she replied. "Are the doors locked?"

"Do I ever leave doors unlocked?" Chou Ma's voice was
reproachful.

"Go and listen," Madame Liang commanded.

She stepped out of the tub, nevertheless, and dried herself
thoroughly. Then she scented her body with gardenia oil.
Her flesh, so scented for many years, had absorbed the fra-
grance until she moved in its atmosphere. Long ago, a bride
in a faraway province, she had thus scented herself for her
wedding night. They had not been strangers to one another,
she and the impetuous young man she had chosen to marry.
Yes, she had chosen him in those days when they had been
students together at the Sorbonne in Paris, and together
they had become followers of Sun Yat-sen. Together they
had returned to Peking to tell him they would join the revolution.

"What would I do without Liang!" Sun had said when
later they announced their decision to marry. "And you,"
he had said to her, "you are the wife I would have
chosen for him. You are strong—and he—well, he is only
too warmhearted!"

Then, turning his head, he had bidden a servant fetch his
own beautiful, newlywed young wife. "These two," he told

her when she came in, "these two are to be married. They love each other in the modern fashion. It is a good match. He is fire and she is earth."

On that same day she had felt her first fear of Sun's death, his skin clinging to his bones without flesh, his black eyes buried in deep sockets. Already he was ridden with cancer in his liver and three months later was dying, angry and unforgiving of the fate that doomed him before his work was done. Perhaps he, too, had known of that day, for he had clasped her hands into Liang Cheng's and had held their hands together in his.

"Carry on the revolution," he had commanded them. "Whether I live or die, I depend upon you to carry on what I have begun."

He was dead by their wedding day, an old-fashioned wedding, for she and Cheng had returned to their families, hers in Nanking, the old capital in the rich central province of Kiangsu, and his in Peking. Marriage contracts were drawn and gifts were exchanged. She had not seen Cheng again until their wedding day.

Chou Ma entered the room. "The footsteps stopped at the door. Whoever it was, he listened. I looked through the keyhole and saw an eye. He saw my eye and went away again."

"Why do you say 'he'?" Madame Liang inquired. "Can you tell through a keyhole whether a spy is a man or a woman?"

Chou Ma answered firmly. "Surely I can tell, lady! This was a bold black eye."

"All eyes are bold nowadays, and all eyes are black, since no foreigners remain among us," Madame Liang retorted.

Not wanting argument, however, she went into her bedroom and put on the white silk night-robe Chou Ma had laid out for her. Then she seated herself before her toilet table, and Chou Ma began to brush her long hair. It was still black, in spite of her fifty-four years.

"This hair," Chou Ma said, "is as beautiful as it was on your wedding night."

"Is it so?" Madame Liang murmured. She had many thoughts to ponder and Chou Ma's chatter she seldom heard.

"That night," Chou Ma continued, pausing to wipe her right eye with the edge of her left sleeve, "is it ever to be forgotten? Your lord stood in the doorway. 'For shame,' I told him. 'You come too soon. Wait until I am gone!' Who could have thought that years later when the third daughter was born he would have—"

"Be silent," Madame Liang commanded.

Chou Ma obeyed. She spoke no further word while she braided Madame Liang's hair for the night.

"Bring me the cashbox," Madame Liang then directed.

The cashbox was of polished wood with strong brass locks at both ends. It was so heavy that Chou Ma pushed it across the floor, lifting it upon the blue and white rug woven long ago in Peking.

"Open it and count the day's money," Madame Liang directed.

Chou Ma obeyed under Madame Liang's eyes.

"Three hundred dollars and fifty-five small coins," Chou Ma announced.

"It was the minister's feast today that made us rich," Madame Liang declared. "Now lock the box and put it under the bed as you always do. Tomorrow move the money into the big iron safe. When they come to ask how much, say that you know nothing. I will say that because of the minister's kindness I shall make a contribution to the Hung-yang Cooperative."

"You are always clever, lady," Chou Ma said.

She waited until her mistress had climbed into the high old-fashioned bed. Then she spread the silken quilts and drew the embroidered curtains. This bed Madame Liang had brought from the faraway province where Cheng had been the governor. There she had lived with him for ten years until the third child, again a girl, had been born.

"I will not leave my marriage bed for him to sleep in with other women," she had said when she left him.

The bed had been brought here to Shanghai by cart and by boat and for years it had stood in the bedroom of the first house she had rented for her restaurant. When she had bought this American house, furnished as it had been left, she brought the bed with her. And why, she sometimes wondered, for this bed held sorrowful memories for her. Here behind these satin curtains she and Cheng, after years of marriage following early happiness, had made their final quarrel. He had come to her on that last night, and she had refused him, her voice cold.

"We agreed, you and I, that our marriage would not be like that of our parents. I said that I would never live as my mother lived, my father taking one concubine after another."

"You have given me no son," he muttered.

"Can I make sons at will?" she had cried.

Later she had read in a Western book that it is the man who determines the sex of his child, but in those days no one knew such facts, and she had been only one more of the women whose husbands made complaint that they bore no sons. At least she had determined her own fate, and at least she had not accepted his blame while he brought other women into the house. Instead she had flamed into instant anger.

"Do you no longer love me?" she had demanded.

"I do love you," he had insisted, "but heed me, my heart. The woman outside the wall is already carrying my child. What if it is a son?"

"You behave as if you were still in Paris," she flung at him.

He had laughed. "I learned many things in Paris!"

There had been quarrels enough before that final one. Yes, it was the last quarrel, for the woman outside did indeed give him a son, and, suddenly all Chinese, he brought her into his house as his concubine, so that the child had his name and a place in the family, a higher place than that of her daughters. Was he not male? She had never made another quarrel with Cheng, not even when she left him.

Chou Ma's voice interrupted these memories. "Shall I leave a light burning since there were footsteps tonight?"

Madame Liang considered. "Leave the small lamp on the chimneypiece."

She never used the fireplaces in this house. They were iron grates that had held blazing coals in the winters when the foreigners were still here. Coming to dine with the Americans, as she had often done, she had admired the glowing coals that warmed the rooms, a charming custom, but who could buy coal nowadays? And even if there had been coal it would have been unwise to buy it. Luxury must be concealed. Yet she could not live without it. Over her satin gown when she went downstairs to the restaurant she wore a robe of cotton cloth, simple though elegant. Her age, she declared, forbade the severe uniform of coat and trousers that all younger women wore. The truth was that she could not live without beauty. She had been reared in the midst of beauty, her father a rich man in a rich city. Ah, she would not think of her father! He had been killed—no, she would not think of that. Let her remember him as he had been when she was a young girl, restless and fretful for freedom from the old ways. He had only been bewildered.

"What have I done, my child?" he had asked her sadly. "Did I bind your feet when you were small? Did I insist that you wed the son of my old friend, to whom you were betrothed as soon as you were born? Have I forbidden you to learn to read, although reading is useless for a woman? Have I not said that you need not marry the one I chose for you when you were a child? What now—what now?"

"Let me go to Paris," she had insisted.

That was when she had been sent to Paris, city of beauty, and there had met Cheng and Chao Chung, who now was a minister, and all those other young men and women who had burned with the fires of revolution. In later years, when beauty was forgotten, years when beauty had been lost in the failures and disappointments of revolution, Cheng had escaped into the governorship of a distant province and she with him. Yet in escape she had found beauty again, the beauty of misted landscapes, of gardens in old walled cities and in the courtyards of vast and ancient houses.

Now once more beauty was lost. The war with Japan

and the conquest of the country by strange new doctrines
had resulted in this utter loss of beauty—ah, here was the
soul's destruction! She knew all the present arguments
against beauty—the people better fed, corruption wiped
clean away, bridges built, floods controlled, even flies and
rats gone—but beauty was dead. She hoarded its remnants,
her jewels, her robes, her house, her music. Downstairs
there was a huge drawing room which she used only for the
private parties ordered by the important few at the top of
the governmental structure, the dinners for which her
chef prepared forgotten dainties, the gourmet foods which
this generation of her people did not know existed, but in
which, when discovered, they secretly delighted. In the
drawing room there was a grand piano, a Steinway American piano, which the Brandon family had left on the day
when they had been compelled to flee quickly and secretly.
For this piano and for everything else they had left she had
paid them from a hidden account in a bank in New York.
Years ago, ever since she had left her husband and had set
up her own business, she had put her profits into that bank.
Money was safe only in America and Switzerland, and she
had chosen America, for it was there that she wished to
send her three daughters, and had sent them. She was glad
she had done so while she could, for now of course she
could not. There her daughters had been safe from war and
revolution and the troubles of the people. There they were
now, safe. Here she was alone.

She turned restlessly in the huge bed. The down quilts
were light, the sheets were of white silk, but she was sleepless. Moonlight shone against the windows for behind the
curtains the moon was full. She remembered this moon,

hanging in the sky above the gardens of her childhood home. On such nights her father summoned the family into the court, where the lotus bloomed in the ponds. There they sat, eating sweetmeats and listening to the music of zither and lute. Among the serving folk there were always musicians. Her father, enchanted by music, tolerated idleness, even disobedience, if there were music. Years later, when he saw a piano for the first time, when he heard its lyric voice, he was beside himself with delight.

"Why has no one told me of this instrument?" he demanded.

They had been on a river steamer owned by the British firm of Jardine Matheson, for that year her father had taken a fancy to go to Kiukiang, in order to travel by sedan up the steep flanks of the Lu Mountains not far away from the city. There had been some delay and disturbance when they went aboard, for it appeared that Chinese passengers could not have first-class cabins. An exception was made, since her father was no ordinary man, and they were given six cabins apart from the Europeans—six, for her father would not travel without his favorite concubines and without her, his only daughter. Her mother, his wife, would not leave her home.

"The winds and waters of foreign places make me ill," she always explained, but Madame Liang knew, even when she was a girl, that her mother's heart was broken because of the concubines. It was only if a wife did not love her husband that her heart did not break when he brought concubines into the house.

Her mother had been a small dainty woman from Soochow, fine-boned as all Soochow women are, her face as pretty and delicate as a child's, and her hair black until the day she died, at sixty, of cholera. For all her smallness and quiet ways, she had the mind of a man, and in the ancestral house she was a ruler, though gentle.

On the English ship, then, there was a piano, and her father, examining its wonders, the network of wires under its heavy lid, the felt-covered hammers, the sounding board, declared that as soon as he went again to Shanghai, where alone such instruments could be purchased, he must have one. Thither they went before the next winter solstice, and Madame Liang, then a girl of fifteen, went with her father to the English shop, for it was only she who spoke English.

Once in the shop she addressed the tall young Englishman who came forward with a languid air to inquire what she wished.

"My father like piano, please, sir or madame, as the case may be," she had told him.

"This way," he had said, astonished but unsmiling, and had led them into a great room filled with pianos. Her father had seated himself and listened gravely to one piano after the other, as a young man tinkled an air on each, and after some hours he decided upon an ebony black piano.

"My compliments, sir," the Englishman had told him. "You have chosen our finest instrument."

The price was high, but money was plentiful in those days, and the steward who went everywhere with her father paid for the piano in rolls of Mexican silver dollars wrapped in brown paper. It was the currency of that time. Why Mexican? She never knew. Now of course the currency was Chinese—or perhaps only Communist. She herself hoarded gold, not trusting the new times. Her stewards

had orders to bring her gold in secret, gold jewelry from
ladies once rich in such things, small gold images from
temples and former priests and nuns, and objects in gold
from curio dealers. This hoard she kept in a secret chest
built in the wall of her bedroom. The chest seemed to be a
place for cosmetics and scent bottles, but behind the trifles
and sunk under the bottom there was a secret pit, half full
of gold. The thought of it comforted her now and at last
she slept.

"Lady, lady!" Chou Ma called.

It was morning. Madame Liang lay in deep sleep, her
beautiful hands crossed on her breast. Chou Ma smoothed
them gently.

"Wake, lady," she murmured. "I call your soul home
to your body. Come home, O Soul! Wherever you wander
as she sleeps, come home now!"

Slowly Madame Liang's soul returned, and as she woke
she perceived Chou Ma's anxious face above her.

"Is it day?" she inquired.

"Alas, lady, it is noon," Chou Ma replied. "The one from
above is waiting for you in the Lotus Room—the Minister
Chao Chung. He is impatient."

Madame Liang prepared to rouse herself. She knew the
dangers of sudden demand upon heart and bone, blood and
brain. She lay silent and unmoving therefore until she felt
thought alive in her skull. Then she filled her lungs with
fresh breath, inhaling and exhaling seven times. Her blood
stirred in her veins, and she moved her feet, her hands, her
arms, her legs, until she was alive and present. Now she sat

up and Chou Ma rubbed her shoulders and her back for a full three minutes. At the end of this time Madame Liang put her feet out of the bed upon the carpeted floor. Once awake and up, she moved swiftly and in a short time she had washed and had put on a long robe buttoned at the throat and reaching to her ankles. It was of a somber color, but it fitted her slender body and set off her fair skin and dark eyes. Meanwhile, as she dressed, she drank hot tea, which Chou Ma served her, and ate a few small sweetmeats, steaming hot, which Chou Ma brought in on a lacquered tray.

"So he is impatient," Madame Liang murmured, when Chou Ma had set the last silver pin in her hair.

"He has come with a purpose," Chou Ma said.

"Then I must prepare myself," Madame Liang said. "I must be strong."

She did not look strong, however, when she entered the Lotus Room a few minutes later, so-called because the white panels were painted in lotus flowers and leaves. Instead she looked fragile and remote, absorbed in private concern. The room was kept for her few special guests. It was furnished in a French style, with here and there a fine Chinese piece, a two-tiered table set between delicate carved upright chairs, a pair of Sung vases, a T'ang pottery horse on its own pedestal. Without show of extravagance, the room had elegance.

Her guest awaited her, a slender handsome man, his hair gray, his dark eyes brilliant and ironical. They met almost as strangers in these new days, speaking seldom of the old days in Paris or of any past life they had lived. She approached him with habitual feminine shyness, a slight graceful figure, her usually erect carriage subdued to appeal.

"Ah, Madame Liang," he said. "Are you well?"

He spoke in Mandarin, and the accent, cultivated and correct, was that of Peking.

"I am well," she said. "And how is the Honorable Person?"

It was no longer fashionable to use such ancient honorifics, but she did so willfully, claiming the excuse of her age and position, in order that she need not speak his name.

"I am well, I am well," he said.

She motioned to him to be seated, and then she seated herself in a chair somewhat lower than the one he chose. The light from the window fell upon his face, and from the shadow in which she sat she looked at him, not fully, for this would have been rude, but glancing and sidewise and drooping her head.

"I come as your old friend," he said. His voice was full and deep, its tones mellifluous, a voice, as she well knew, which he used as an instrument and sometimes as a weapon.

"I know your good heart," she said gently.

"In high conference two days ago," he went on, "your affairs were discussed."

"I am honored," she said in the same tone, again inclining her head.

She did not allow her eyes to observe now beyond the upper part of his uniform. He wore the usual costume of black trousers and buttoned jacket, the collar high. The style was like those worn by all men, but the cloth was the finest English wool and the tailoring conveyed an air of elegance. Even his shoes were elegant, imported doubtless from English shops in Hong Kong. She allowed her gaze to wander to the windows. Outside in the garden the bamboos waved in a slight breeze.

"We have been friends for a long time," he said, "and I told them I would convey their thoughts to you."

"Thoughts?"

"Nothing more," he said. "We appreciate your steadfastness. We know that you must often be lonely here, without your daughters."

"I have no time to be lonely," she replied. "My business is my life. May I ask if the feast last night was to your taste?"

"Each dish was"—he held up his thumb to express excellence—"superb. But we missed you. When we were drinking wine after the meal was over you did not join us as you usually do."

"I had a headache," she said.

"And this morning?"

"It is gone."

"Then I may proceed?"

"Of course."

He cleared his throat, he folded his hands on his crossed knees. "What I have to say, Comrade Liang, is in no way a reproach. It is an appeal—an appeal to your patriotism, which we all know so well, to your loyalty to the Party, to your—"

She lifted her head and looked at him full. "What do you wish me to do, Comrade Chao?"

He replied abruptly. "Your eldest daughter is to return from America at once."

She hid the sudden rush of fear that clutched at her heart

and made her voice calm. "Her education is not complete."

"She can finish here. She is needed."

"She is in the midst of her research."

"We know everything she is doing and where she is." And then, as though to prove to her that nothing was hidden from him, that indeed he did know everything, he proceeded to speak of her daughter.

"Your eldest daughter, whose personal name is Endien, although abroad she is called by its translation, Grace, is indeed a remarkable young woman. She combines beauty and a brilliant scientific mind. She is a Research Fellow at the Harvard Botanical Museum, where she is a botanist and a pharmacologist. But she is also a fashion model. We know that she earns much money—indeed, we have an exact accounting of her weekly salary. She sends you no money—"

Madame Liang interrupted. "I need none."

"We know that, but it has been suggested to your daughter, nevertheless, that she send a portion of her ample salary as a contribution to the cause. Ours is a vast country, our people beyond numbering. We have many zealous young men and women who must be sent to the villages to teach and to work. They must be fed and clothed. Our great scientific projects are costly. This has all been explained to your daughter. She does not reply, she pays no heed. It is time that she came home."

Madame Liang controlled her trembling lips. "Will this not waste the years in which she has been engaged upon valuable medical research?"

"No, for we can supply the materials for her. You know, doubtless, that she is completing her thesis on the characteristics and uses of an intoxicating plant, found in the jungles of South America. I do not need to remind you that she has spent two summers in that continent, in search of this plant. But we have this plant also in our own southern jungles. I myself have seen it growing, a tree much like mimosa."

"She is working under a famous professor who—"

"She does not need him."

"But she is gathering together into a book all her knowledge—"

"Our ancient Chinese books of materia medica contain more than she can find anywhere else. It is for this indeed that she is asked to return. We wish her to study our own medical books and to compile from their rich and ancient lore modern textbooks which can be used in our new Institute of Chinese Medicine in the capital. She has her tools and her techniques. Why should they be wasted on Western materials when here we have the accumulations of centuries? Our physicians have always relied on herbs. Doubtless it was from us that the people of the West Indies first learned of this plant, which they call cohoba. It was here when Columbus made his second voyage during the years of our Ming dynasty. In that same dynasty, you will remember, the vast *Encyclopedia of Materia Medica* was compiled by the great Li Shih-chen. If your daughter made a lifework of study in this treatise, it would serve our country well. Certainly our encyclopedia is better organized than the confused literature of the West, even on this plant alone."

Madame Liang touched her pink silk kerchief to her lips. "I believe she is also making certain tests on ill persons—"

He interrupted her again. "Yes, yes, less than ten years

ago it was discovered that the plant has medicinal values beneficial to the treatment of the insane. It is well known that many Americans go insane and this is no cause for wonder. While we are not so afflicted, yet there are occasions when we need narcotics. I myself have hope that cohoba can be used in surgery. But I am not a scientist. I am only a humble patriot, wishing to serve our country!"

She tried to answer his smile. "You will convey the news to her?"

"She will be officially invited to return."

"What then can I say?"

He rose. "Write to her as a mother. Tell her that we are beginning our greatest era. Tell her that we need young women like her. We cannot afford to waste half our national brains as the Americans do, by excluding women. We bring women out of their homes to serve the nation, especially women like your daughter."

"Then she will not live here with me?"

"We will see—we will see. Certainly it will be her duty to visit you."

He was affable and smiling, his handsome face smiling as he bowed his farewell. She said no more but followed him to the door. Suddenly he turned.

"One more suggestion. Do not communicate with her through your usual chain! An important link in that chain was found dead, eleven days ago. Some unknown person had stabbed him in the heart as he walked down a street in Hong Kong."

He smiled, nodded and was gone before she could speak. She returned to her seat and sat there awhile, pondering what she had heard. The dead man was unknown to her.

What part he played in "the chain," as Chao Chung called it, she did not know. But this man Chao knew exactly what she had been doing. Her letters to her daughters, written openly and freely, were of course read. But there were the other letters, the few words hidden in a gift sent through her sister in Hong Kong—a scarf, a length of silk, a pair of silk stockings. She must devise a letter warning her sister and asking her somehow to let her eldest daughter, far away in America, know that she must go into hiding in Europe, in Africa, somewhere and anywhere. She must not come home. As soon as she had this thought she gave it up. Wherever her daughter might hide she would be found— and punished. But she would not hide. She had been reared to love her country and to be proud that she was Chinese.

Dr. Grace Liang was not in her laboratories when at last the summons reached her. Three months it had been on the way, arriving quickly enough at its first address, but en- closed in another envelope and readdressed to this botanical station on the edge of the South American jungle. She had only just returned from a collecting trip in a search for co- hoba, the tree resembling mimosa. For many weeks she had traveled far beyond the reach of letters and communica- tion, but tonight, returning weary and in need of a bath, she saw upon the unpainted table of her small bedroom in a poor hotel, a bundle of mail. She sat down, travel-stained as she was, cut the string and let fall the scattered letters. None from her aunt in Hong Kong? Then there was no word from her mother. She was always anxious about her mother, living her precarious, capitalistic life in the Com- munist desert. No, wait—here was an envelope—only why from Peking? It was addressed in both English and Chinese —the letters of the English unformed and straggling, but the Chinese characters very beautiful and skilled. She tore it open and drew out a sheet of thin rice paper. It was covered with Chinese characters, written in the same clear brush writing that had addressed the envelope.

"Comrade Doctor Grace Liang," the letter began brusquely in the new fashion. There were none of the honorifics nowadays, no compliments of the old stylized approach even in letters.

"You are invited to return immediately to your native land. Our new China has need of its young men and women. You will sail on the twentieth of the third month, leaving by steamer from the port of San Francisco. Your fare is paid. The vessel sails at one o'clock. Upon arrival at Hong Kong you will leave immediately for the mainland. At the border you will be met by a guide whom you will not know but who knows you. He will give you a pass on the railroad directly to the capital. This invitation is not to be refused. Your mother has been told that you are coming. You may arrange for a stopover of two days in Shanghai to visit her and thereby fulfill your duty as a daughter. Should you prefer to proceed at once to your post, however, we will approve."

The letter was signed by an unknown name.

She folded it slowly. Around her the jungle darkness deepened after the short twilight. She had been expecting the summons. The wonder was that it had not come before. She had known when she chose to become a scientist that sooner or later the summons would come.

"Oh, why will you insist on being a scientist?" her sister

32

Joy had cried. "Why will you not choose your music instead? They'd never force a concert pianist to come back. You'd not be productive in the new society. That's why I've chosen to be an artist. In the new society who wants a pianist? Anything—anything but a scientist!"

Yet, dearly as she loved her piano, she had not wanted to be anything but a scientist. And there was also the matter of conscience. Whatever the new people were politically, however profoundly changed, were they not her people, and of her people her own generation? Did not her duty lie with them rather than with Americans? She had consoled her conscience by reflecting upon the future. Whatever that future was to be, she would only be of more service if she became a good scientist. For a full year she had argued against her own indecision as to whether she should not be a doctor, or perhaps a surgeon. She had clever hands, suited equally to the piano or to a surgeon's scalpel. Then, remembering the reluctance of the Chinese to allow surgery, she had chosen pharmacology and finally the study of healing plants. Much of Chinese medicine was based upon such plants.

Her mood of reflection was broken now by the sound of fluttering wings. Against the wire netting of the window a great green moth, drawn by the lamplight inside her room, beat its delicate head. She rose, slipped aside the screen and let the moth enter, then caught it in her cupped hands to save it from death against the glass chimney of the oil lamp. It lay quivering upon her palms, its antennae drooping, the extravagant tails of its filmy wings limp. She stood gazing at it for a moment and then went to the opposite side of the room and released it into the moonless night.

"*Hu tieh*," she murmured. That was the Chinese name for butterfly. But this was a moth. She could not remember if there were another word in Chinese for moth. Was she forgetting her own language? It was time to go home to her own people. She had been only fifteen when her mother sent her to America to learn music, and until three years ago she had never thought of being anything else than a musician, a pianist. In the girls' school in Shanghai, which she had attended, as did all the daughters of the rich, she had been the one most talented. Her teacher, an American woman, had been embarrassingly proud of her. "You must go to one of our great American schools of music," she had insisted. "Perhaps Juilliard, in New York? I'll get you in. It won't be hard. They'll need only to hear you." It was her father who insisted, as soon as the piano came, that she must first have lessons from the Frenchwoman in their city who had married a Chinese during the world war. Then her mother had left her father and she followed her mother's wish and crossed the ocean to study at Juilliard. Yet, when she had finished there, she had gone to the Harvard Botanical Museum.

Just how or when the decision to become a scientist came, she scarcely knew. Perhaps it was her voracious reading; perhaps it was her friendship with a young American scientist who was also a violinist.

"Most scientists are musicians of a sort," he had told her. "Why? I suppose because music is an exact art—scientifically exact. Anyway, you'll find that most of us have an interest in music."

She had decided finally and had ended by becoming a Research Fellow. And because her mother might one day need the money stored in a New York bank, she had begun to earn for herself as a model. Her slim figure, tall for a Chinese girl, although the girls of the north were tall, happened to be of the right proportions for fashion, and her Oriental face—well, she was, she supposed, to be considered beautiful, but to that she was accustomed. Until she had been sent on this expedition, she had so continued.

She was stripping herself now for the first hot bath she had been able to take in weeks. In the small bathroom a long tin tub, filled with hot water, stood waiting, and towels were laid across the back of a chair. The silent Indian woman who had been detailed to wait on her withdrew when she entered. Strange how Asian these South American Indians looked! The Asian strain was surely the strongest in the world, the most prevailing. And now, though her own people were enemies to Americans, who had done so much for her, even to Mr. and Mrs. Brandon, who had let her come and go in their home exactly as though she were their daughter, she was glad she was Chinese. All Chinese were glad so to be. She laughed softly to herself as she lay in the warmth of the water. She was remembering her first teacher, a Confucian scholar, very old, his little beard a wisp hanging at the edge of his chin. Those were the days when her mother had not yet left her father and they lived in Szechuan together. The scholar was her tutor; she, the eldest of the three daughters.

"We who are Chinese," the old man had declared, "must remember at all times that we are the superior people of this earth. All peoples look up to us. We are the most civilized, the nearest to the gods. All others are barbarians in varying degrees."

Upon this premise he had instructed her in the arts and graces of learning and behavior. Yes, in honesty he had taught her, she thought, as she soaped her smooth slight body, and she had not forgotten. In her secret and innermost being she too believed that her own people were superior to all others. Theirs was the most profoundly civilized among peoples. She carried herself always with acknowledged pride because she was Chinese. But, stay— were these new Chinese the same?

"You would not recognize our country," her mother had written in one of her secret letters, hidden in the folds of a length of white silk. "We are ruled now by the children of peasants. Heaven and earth are upside down. Those who were high are made low—or are dead. Those who were low are raised up and they rule. We must wait, perhaps for a hundred years, until the times are set right again. Did not Wang An-shih, in the Sung dynasty, also upset the nation? 'The state,' he said, 'should control commerce, industry and agriculture, in order to protect the poor and prevent the rich.' He caused much disturbance, but at the end of a decade after his death the nation righted itself, for the people themselves refused to follow Wang. He died in the second Christian century and though, twenty years later, his name was raised in the Hall of Confucius as a great leader and a profound thinker, it was soon removed. Who thinks of Wang An-shih now without ridicule and scorn? So it will be again—"

Grace had smiled. She knew that her mother had become a student of Chinese history, finding consolation for the present in the excesses and follies of the past. Then, feeling the water growing chill, she rose from the tub and dried herself and put on the garments the Indian woman had left on a chair. By day she wore a khaki suit as severe as a soldier's uniform, but in the evening she laid this aside and put on a soft silken Chinese robe, fitted to her slender body but unconfining. Now, thus garbed, she ordered her solitary dinner sent to her room. She ate the somewhat unappetizing meal and when she had eaten she went to bed but not to sleep. Instead she lay hours awake, her hands clasped behind her head, her mind busy. Which should she follow, the warnings her mother and her aunt in Hong Kong had always sent her or the summons she had received from Peking? It was near dawn when she finally made up her mind. She longed for her own country, her own people. Kind as the Americans had been to her, she wanted to go home. And this was her duty also, was it not? China had need of her young and strong; in her struggle to come out of the past she had need of her youth, educated in Western ways, especially in science. She remembered the villages of the distant province in which she had been a child. Even then she had been troubled by the sight of little children who were wasting in illness, or whose eyes were blinded by pus from infections, and she had turned to her mother.

"M-ma, why don't they call the doctor?"

"Because there is no doctor here," her mother had replied. "Do you not remember last year when you had a dysentery that I took you all the way to the great American hospital in Peking? It was they who made you well."

"Why don't these go to Peking?" she had persisted.

"They are too poor," her mother had said. "It costs money to go to the hospital in Peking."

"M-ma," she had continued, "why don't we give them our money?"

"There are too many of them," her mother had said.

Perhaps it was the villagers who in the end persuaded her. She did not know until now, lying awake in a small hotel in a distant city of South America, that she had never forgotten the faces of those people, her people. Yes, she must go back to them. She would never be happy until she went back to them.

It was night in the great restaurant. Not a table was empty and the guests were gay. Most of them were Chinese, but there was a sprinkling of Europeans, Scandinavians and Africans, a few of them businessmen and their wives and the others delegations. At one table sat a group of men and women from India, the men in Western dress, except for turbaned heads, and the women in brilliant, soft saris. Madame Liang was pleased to see peoples from other countries. It was almost like the old Shanghai, she thought, pausing here and there to greet her customers, as she came and went among the tables. In those days now past Shanghai had seemed to be the center of the world in a constant ever-changing flow of travelers from everywhere about the globe. Now of course the walls were up. She had protested the walls, at first, even to Chao Chung, the Minister of Foreign Affairs, who had been her friend, although Cheng had repudiated him long ago when Chao Chung encouraged her to leave him. Cheng had accused her of still being in love with this friend, but she had denied the charge.

"I have had enough of love and even of the talk of love," she had told her husband.

She had looked him in the eyes as she spoke, knowing that he could not endure that gaze. How changed he was, she had thought that day, remembering the intrepid, impulsive young man she had loved and married! He had turned his head, avoiding her look, and he had remained silent. In silence he had let her go, and Chao Chung, whom he had accused, had remained her friend. Throughout the years she knew his voice had spoken the right words at the right place and time and to the right person, words that enabled her to continue to live in her palatial house and keep open her famous restaurant. He was here again tonight, at the head of a long rectangular table which she always reserved for him and his associates, whenever he came to Shanghai. He lifted his head at this moment, as though her eyes upon him had been a summons, but she only smiled at him slightly and turned away to pursue her leisurely stroll through the restaurant. Between the tables she passed, her black gown, cut long and close to her slender figure, plain and yet elegant. Not that most of the guests here would or could recognize elegance when they saw it! He, of course, was the exception. He had been reared in luxury and educated in Europe; yet he had given up his past gracefully and with seeming nonchalance. In his heart, as she knew, he was cynical and melancholy. None could have guessed this, however, from the brilliance of his smile and the liveliness of his black eyes under their heavy brows.

She managed to pass his table last, before she drifted out of the restaurant and to her own rooms upstairs. Once every hour or two until midnight, depending on how swiftly people came and went, she walked among the tables to show her concern for her guests.

"Be happy," she murmured. "You like the food? Thank you. Alas, that I cannot make it as delicious as I wish!"

She paused at his table now with the same words, adding only his title, Comrade Minister Chao. He nodded in his usual cheerful fashion, and then raised his voice slightly.

"I congratulate you, Comrade Liang," he said, clearly enough so that all the guests at the table could hear him. "We have received a letter from your eldest daughter telling us that she wishes to return to her country to help our people in medical science. This is patriotic indeed, but of such a mother I expect only patriotism in the daughter."

It was the first time she had heard of her daughter's decision. Then her sister's letter, too, had been intercepted! Her sister was being watched. The walls went higher and the gates, one after the other, were locked. Perhaps this was even the last gate. There was nothing for her to do now but to wait for her daughter's return. Let the gods be thanked, the Christian as well as all others, that she, the mother, was here. She could protect and warn, explain and save, if need be, and how could there not be need? Her daughters had not been reared as Chinese girls were reared. She had taught them that independence and resourcefulness are not to be hidden because one is a woman. Had she not been independent and resourceful, and could she have hidden her own example? She was safe now only because she had succeeded in what she was doing. This was the lesson she must teach her daughter—"Succeed, and you are safe."

"Thank you," she said quietly to the smiling minister.

Their eyes met, but she did not permit his challenging gaze. As coolly as though what he had told her she had already known, she turned her head to speak to another guest and so went her usual way, moving gracefully, always gracefully, among the tables until she reached the door to the kitchens. No one except her faithful chef and her woman servant knew that from the entry to the locked storeroom, where seldom used dishes were kept, a hidden elevator ran directly to her own rooms.

She lived thereafter in a fever of expectation. There was no one of whom she could inquire, "When will my daughter arrive?" She dared not write again to her sister in Hong Kong about Grace nor indeed to Grace herself. Nor did she wish to allow the minister to know that she knew nothing. Let him imagine that she had many ways of private communication, none of which he could discover! Let him believe that she was more clever than he and let him be afraid! Then it occurred to her that he might wonder why she did not write her sister, and forthwith she decided to write one of her usual amiable letters, containing no news, no report, no comment.

"Summer is here," she wrote. "In the garden the lilies are in bloom and in the pool the lotus is in bud. My business is good, thanks to many friends. My old chef has learned how to make good soup without the imported gelatin from birds' nests. Nor does he use sharks' fins. Instead he has devised substitutes made from soybeans. You remember he was once cook in a Buddhist monastery, where the monks, though they could eat no animal meats, nevertheless enjoyed deceiving themselves with vegetable foods made to look like meats . . . News? I have no news. My life is very peaceful. Please do not worry about me. Your sister, Siu-lan."

The days moved smoothly into late summer. There were hours, even days, when she could imagine that nothing was changed in Shanghai. Business was good; her dining rooms were crowded; and the markets were better than they had been since the years before the last famine. Nevertheless, on a certain afternoon in the fifth lunar month she felt restless with waiting in silence for her daughter's coming, and she resolved to leave her house, which so rarely she did, and engage a horse carriage and ride for an hour or two about the city. The sky was clear and a clean wind blew in from the sea. The city did not stand by the shore of the Eastern Ocean but upon a river which flowed into the sea, its yellow, earth-laden waters staining the blue for miles beyond the coast. In a few minutes, with the help of her woman servant, she sat in the carriage, wrapped in her light silk gown but the silk hidden under a covering of gray cloth.

"Drive along the Bund," she directed, and the man obeyed.

This city, which she knew so well through all its several lives, she now saw with sharpened perception. How would it appear to her daughter, accustomed for years to living in great American cities? She felt a pang of jealousy for the sake of the city of Shanghai, which she loved. Would her daughter be able to comprehend and appreciate its present life? Would she remember that once these streets had been crowded with beggars and refugees from famine and flood? She saw with reluctant pride that the streets now were filled with other crowds, not the rich, not the poor, not the foreign, but people plainly dressed and clean and not one a beggar. On Nanking Road, the great thoroughfare, there were shops selling many different goods, and it was filled with quiet people—no cars, or very few. Her daughter had written of American streets crowded with swiftly moving motor cars, but here there were only buses, and ascending and descending people, silent in all they did.

When the carriage rolled to the Bund itself, she saw the change in its present life. Here were no shops, but the great banks still stood, though the foreign gold was gone. Instead of being the center of the vast international business it had once been, it was now a park, and along the river's edge were benches and shading trees.

"Stop," she told the driver. "I will sit here for a time of contemplation."

She came down from the carriage then and sat on a bench at the other end of which was already seated a very old gentleman. It was clear that once he had been a rich man, for his skin was pale and fine, and his hands were those of a man who has never worked. That he was no longer rich could also be seen, for his satin robe was worn and the silk with which it was lined was frayed at the wrists and at the edge of the skirt. In other days she would have greeted him, but nowadays one did not give greeting to a stranger. The quiet of the city, the silence of the nation, was everywhere. Yet the old gentleman seemed not afraid, or else he was senile. When she sat down, he smiled and spoke.

"*T'ai-t'ai*, it is a pleasant day." He addressed her as "Madame" in the courtly manner she liked. She nodded and made a small answering smile but she did not speak. Instead she gazed over the river, whose waters were busy with

43

boats bearing three-cornered sails, with ponderous junks and slow barges.

"I come here every day that it does not rain," the old gentleman continued.

"Do you indeed?" she murmured.

"It is quiet nowadays, and gaiety is gone," he went on. "Yet I can remember when this was the busiest place in the city. Many capitalists lived in Shanghai at that time and they caused much confusion, coming and going. Great ships came up this river, and dock workers carried loads to and fro on their shoulders. And there were beggars and thieves darting everywhere, snatching and purloining—"

He paused, and she murmured courteously, "Was it so—"

He removed his small round old hat and scratched his scalp with the long nail on his little finger. Then he put his cap on again, looked about carefully and spat on the ground. How well she understood that cautious look! It was forbidden nowadays to spit where one would, but for the old this was a hardship, accustomed as they had been to spitting when they felt the need. He ground his spittle carefully into the dust with the heel of his worn velvet shoe. Suddenly his amiable look changed. A sourness came over his ancient face.

"It is very fine here," he said in a low voice. "But at our age, *T'ai-t'ai*, we remember other days. And let me tell you, if you go behind that part of the city which was once Japanese, even now you will see many poor people, swarming like flies on a manure pile. And there are no buses there and no carriages like yours. No, the streets are busy with carts still pulled by human beings."

She began to be afraid of the old gentleman. "Every-

44

thing cannot be done at once," she said. "At least the rich are not so rich and the poor are not so poor."

"Give us time," he retorted, "and some will be rich again and some will be poor. It is man's fate."

To this she did not reply. Instead she rose, and bowing slightly, she walked away. One never knew, these days, who, for a little money, might act as spy. But the old man's words held in her mind. Was it true that the day would come when again the rich grew more rich and the poor more poor? This city she had seen in all its several lives. Twenty years ago she had come here with her three daughters, then small children. The city at that time had been one of the centers of the world. Indeed, the world was here, France and England and Japan, each with its part. The streets had been clean in these foreign concessions, the traffic swift but controlled by uniformed policemen, all foreign. In the park dogs and Chinese were not allowed. How angered she had been when she found, newly come, that she could not take her children to the park on a holiday because she and they were Chinese!

"Is this not China?" she had demanded of a policeman at the entrance to the park.

"No," he had replied. "It is a piece of England, a bounty after the last opium war."

And yet beyond those foreign parts the Chinese city had festered in a maze of small narrow filthy streets and open gutters.

She remembered next another Shanghai upon which the Japanese bombs were falling, but only on the Chinese sections. From thence the people ran out like rats and took shelter in the foreign streets and made huts of matting and old boxes and any cover for themselves. Into the Japanese victory parade a Chinese youth had thrown a bomb and then had leaped from the top of a high foreign building, and she saw his spattered body on the sidewalk. And dead Chinese soldiers lay everywhere, the dead of the Nationalist Army, left behind when their leader fled, until the city stank with their rotting flesh, and wild dogs grew fat as they cleaned the dead away.

That city had lived through agony. Beautiful girls were sold on the streets for a dollar or two a night, and then even the dollar became worthless and the wind blew money about the streets like wastepaper, and men squatting by the gutters in the alleys cleaned themselves with bills that bore the likeness of the escaped leader. In the shops there was every kind of American merchandise, for in those days Americans were the visitors, and the goods belonged to them, but they were stolen and sold in private markets. Corruption rotted the entire city and none was innocent. So sickened was she that she had welcomed the attack of Those who laid siege. Rich men and their families in the beleaguered city fled to other cities and countries, and any suspected of being one of Those was butchered in the streets, until the people, able no more to endure, cried out that the war must end, even though victory belonged to the enemy.

And then They came in, the silent army, their cloth-shod feet noiseless as they marched, peasant men and angry. They did not rob or rape, but, grim as the the gray tide of the sea, they flooded into the city. They took possession of everything, even to the very soul of man.

"I will return to my home," she said now to the driver. "I have seen enough."

*   *   *

46

Grace Liang entered the dining room of her aunt's house in Hong Kong. It stood on a rocky hillside, overlooking the sea and the harbor, its low Chinese rooflines melting into the landscape. The large central hall faced the water, but the dining room, behind it, gave only a view of the crowded city and above it, on the hills, the homes of the wealthy, both Chinese and Western, half hidden by trees. When she entered, her aunt was already at the table, but she was waiting. Several dishes stood on the table before her, but the lids had not been removed.

"I hope you are not waiting for me, Auntie," Grace said, smiling. "The truth is that I slept too well. The air is so mild, I had forgotten."

"Sleep while you can," her aunt replied. "You may not be able to sleep so well in a few days, after you have crossed the border."

They spoke in English, which the servants did not understand, even in simplest words. Grace took her seat. Her aunt lived alone, except for servants, for her husband had been killed in an earlier purge in the province of Kiangsi. He had been a landowner there, inheriting his family estates, and the peasants who had for generations tilled the soil for his ancestors rose against him, urged on by the new rulers. He had not been a cruel landowner, merely a negligent one, and prudently he had built his house in Hong Kong in the last years of the republic, foreseeing, when Communists were invited to come in from Soviet Russia, that men like him must one day choose between capitulation, exile or death.

Alas, the choice had not been given him. On a sunny morning in early summer, ten years ago, he had been summoned to his own front gate, there to face a strangely silent mob of his own peasants. When a handful of angry young strangers had demanded that they condemn him, the peasants had remained silent. He had been too proud to speak in his own defense, for he had done no wrong, or so he believed. He had merely lived as a gentleman and a scholar, enjoying his ancestral home with its many courts and gardens. In this mutual silence he was summarily shot by the angry young man who led the peasants. When they had dispersed, his family lifted his body up from the dust and buried it in the family burial ground on a nearby hillside, taking the precaution of performing the rites at night. That same night his wife, Madame Liang's younger sister, accompanied by her servants, left for Hong Kong, and this at the urgent pleading of her only son, who remained behind to protect the family estates, if possible. It had not been possible. In less than a month lands and houses were seized by the new rulers, and her son was sent to hard labor at some distant place whose name she did not know. She had never heard of him again. All this Grace knew, but she was too kind to inquire if her aunt had had any news. Ten years had passed.

Her aunt was lifting the lid of one dish after another.

"I suppose you will like a Western breakfast," she said. "Both Western and Chinese have been prepared."

"I have been looking forward to a Chinese breakfast," Grace replied.

"Then there is the rice congee, and here are the small dishes to accompany it," her aunt said.

They filled their bowls and ate for a few minutes without talk, this in deference to good manners. Long ago her mother had taught her daughters that one does not begin conversation until food has been served and the first pangs of hunger satisfied. Then Grace put down her chopsticks.

"My mother seems to do very well in Shanghai, Auntie," she observed.

"You will see with your own eyes how well she does," her aunt retorted. "Naturally she will not put down in writing what she endures. She is no fool."

"You really think—"

"I do not think—I know. For charity I spend some hours each day in the refugee camps, where our people come over the border from the mainland. They do not wait for me to ask questions. Suffering pours from them. They are surfeited. These communes—"

She looked cautiously about the room. The servants had left, all except one old man.

"Lao Erh knows," she said, in lowered tones, but in Chinese. "He knows everything. He came over."

The old man nodded but did not speak.

"Lao Erh, go and fetch hot tea," his mistress commanded.

He obeyed, and her aunt leaned closer across the table. "They tell fearful tales, these people! Families are divided, the children put in one place, the parents in another. Old grandparents are put in still another. Is this not to disturb the very harmony upon which heaven and earth are based?"

"Perhaps they do not believe in this harmony," Grace suggested.

Her aunt nodded. "There you have said the truth! They do not believe in anything that the ancestors teach us. Therefore they cannot endure. It is merely a matter of waiting."

Grace smiled, without reply. She had made up her mind that she would see for herself this new China, her country.

49

Whatever it was, it was hers, for good or evil. On that last day in San Francisco, she had met with her two sisters, and they had talked long together, the hours mounting until midnight before they parted.

"I do not fear for you. I am glad you are going home," Mercy had said. "Our mother is alone there."

They were very different, her sisters and herself. Mercy, the singer, was the strongest perhaps, stronger even than she, more volatile, more talkative, more emotional. Joy was the quiet one, the youngest, the dreamer, the artist.

"I cannot believe that I have anything to fear, not from my own people," Grace had said firmly.

Joy had said nothing. She was a small slender girl, silent perhaps because her two older sisters had much to say. Her paintings were strangely unlike her, and Americans, seeing her dainty frame, her gentle Chinese ways, expected paintings of blossoms and willows. Instead she painted upon enormous canvases, her brushstrokes bold, her colors strong. Her subject was human, always human—men at work, children at play, women—no, her women were idle, decorative and predatory.

Grace had continued. "Of course I expect to find changes. But our people have always been capable of change. They accept change with aplomb. I remember—"

When she smiled her cheeks dimpled.

"Well, go on with your remembering," Mercy had urged.

"An old farmer was getting on an airplane, one of the very first to fly between Shanghai and Peking. He carried on his shoulder a basket of hens, and he insisted upon keeping them with him. He was not in the least surprised when the plane lifted itself from the ground. One would have thought he had traveled every day by air—with hens!"

They had laughed together with the tenderness habitual to them when they spoke of their own people.

"I miss them," Mercy had said. "I don't just miss our mother. I miss our people. There's something about them different from every other people on earth. They are always gay."

They had fallen into mutual silence for a brief space, each with her own memories. Then Joy spoke. "Perhaps it will be better than ever. Perhaps we shall all be happy together again."

"Perhaps," Grace had said, "perhaps—"

An hour later they had parted for time unknown.

"And now will you go with me to visit my refugees?" her aunt was saying.

"Of course."

She rose as she spoke, and while her aunt gave directions to a servant, she went to the window and stood looking out over the city. Beyond the mountains, across the barrier, her country waited.

"But these people have left everything behind them," she exclaimed. "It is natural that they are full of hatred. I must not be influenced by their hatred. I must make up my own mind."

They stood on a street corner in the Chinese section of Hong Kong, a swarming, busy street. Tall cement buildings rose on either side, the new housing. Her Majesty's Government had provided for the refugees. On every floor the verandas were lively with fluttering clotheslines.

"You had better heed what these people say, nevertheless," her aunt replied. "They are the ones the new regime is supposed to help. Yet what do they do when they escape? They begin at once to live as they did in the old days. They begin to be independent and set up a small business somewhere. See that hillside yonder between the two buildings across the street? It is covered with shacks, made of cardboard sheets and scraps of wood, anything that can be picked up. That's where they live at first. A refugee family works in a unit, young and old, to build that poor shelter. Then, as soon as possible, they move into one of the two-room apartments in a housing unit and they wash their rags of clothes—as you see by those fluttering clotheslines on the verandas. Next they buy a few boxes of matches, a handful of candy, a pound of peanuts—any small something which they can package and sell on a street corner. They prosper—of course they prosper. Did you ever know any of our people who don't prosper if you leave them alone? We're hated all over Asia because we always grow rich from just such pitiful beginnings. The richest man in old Indonesia was a Chinese coolie who went there with nothing. His daughter became the wife of the Chinese Ambassador to the United States! Who else but a Chinese could achieve such a change in a single generation?"

"An American," Grace murmured, laughing.

Her aunt stared at her. "I don't know Americans."

"No, Auntie, but they're the same as we are."

"Anyway, no one can do it under these new people," her aunt retorted. "Chinese or Americans, they can't."

While they talked a cloud, ominous and black, drifted over the mountain, and now it released a sudden rain.

"Get in the car," her aunt ordered. "We'll drive to the barrier."

The barrier was crowded with relatives and friends, all Chinese, waiting to see who that day might come over the border. Not only people came, but carriers with vegetables and fruits, fowl and eggs in baskets swinging from poles on their shoulders.

Her aunt murmured, "We are dependent upon the enemy mainland for the very water we drink and the food we eat! We live on this rocky island and—"

Grace did not hear her. She was watching the people who pushed their way across into British territory. Many were old, but most were young, men and women beyond adolescence but not far past thirty. Why did they wish to leave their country? And not all were working people, she was convinced. Disguised by the drab clothing of faded blue cotton, she saw keen intellectual faces, men and women. Would they, too, live in the huts on the hillside, waiting until they could rent two rooms in a cement beehive? Would they sell matches on the street corner, cigarettes or beancurd squares at the gateway of a park? She could not imagine it, and she turned to her aunt.

"Not all these people are peasants, Auntie! So what will the others do?"

"They will disappear," her aunt said. "They will melt into the city; they will find their friends; they will live in silence, waiting."

"Waiting for what, Auntie?"

"Whatever your mother is waiting for—"

"Will there be change?"

"There is always change, for better or worse. And can there be worse?"

"I don't know, Auntie."

"I tell you, there cannot be worse. But you will see for yourself."

"Thank you, Auntie."

She was restless, she was restless. Not knowing whether what her aunt hinted was truth, not knowing why her mother had not written her, she was eager to leave this crowded island of Hong Kong standing upright in the sea, the houses clinging to its steep slopes so that when a typhoon struck, as it did one afternoon, she could imagine that all would be washed away and the rock left bare again as it had been created. The wind tore at the rock and the rains drenched its cliffs. She thought of the miserable shacks on the hillside, the cardboard walls, the corrugated tin roofs and the wretched people huddled within. Could what they had escaped be worse than what they suffered? Yes, for here they had the chance to better themselves. But better than what? Such questions ate into her mind, and she left her aunt's house abruptly, two days earlier than she had planned and indeed as soon as the typhoon had swept into the mainland.

"I shall write you everything, Auntie," she said in farewell.

"Write me nothing," her aunt cried in alarm.

"But why, Auntie?"

"You will find answers to all your questions," her aunt said with decision, "but I have my own answers."

She left her aunt at the border then, one clear morning,

and was met by a man who came forward and presented her with a letter. Opening it, she found it was from Comrade Chao, as he signed himself, and it bade her welcome.

"We have long awaited your arrival," the letter said. "You are needed and you will be given every aid. But do not hurry. Linger if you like for a day or two in Canton; observe the masses there, and how the ancient crafts have been nourished. You will then take the train to Shanghai and there you will visit your mother for two days. On the third we shall expect you to leave for Peking, where all is ready for your coming. You understand that our native medicines are receiving the utmost aid from the government. They were long neglected by the imperialists, but now our doctors are freely reviving their own practices, to the benefit of our people. It is to help in this important work that you have been summoned."

With this permission, she decided indeed to stay for a day and perhaps two in Canton, a city which she remembered as the home of delicate and beautiful crafts, especially in ivory. She had read in Western journals that beauty, the ancient beauty of China, had left that land and was no more. Now she would see for herself. With this decision she gave herself into the hands of her guide and proceeded on her journey.

She had lived so long abroad that she had forgotten that a city can be gray. Or perhaps she had wandered too long in the lush jungles of the Amazon, where she had grown used to the varied colors of the orchids against the vivid green. She had grown used to the opulence of American cities, the magnificence of buildings, of churches and shops, of apartment houses circling Central Park in New York, of rich old town houses in Philadelphia and Boston, or perhaps it was only the British grace of Hong Kong. But Canton? It was now a city of meager charm. She felt a vague disappointment, a subtle discouragement. The people were poorly dressed, many were barefoot, which she had not remembered in cities when she was a child. Here and there a fairly well dressed man rode by on a bicycle or a woman in a neat long gown paused at a vegetable stall. Yet even the poor were clean, she observed. Much had been said about the cleanliness of this new China as compared to the filth and flies of the old, the streets overflowing into gutters. The streets were clean now, even in the poor areas, though the small shops of craftsmen were gone.

She approached an elderly woman in a neat costume of gauzy black. "Elder sister, will you tell me whether the ivory workers are still to be found in this city?"

The woman stared at her. "The proper address is 'comrade,' " she said without smiling.

"Forgive me," Grace stammered. "I have only just come from across the border."

"And the ivory workers are yonder." The woman pointed with outthrust chin.

"Thank you."

She tried to say "comrade," but the strange word would not be said. I shall have to learn, she thought.

And yonder, when she reached it, was still not the street of many small houses in each of which an ivory carver lived and worked, surrounded by his family. Instead it was a factory, not tall or imposing, within which she found not only a fine exhibit of ivory pieces but the workers in ivory as well. As she walked about she saw many exquisite objects made from precious and semiprecious stones sent from the southeastern countries of Asia. But ivory she had always loved best, that cream-white substance, hard as bone and yet somehow soft as living tissue. Each craftsman, sitting in his place, was given his material, no single piece larger than the tusk of an elephant, yet whole or in part, whatever its shape, he must study it and meditate until out from the shape he held in his hands he saw another shape, suited to its lines, but a new shape, his own creation. True, she saw, too, the show pieces she remembered, the ivory balls, one carved within another until there were as many as twenty-six, each perfect and free of every other, but this was not what caught her gaze. Art, so she reasoned, does not announce itself, does not boast of what it is, but, like a misty landscape, its meaning steals into the perception. She saw such a landscape carved in ivory which breathed of spring in its blossoms and weeping willows. She saw galleons with sails set full, pennants waving and tiny figures bent to the wind. She saw an ivory fisherman casting his ivory net, every mesh perfected by a fine electric drill.

"A drill?" she inquired of the carver. "And what if the point slips and your art is destroyed?"

The man smiled, a bronze-faced old man.

"It never slips," he said.

She wandered among the ivory pieces, examining each in its perfection. She saw ivory junks with twisted ropes of ivory; she saw dancing girls of ivory, their ivory scarves whirling in the dance; she saw old men and women with ivory wrinkles, and laughing Buddhas all of ivory. Such were for export, through the gate of Hong Kong, to the Western world, but certain ones were too rare for export. She saw a pagoda, within its tusk confining thirteen stories, each corner tipped with a freely swinging bell. She saw palace gardens with every tree and flower perfected, and she saw wild rocky mountains in a landscape and such varied sights that she was awed by all she saw.

From ivory she went to jade, and now she saw how a clever carver had used the natural color of his jade to portray purple grapes, green leaves, gray rock, and she saw jade panthers and tigers and small pet dogs, their natural hues the colors of the stone. Yet beautiful as jade was, she found beauty too in the humbler materials of wood and bamboo and even paper, for in paper the clever scissors had cut large designs of most intricate patterns, scenes of land and waters. She remembered as a child how on feast days her mother used to bid her servants paste on the doors and gates these cut paper pictures for good luck. All those, like the ones upon which she now looked, were cut from a single piece of paper without joins.

When she had satisfied her eyes, she turned to her guide. "Somehow I am heartened to see these old crafts kept alive, though I confess I am amazed that the new tools can work as well as the old ones."

"Better," the guide replied. "Look at these prawns in stone!"

He pointed, and, her eyes following his outthrust chin, she saw prawns, gray as they are to be found in the sea, but the main carapaces were darkened over the brain, as they are in life, and the stone antennae were fine enough to tremble at her touch.

"Truly I am amazed," she murmured.

That night she slept in a Chinese inn, preferring it to the fine hotel built especially for foreigners, those businessmen who gather in Canton for the huge Export Commodities Fair, and she ate such cooking as she had forgotten could be, though the dishes were simple. She went to bed at last, deciding to linger no longer in this city so gray and silent, for she remembered, now at the end of the day, that everywhere the new people were silent. In the old days of her childhood, she remembered, the streets of a city were always gay and noisy, neighbor calling to neighbor, vendors shouting their wares, children's voices laughing in play. Now the people came and went in silence, or if one spoke it was with few words and in low tones. A gray city, she would have said, except that she remembered the beauty she had seen, set forth in jade and stone, in bamboo, wood and paper. Therefore in the midst of the new silence something, and something very much, remained of the past she had once known, and it was beauty.

The land was tended, that she could see even from the train window. The land was still the source. Now, as far as she could see, the fields were green with young rice, and not only fields but every bit and parcel of land, odd corners and narrow spaces, were given over to vegetables, as though the people could never forget how they had starved in other years.

Yet even the land she saw was changed. No longer were there the small fields of the past. Boundaries had been torn away and ditches filled and paths removed, so that vast areas of waving green promised a good harvest. Who had taken away the boundaries and who had filled the dividing ditches and done away with the narrow paths between small old fields, until now the landscape was a great garden before her eyes?

She longed to ask someone how it had happened, but there was no one in her compartment whose looks invited such conversation. Of the four that it contained, the other three were men, one her silent guide, who stared blankly at the wall opposite him, and the other two young men in the ubiquitous uniform of the country, jacket buttoned to the narrow upstanding collar and trousers of the same dark cotton. These two were studying small books, in which now and then one and the other would pause to write a note on a margin. Thus isolated, she turned again to the window and watched a golden sun sink into the twilight of the land.

Her journey had obviously first been planned directly to Peking, for instead of turning eastward toward the coast for Shanghai, they were headed for Hankow. She had inquired of the guide and had received a short answer.

"At Hankow you will take a river steamer for Shanghai. And at Hankow you will see the new bridge."

She had not protested the delay for she was curious to see this great bridge, this famous bridge, which engineers of half the Western world had said could never be built across the wide stretch of the Yangtse river. It had been built, nevertheless, and now she was to see it. But first she must see the provinces, lying green under a rain-washed sky. The young rice was here, too, brilliantly green, and the villages, those clusters of human life, were not changed, so far as she could see from the window of the train. In the fields now she saw the gray water buffaloes pulling the old wooden plows. Nothing was changed here —no, wait, the hills, once bare except for fuel grass, had been planted to young trees and there were new reservoirs for irrigation. Next she saw farmers scattering something white over the fields and she recognized the substance. It was chemical fertilizer, furnished them doubtless by the new government through the communes. The nation was making its own fertilizer! This meant chemical installations and perhaps chemical medicines for human beings.

In Honan the houses were no better than they had been but the people were better dressed, their clothes less faded and seldom patched. Here in this province Mao Tse-tung was born, the son of a farmer but not a poor one, a father who tried to force his son, the rebellious boy, to be a country schoolteacher. Mao Tse-tung a country schoolteacher! She saw a placid river, junks sailing slowly down its smoothly flowing waters, junks for carrying goods and junks for fishing. Ah, now here were the cooperatives, doubtless! Not individual farmers pushing a plow behind a slow buffalo, but groups of twenty or so men and women worked together in a wide field. Only in small plots did she see children working, and these, she decided, were the bits and scraps of land allotted to families for their own use.

Another day and the landscape changed again, now to the red clay and bare hills and still ancient villages of the next province. The barley was ripe, and it had been cut and was being threshed on village threshing floors. In the old days, as she remembered when she was a child, many birds flew above the threshing floors and boldly pushed their way among the flocks to eat the grain. Now there were no birds. They had been killed by government orders, and too late this government discovered that without the birds insects became rampant.

Suddenly on the next day at evening she saw the great bridge, that symbol of the people's pride. The train made its last stop at the station in Wuchang and soon it rumbled toward the river. She opened the window and looked out. The bridge stood upon eight great piers, based deep into the earth beneath the river, a huge bridge with three levels; above the train tracks a roadway for trucks and buses and a walkway above that. High over the river, between two and three hundred feet, she guessed, the train slowed to caution and she looked down upon the magnificent river, its source in western mountains and its mouth emptying into the sea, a thousand miles away. Slowly, slowly, the train crept the mile-long span of the bridge—yes, the bridge that engineers of the modern world had said again and again could never be built! Now it was built. She saw it with her own eyes; even now she was upon it, gazing upon the mighty river below, and she felt a great pride in her own people swell into her heart. If her people could build this bridge, was there anything they could not do?

She dreaded the meeting with her mother, and at the same time she eagerly longed for it. Would she find her mother aged and changed by hardship? In America the news had been all of hardship and cruelty in China. She had studied her mother's usual letters to discover the hardship and had found neither joy nor sorrow in them. Calm and bland, the letters had told only of small daily affairs, the garden, the house, the servants, the weather. There was not a hint of the vast and monumental changes surrounding this single life. Of illness her mother never wrote nor of hunger or deprivation. She could only imagine her mother continuing her usual life in the new world about her. Somehow she would continue her usual life.

Nevertheless, in Shanghai at last, she stood before the gate in considerable excitement. Her guide was always with her, a silent though courteous presence.

"We are directed to go at once to your mother's residence," he had said when they left the ship that had carried them down the great river. It was a vessel that had once belonged to Jardine Matheson, but belonged now to the Chinese. In the old days when her mother would take them to the mountains of Kiangsi to escape the heat of the river delta, they had always traveled on English ships. Yet, though the furniture was somewhat worn and the ships needed paint, it was run as well as before, its Chinese captain efficient and silent, as everyone seemed efficient and silent. In silence she had passed the three days on the ship, absorbing alone the magnificent scenery on either side, remembering one place and another where as children her mother had taken them for pleasure trips—the island of the Big Orphan, the island of the Little Orphan, Golden Island, now embedded in the shifting riverbank, its pagoda visible nevertheless from the ship.

"Does my mother know we are coming?" she asked.

"Assuredly she does," her guide replied. "Everything is prepared and in order."

He was a mild colorless little man, she thought, casting him a sidewise glance. They had been together for days; he had been always polite and quick to supply her needs, but she continually forgot him. He disappeared now and then, or so she thought, but when she moved or so much as turned her head, he was there again. Had he orders for her every movement, the hours for her meals, the food to be prepared, where she was to sleep, where she was to go, what she was to see? She smiled at her own vanity. Surely she was not of such importance! Yet so smoothly was all prepared that she could not have improved upon anything, except that she decided nothing for herself. Before she could express a wish, arrangements had been made and it would have been troublesome to change them.

He knocked on the gate again and it opened. The gateman was a stranger to her, but this was to be expected since her mother had told her that their old gateman, the one who had served in her childhood home, was now in a rest house for the aged. That, too, was something new, such rest houses. There had been no such places when she was a child. In those days each family had taken care of its own aged members. But perhaps he had no son?

"Comrade T'ai-t'ai is expecting you," the gateman said, thus combining both new and old address.

He led the way, a slim old man, his shoulders bent, and she followed, the guide behind her. At the house the gateman called and the door opened. Another servant, a young man in the usual blue cotton suit, bowed his head in invitation.

"Please enter," he said.

Even the language was new to her. In the old days he would have called her "Young Mistress," or as the phrase had been, "Eldest Sister," with the proper honorifics.

He led the way through a square entrance hall, strange to her, as the house was strange, for she had not lived here, and only once or twice had visited the Brandons in Shanghai, although she had visited them before she sailed to Hong Kong, spending a long weekend with them in their home in San Francisco.

"Write to us, dear," Mrs. Brandon had urged. "Your dear mother never writes to us. Probably she is not allowed."

"Nonsense," she had replied. "I am sure it is only that she is busy. And she never liked writing letters. Even we, her daughters, seldom hear from her more than twice a year. She always seems quite happy."

"I hope you're right," Mr. Brandon had growled. "I don't like some of the things I hear."

The servant opened a door. "She has come," he announced.

Madame Liang was sitting in a large carved wooden chair, her hands folded in her lap. Her eyes had been fixed on this door for the last ten minutes. She had been told the exact hour when her daughter would arrive and she did not doubt that at the stated moment, which was now, the door would open and Grace would be there. Now she saw a tall young woman, taller than she remembered, very slim and wearing a Western suit, jacket and skirt, of a soft gray wool material. The face had not changed, except that it was no longer childish. It was the face of a strong and resolute young woman. The dark hair was short and slightly curled, the dark eyes were calm.

"Mother," Grace said in a low voice.

Madame Liang rose but she did not come forward. She stood waiting, her eyes upon the guide.

It was the guide who spoke. He coughed slightly and took two steps forward. "Comrade Liang?" he inquired.

"I am she," Madame Liang replied.

"According to instructions, I have brought your eldest daughter here to you. I deliver her to you. Please confirm!"

"I will confirm," Madame Liang said.

"Then I take my leave of you," he said with a short bow, scarcely more than a nod.

With the same nod, he turned to Grace. "In three days, I return for your journey to the capital," and without further speech he left the room. The servant closed the door and mother and daughter were alone.

"Mother," Grace said again. She felt a strange hesitation; her impulse was to throw her arms about her mother, and yet she hesitated. Madame Liang moved forward and took her hand and smoothed it gently, gazing into her daughter's eyes as she did so.

"You have not changed and yet you have changed very much," she said in her soft voice and very low, so that Grace could scarcely catch the words.

"But you have not changed, Mother," she said. "At least very little."

"I live here," Madame Liang said vaguely, almost evasively. "I live here," she repeated, nodding her head.

"You are thinner, I think," Grace said.

"I am growing old," Madame Liang replied. She drew her daughter by the hand to a sofa and they sat down, still hand in hand, and so they sat looking at each other. At last Madame Liang spoke again.

"I want you to know," she said. "I want you to know that I forgive them everything."

"Mother," Grace cried. "What do you mean? Whom do you forgive?"

It occurred to her now that her mother was not well. This strange vagueness—what did it mean? And they were speaking in English, she suddenly noticed. She had not noticed it until now, so accustomed had she grown to this tongue, but never in the old days had they spoken together in English, her mother, her sisters and she. True, she had spoken in English when she met her sisters in San Francisco—they had all grown accustomed to that tongue—but why did she continue it here, and why did her mother accept it?

"We are speaking in English," she exclaimed in astonishment.

"It is safer," Madame Liang replied.

Yet after a moment of silence, in which each had examined the other's face anew, her mother began to speak in Chinese, easily and as though the last few minutes had not existed, as though they met now for the first time since they parted so many years ago.

"You must be weary," she said. "You must be hungry. On the train, on the ship, how do I know what hardship you have suffered?"

Grace replied in Chinese, not so easily after the years of harsh English. "I have been well treated. My guide saw to that."

"Ah, doubtless," Madame Liang replied with seeming

negligence. "He attended to everything as he was told to do, I daresay. It was his duty. Let us go to your room. It is waiting for you." She rose as she spoke and led her daughter by the hand up the great staircase to the second floor. Now she opened a door.

"I have put you in the room next to mine," she said. "If you call me in the night, I shall hear."

Grace smiled. "I am too happy to be with you, Mother. I shall not wake."

"One never knows," Madame Liang said, still vaguely. "Sometimes there are noises in the night—street noises. It is better not to open the window." Suddenly her vagueness melted away. "Refresh yourself, my child. Then come into my room. Tonight I do not go to my restaurant. Instead, our meal will be served in my small library, adjoining my bedroom. We will talk. Three days will not suffice for all we have to ask and to tell."

The two women looked at each other with searching eyes, then embraced. In her arms the daughter felt the slight and delicate frame of her mother. In her arms the mother felt the strong tall shape of her daughter. Both knew an instinctive trust, each in the other.

"Tell me," her daughter said, "tell me, now that we are alone, what you meant when you spoke of forgiveness."

The hour was come for deep, understanding talk. Their meal had been served by Chou Ma, delicacies sent up from the restaurant, dishes chosen that day by Madame Liang herself. She had considered these dishes. Should she serve such gourmet food as only a few could afford to eat, or should she serve those simple supplies which the people must eat? After thought, she decided upon the rich dishes, the hidden ones, and this for two reasons: the first, and the more important, that her daughter might make her own discoveries; the second, that such discoveries could begin through food. Let her daughter be introduced, day by day, to whatever she was to meet! Therefore, Grace ate the delicious dishes in ignorance and innocence, exclaiming and declaring that she had not eaten such food since she was last in Shanghai.

"Why are there such reports abroad of famine here in our country?" she exclaimed. "Surely there is no sign of it. The peasants do well."

"They are no longer peasants—that is, men and women who work only with their hands," Madame Liang replied. "Today we all work with our hands. The scholar, the intellectual—"

Grace broke into laughter. "M-ma," she said in Chinese. "Are you making propaganda? Do not, please! It is not necessary. I am prepared to believe. I only ask that first I see."

Madame Liang smiled and stirred a dish of chicken and mushrooms with her ivory chopsticks. "You will discover both good and bad," she said in her calm voice. "Here's a bit of liver. You used to like chicken liver."

"And you remember everything, M-ma!"

Yet when the dishes had been removed, Grace remembered the question she had asked that had not been answered. She began again in English.

"Mother, you did not tell me what you meant when you spoke of forgiveness. We became involved with chicken livers."

The room was quiet, the doors were bolted, the windows closed. From far off, if she listened, she could hear the murmur of voices from the restaurant downstairs, but she did not listen. There was something rare, even precious, in the atmosphere of the spacious room, and to it her mother lent her own grace. Neither of her sisters, nor she herself, had the full measure of her mother's beauty. At fifty-five Madame Liang was slender and strong, her close-fitting gown of pale green satin revealing slight hips, a narrow waist and small firm breasts. Her neck was smooth and her skin without lines. Into this room she had created she fitted as a jewel fits into its setting. Somehow she had not expected to see her mother still exquisite.

"I should have to go very far back in the years to answer your question," Madame Liang was saying.

She was speaking English again, unconsciously, as though her daughter had become a foreigner, a flawless English, almost without accent.

"Then go back, please," her daughter said.

"When you have not told me about your sisters, or your aunt in Hong Kong?"

"Answer my question first and then I will answer yours."

Madame Liang lit a fragrant cigarette. Such luxuries were smuggled into the country, but she did not ask how. Minister Chao kept her supplied.

"I forgive my people," Madame Liang said slowly, "first, because they are trying very hard, piteously hard, to achieve stability; and second, because all that they do and feel and say, all indeed that happens, is the result of what has gone before—that is to say, the result of history. Nothing is happening today that is not the result of history."

"I have read the history of our own country but I found no answer there," her daughter said.

Madame Liang was silent for a space of minutes, smoking thoughtfully and flicking away the ash with her little finger, while her daughter watched her beautiful and wise face. Suddenly she crushed her cigarette in the porcelain ashtray.

"I will pluck out the heart of the matter," she said. "Through our thousands of years our weakness has been in our pride. We believed and do still believe that we are the superior race, the best people. We grew accustomed through centuries, and with reason, to being the first nation in the world, our civilization above that of any other. We became the most ancient of days. While other peoples rose and died and nations flourished and passed away, our nation and our people continued upon the earth, the center of all. We knew this, and the knowing of it, the certainty of it, has been our undoing. We could not believe that the time had arrived for us to change, because a new power had come to mankind. It is the power of science, first manifest to us in new weapons. The new weapons, devised by the few, were soon used by the many. One man, devising a weapon, gives power of life and death to the many who know nothing except how to pull a trigger. This science was our undoing, and all the wisdom of Confucius could not save us."

Her daughter stared at her with surprise. "You sit here alone and think such thoughts!"

"I sit here alone and think such thoughts," Madame Liang agreed. "What company have I now except my thoughts? Yes, we are at the same time the wisest and most stupid of people—wise because we are right in what we have believed. We had these clever men, too. One such devised explosion by gunpowder, another such devised a flying machine, another the art of printing, another—but why should I repeat such truths? We were first, even in inventions."

"Where was our fault that we invented and did not continue?"

"Our next fault," Madame Liang replied, looking her daughter full in the eyes, "was that we put our faith above all else in the wisdom of our good men. Not to kill, but to create, our good men taught us, was the basis of continuing life. To behave toward others as we would have them behave toward us, to care for the aged as we would wish ourselves when aged to be cared for; reciprocity in all human relationships, in this is the secret of life, our wise men taught us. And so long was this true that we continued to live while others died in wars and strife. Yes, and we were right. Then our good great men failed us."

"What do you mean, Mother?"

"They did not see that even the good and the wise are at the mercy of the man who carries the weapon. Alas, alas! Now I know this is true and so I keep silence. I go about my business in silence. I confide in none. The old teachings no longer serve, not because they are wrong, but because the world around us is barbarian. Must we, too, become barbarous in order to live?"

She stopped here to sigh and shake her head. "It is the

question now. Must weapon match weapon? Must we who are old and wise become like the young, the lesser peoples?"

She lit another cigarette, the great jade ring on her left forefinger gleaming in the light of the flame. "Yet even so we might have prevailed—for truth remains truth—if the events in history had not combined against us."

"M-ma, what do you mean?" Her daughter was leaning forward in her chair, hands gripped, her eyes upon her mother's face.

Madame Liang took two puffs more on her cigarette before she replied. "I cannot put into a few sentences what has taken centuries to pass and yet I can, even as the kernel of a nut, the seed in a fruit, expresses the effort of the whole tree, the essence of its life. Consider this: I sent you, my three daughters, far from your own country because I foresaw the concatenation of events which would bring disaster to our people. I wish you to survive."

"The events?" her daughter inquired.

Madame Liang put down her cigarette upon the ashtray in order to be able to count upon her fingers, beginning with the small finger of her left hand and progressing to her thumb. "First, our country was approaching the natural end of a dynasty. The old Empress Dowager was near death and without an heir. At such times our country breaks into sections, each section held by a strong young man, upheld by his own private army. It has always been thus. One of these men wins over his rivals; he becomes the final victor and therefore the first emperor of the new dynasty—a healthy process, for he is a man of the people and he proves himself a natural leader. But now, and second, suddenly there was no throne upon which such a victor could sit. What confusion, therefore! And why was there no throne?"

Here she put forth a third finger. "Because a young Christian, Sun Yat-sen, and his followers had overthrown the very structure of our government! We were without a throne. Those were the years when I was young and you were far away in the shades of the future. But he was our leader. Your father was his friend and I was his follower among thousands of the young. We dreamed of a new government through which we could serve our people. We dreamed of a new country, one strong enough to hold back the greedy Western peoples who coveted our land. Oh, we had such dreams! And the country held firm. Family tradition and our age-old civil service kept our people steady while we made the change."

"But, M-ma, why throw away all the past?" her daughter asked, and in reproach.

Madame Liang interrupted with some impatience. "Because it was the only way we could take power, or so we thought! We had all been educated in the Western schools of the Christians and therefore our young men could not pass the ancient Imperial Examinations, from which our civil administrators always were chosen. I see now how wise were those tests, which discovered for the use of our people the minds which were the most quick, the most profound. Did you know that England based her civil service upon ours? And that Americans took their civil service plan from England and so from us? In reality all good things began with us!"

"Mother, how can I know? I have not studied these matters."

"Ah, but I have! I have had plenty of time to study in these years since I left your father to his concubines! Yes, we were a part of that revolution, but what we young people did not realize was that a government is created only by the people. Through centuries they create out of themselves and their own needs the ruling structure which alone can insure peace and order. How then could we, dreamers that we were, borrow a government from the West or even fashion a government as a woman cuts a garment or a man builds a house? There was no time for growth. We said that we would make a government for the people, by the people—yes, we had that dream from America—but our people had their own dreams and their own memories. They did not understand; they did not accept what we discovered, though for ten long years we struggled to persuade them. Alas, in those ten years the Russians destroyed their government, too, and set up another! Upon bloodshed and destruction they created a new structure, frail and unsteady, but a structure. And we were in chaos and our leader, Sun Yat-sen, was in despair. The Russians—oh, yes, it was crafty, for we knew that for centuries they had cast their eyes in our direction—but we needed to believe, and we who were young believed their young, and had not our ancient ways failed us? 'Let us help you,' they said and we said, 'Help us.' They came then, with advisers and weapons—and here they are. I have led you too hastily, for the Japanese attack came upon us, too, and the defection of the Nationalists. But you can see the coming together of these mighty events. And I should also mention, meanwhile, those two great world wars that weakened the Western powers and hastened the independence of their colonies here in our East, increasing the turmoil, so that we dreamed even more dreams than before and ones more vast. We dreamed of the rise of Asia, with ourselves as the leaders of the future even as we have been in the past."

She had continued to count off one finger and another until now she had arrived at her thumb, and her daughter marveled at the swift clarity of her mind and her cool reasoning.

"Here we now are," Madame Liang repeated, "and thus our people are engaged. Without hope of other leaders, they have been persuaded to these and they have lent themselves with whole heart to the new effort. They are good people, but desperate, for all roads save this one have been destroyed. Yes, we began the destruction and the Japanese finished it. I remember the very day when we began it. It was in the city of Canton, where the long arm of Peking could not reach, and in an old building where a school had once been. We sat on the floor because there were no chairs, and our leader spun out dreams for us. Who could have thought— Who could have thought—"

She forgot where she was and to whom she spoke and her hands dropped to her lap, and her daughter did not interrupt her memories. It was minutes before Madame Liang spoke again, and when she did she made another heavy sigh. "Such a task as we have now! For the real revolution must take place in the hearts of the people—in the deepest thoughts, in the habits of mind, in the accustomed principles. In a few years we are trying to change the thoughts, the habits, the principles—to make a new people out of the oldest in the world. What is that saying of the Christians?

Something about new wine in old bottles, is it not? And so we cannot be surprised when the new wine is too strong and destroys that which tries to contain it—the new wine—"

Suddenly she lifted her head and with a bemused look she put a question which seemed to have no relation to what she had said before.

"Tell me, did you hear Americans say why they will not have us in their United Nations?"

Grace was unprepared for this surprising question, and she answered as best she could. "M-ma, it was because they think we are an aggressor nation."

Madame Liang was shocked. "We? An aggressor nation? But we have fought no aggressive wars in two thousand years!"

"It was because of Korea, M-ma. We sent a volunteer army."

"But that was our duty! Korea is one of our tributary nations and has been for many centuries. It was our responsibility, always, to send a volunteer army if any of our tributary nations was attacked by a foreign power."

"M-ma, they don't know that."

"Do they not read our history?"

"No, M-ma, I don't think so."

Madame Liang was too astonished for a while even to speak. Then she shook her head and murmured something that her daughter could not hear.

"What are you saying, M-ma?" Grace asked.

"Our friends—" Madame Liang spoke with difficulty. "The Americans—our friends—"

To her daughter's shock and surprise, Madame Liang began to sob softly, shaking her head and sobbing.

"M-ma!" her daughter cried in alarm. "M-ma, why do you weep?"

She hastened to her mother and knelt beside her, and with her handkerchief she wiped her mother's pale cheeks. Madame Liang tried to laugh and moved away from her daughter.

"I am sure I do not know why," she said unsteadily. "Very foolish, of course, for I have nothing to weep about —except, somehow, everything!"

Her voice dropped on the last word, but her daughter put no further question. "You are tired, M-ma, that is all. This day has been an excitement for you. It has been so long since we were together and you have been alone too long. I blame myself. I wish I could stay with you. I will ask—"

Madame interrupted in haste. "No, no—ask for nothing! I am quite accustomed—in fact, it is better for me if you ask no favors. You are needed elsewhere. One must think of our people now, not of a single person."

She seemed so alarmed that her daughter said no more. But why alarmed, she wondered.

"It is time for us to sleep," Madame Liang said, regaining her usual voice. "There is always tomorrow."

And upon this they parted for rest, Madame Liang to her own room and her daughter to one adjoining.

"But shall I not leave the door open between?" Grace asked.

"If you wish." Madame Liang was now quite calm.

"I feel strange in this house," her daughter said.

"Then leave the door open," her mother replied.

"So now," Madame Liang continued the next morning, "you see why I said I forgive the people. They are not responsible."

"Do you also forgive the leaders?" her daughter asked.

Madame Liang nodded. "I forgive them," she said simply.

They were sitting at breakfast in a small pleasant room which faced south toward the garden. Here Chou Ma brought their bowls of rice congee and the appetizers of salt fish and salted duck eggs and a dozen other small dishes.

"You used to eat an American breakfast, M-ma," Grace said irrelevantly.

"It is not possible now," Madame Liang replied with tranquillity. "It would not be understood. Moreover, I like this better."

"So do I."

"Then without fault we may enjoy what we must do," Madame Liang said, laughing.

"Do you feel guilty, Mother?" her daughter asked.

"Never," Madame Liang said.

The morning was mild, the sunshine flickering between the leaves of the plane trees which lined the street outside. The garden was subsiding into summer calm, the lilies coming into bloom, their heavy heads upheld by thin bamboo supports.

"Except that you are living in a house strange to me, Mother," Grace said, "I could imagine that nothing is changed."

"Yet everything is changed," Madame Liang replied.

79

She took a small fish delicately between her chopsticks and put it into her congee.

"I suppose I shall find it so," Grace agreed.

She waited to see if her mother would speak further of what the change was, but Madame Liang was silent, her thoughts far away. At last she spoke.

"Everything in America is changed also."

Grace looked up surprised. "Why do you say so, Mother?"

"We are told of their troubles."

"What troubles?"

"The Americans are distressed by poverty and strikes and the revolution now being waged by the black serfs! I feel sad for the Brandons. Doubtless they think with regret of this house in which they were so happy."

Grace put down her chopsticks. "Mother, what are you saying? The Brandons are very happy. They live in a beautiful house, bigger than this one, in San Francisco. Mr. Brandon is the president of a great bank in the city."

Madame Liang stared at her daughter. "But the banks are now all ruined!"

"Mother, why do you say such things?"

"But we have been told—"

"Still it is not true!"

"Then I am deceived! Indeed, I have wondered whether you three daughters of mine were safe in America. But I supposed you had friends. And I did not want you to come home unless you were invited—and certainly not for my sake. Then America is not changed?"

"Only for the better. The black people are asking for their rights and they are being given them—too slowly in some places, but surely. But such disturbance never touched me or my sisters. We have been busy with our own lives and our work. Why, one of the most respected scientists in the laboratory where I work is a Negro, Dr. Cadwall. Why do you look at me so, Mother?"

"I am wondering."

"About what?"

Before Madame Liang could reply, the door was opened by Chou Ma, who ushered into the room a tall Chinese man in a uniform of fine English wool, blue in color. He put out both hands and his voice was rich and deep.

"You are early, comrades! But you, Comrade Liang, are always early and filled with zeal for the day's work. And this is your daughter, your eldest? How we have expected you, Doctor Liang! You are 'comrade' also, but let me use at our first meeting the title you have so deservedly won!"

He spoke in smooth Peking Chinese, and Grace, rising to her feet, looked into a handsome oval face, the features finely cut and the eyes large and dark and vivid. She recognized him instantly from his pictures.

"Captain Li—"

He put up a graceful hand. "No, no, we have no titles now. Even officers in the army are simply 'comrade.'"

"You have not breakfasted?" Madame Liang interposed.

"Yes, yes, I, too, rise early. Please continue."

"We are finished," Madame Liang said and with a gesture so slight that it was scarcely noticeable she summoned Chou Ma, who stood at the door, to clear the table.

"Fresh tea," she murmured. Chou Ma nodded.

Captain Li seated himself and beamed at Madame Liang and her daughter. "What a happy day for you and for us all! We have waited for your return, Comrade Liang. It is our purpose to revive the original medicines and medical practices of our own people, so long derided and scorned by the imperialists. Not that we refuse to recognize modern sciences! We make our own contribution there, also. But the two must proceed side by side, each correcting the other. Your laboratory awaits you. Your staff is ready. We have chosen some of our best young minds."

She observed his face and manner as he spoke. There was nothing to rouse alarm, no obvious change. He might have been a Chinese gentleman of her own age, except for his garb. "I shall want to learn, too, and from my elders in Chinese medicine," she said.

A flicker passed over his face, faint and impenetrable, to be wiped away by his generous approving smile. "They also wait to welcome you," he said.

She was aware somehow of an uncertainty in him, not strong enough to imply distrust, and yet it was there. His eyes, so clear in black and white, did not meet hers frankly; his laugh was too ready. Yet this might mean nothing except a natural shyness, left from the teaching of his youth, that a gentleman does not look a lady full in the face. But her mother, too, was behaving with something like constraint. Or was it merely the old-fashioned silence of a lady in the presence of a man? Even for her mother this seemed an impossibility in these days when, as far as eye could see, there was little difference left between man and woman in garb and behavior. That, it now appeared to her, was the most apparent change between the China she had known and the one to which she had come. Even on the train, even on the country roads, the women looked like the men, and especially the young ones, those who had been born in the midst of revolution.

"You will find," he was saying, "that a full schedule has been prepared for you. It will be necessary for you to spend a preliminary time in the hostel for those who enter from overseas, and especially for those who returned from America, where the people know nothing of what is taking place here. Indeed, their thinking is medieval and unenlightened by true knowledge and correct understanding. It will be necessary for you to empty your mind of all past concepts and prepare yourself for the new and the present. But you are intelligent and the process will not be long. Meanwhile you may begin your work by writing a full report of your scientific findings, and the sources from which you have derived them. Our own experts will examine this report and determine what is worth preserving."

She felt a slight indignation. "I can assure you that my work has been done under the most careful, scientific—"

He put up his hand to silence her. "Comrade, it is not necessary for you to defend yourself. We proceed according to our own methods."

"I am not defending myself," she protested and stopped.

Fire lit his black eyes. "Proceed no further," he said brusquely. "I see it will take time for you to understand. Everything you write will be judged on its own merits. We are entirely scientific."

She looked at her mother, bewildered. The beautiful face was without expression. Madame Liang had lit a cigarette and was smoking it with delicate grace.

"Mother," she urged, "you understand I am not defending myself."

Madame Liang smiled. "As Comrade Li says, you need not."

For a moment Grace felt herself with two strangers. Was her mother siding against her? No, no, it was not a question of for or against.

"You have let her be away too long," he was saying to her mother.

"Perhaps you are right," Madame Liang said.

He rose and lifted his left arm to glance at the watch on his wrist. "If you will excuse me, I have an important appointment with—" He lifted his eyebrows to suggest importance.

"Of course," Madame Liang said. "Why not?"

It was evening again, and at the end of the day they were alone, mother and daughter, the day incredible because so far as she, the daughter, could see, her mother did exactly as she had done since she opened the restaurant in Shanghai.

"Nothing has changed, M-ma," Grace exclaimed.

Madame Liang sat down in her favorite chair in the sitting room next to her bedroom. It was a place of mixed decor, the floor covered in the Western fashion but with a Peking rug in a pattern of pale green and rose. The furniture was Chinese except for two comfortable armchairs of rose velvet. The walls of a pale ivory were bare except for one exquisite scroll painted of a landscape some two centuries earlier. The rose-colored curtains were drawn and the room was silent except that, if one listened, a distant music could be heard from the restaurant. This music was also mixed, a piano accompanying a girl's voice, singing a revolutionary song.

"Everything is changed," Madame Liang replied, lighting a cigarette. Though it had been bought in Shanghai, it had been made in America.

Grace laughed. "You even smoke an American cigarette!"

"We have not yet learned how to make them properly," Madame Liang replied. "But we shall, of course. Now tell me about your sisters. You don't smoke?"

"Thanks, no."

"You believe the doctors?"

"I want to live long."

"Ah, since I cannot live long enough, in any case, why should I merely live?"

Grace contemplated the enigmatic half smile on her mother's beautiful face. "What is 'long enough,' my mother?"

"To see the end of—everything!"

"In the world?"

"What do I care about the world? No, this country of ours."

"There will be an end?"

"That is what I would like to know. Since I cannot, tell me about your sisters. You saw them just before you left America?"

"We met at the Brandons' house. Mrs. Brandon, knowing it was difficult for us to meet, arranged this, my mother. Do you know she has never forgotten you? She thinks it better not to write to you—"

"She is right," Madame Liang interposed. "Better for her, better for me."

"You really think so, M-ma? But why should—"

"Come, come. You and your sisters?"

"Yes, Mother. We met in the Brandons' home. It's a big house, and since the Brandon children are all at school and away from home, Mr. Brandon at the bank and Mrs. Brandon here and there the way American ladies are, we had three long quiet days together. M-ma, my second sister wants to come home to China. Joy wants to see you, but —well, she's tenderhearted, remember? Of all of us, she has missed you the most. Mercy wants to come back because she thinks that all loyal Chinese belong in their own country. But singing? What would she do? Unless she could start a school of music?"

Madame Liang crushed her cigarette in a small jade ashtray and lit another. "Let them stay where they are, unless they are summoned as you were."

"I was invited, and I came because of you and because I wanted to serve my people!"

"Invitation or summons, they are the same. Tell me about your sisters."

"You wouldn't know them, Mother. Both of them have grown so pretty—very different, of course. Mercy is tall, like me, but Joy is small. You'd think she was still a child. But she paints such pictures. I never know quite what they are, but somehow one keeps looking at them. And she was making the illustrations for the book I wanted to write— such perfect pictures, every detail correct. She's a meticulous little creature, infinitely patient, very delicate."

She smiled, thinking of that tender, younger sister.

"She had better stay where she is," Madame Liang said.

"I don't know whether she will stay alone in America if Mercy comes here," Grace replied.

"And why, pray"—Madame Liang's voice was an urgent whisper—"why did you come when I bade you to stay?"

Grace stared at her mother's suddenly tense face. "Did you bid me stay?"

"I wrote a secret letter, to be sent from Hong Kong, hidden in a silk gown. I said 'go into hiding—anything but stay where you are.'"

"But I got no such letter, M-ma!"

"No silk gown?"

"No, nothing! Only the—invitation."

She saw terror in her mother's eyes. "Perhaps it was sent too late, M-ma. It will then merely be returned."

"It was not sent too late. If you received my last letter—"

"A week before I left, and since it said nothing against my return—"

"But I counted on your having had the secret letter! I thought you would understand—"

"Understand what, my mother?"

"Nothing—and everything," Madame Liang replied, and the look of fear crept over her face like the shadow of a cloud.

Sometime in the night Grace heard a stealthy step in her room. Or was it imagination? Her ear, oversensitive from the many months in the jungle, caught the sound of a creeping footstep, a breath, a stir no greater than the flutter of a leaf in an autumn forest. She reached for the flashlight on the bedside table.

"Always keep a flashlight near your hand," her mother had said when they parted for the night.

"Who is there?" she cried.

She heard a slight cough and then Chou Ma's voice.

"I came to see if your mosquito net was fastened."

The flashlight sent a beam upon her round face, smiling but abashed. Grace felt a tremor of alarm.

"Trust no one," her mother had said.

"It is fastened," she replied. "I have not forgotten the mosquitoes of my childhood."

But Chou Ma was in no haste to leave. She came near to the bed and lit the candle on the small blackwood table.

"Eldest Sister," she whispered. "Has your honored mother told you?"

"Told me what?" Grace asked. Unconsciously her voice, too, was a whisper.

"Of my troubles," Chou Ma said.

Grace sat up and smoothed back her short hair. "We had many matters of which to speak."

"I will tell you," Chou Ma said. She sat on the carpeted floor, her legs crossed like a Buddha, and as a preliminary she wiped her eyes with the edge of one sleeve and the other before she proceeded. "Doubtless your honored mother did not wish to disturb you with sadness upon your homecoming," she began. "And I must not keep you from sleep."

"I am awake," Grace said. "If you do not tell me, I shall be sleepless with curiosity."

88

Chou Ma rocked back and forth in a moment's silence, her face dark with woe.

"I had a son," she said, and closed her eyes, remembering. "He lived in the village of our ancestors. It is a small village but we had two acres of good land and we could eat. Had it not been for my duty to my mistress, your mother, I would have lived there with my son, his wife, and my two grandsons. Yet from what sorrow I was saved! For when They persuaded my son to join the commune—why do I say persuade? When do They ever use persuasion? They came down on our village like locusts on our fields in a bad year. They would not go away. They argued with my son's wife, a good woman but without words to answer them. When they talked of their new doctrines she heard only that every day in the commune free food would be given them, food which she need not even put out her hand to cook. The fields, too, They would tend.

" 'Will I still be hitched to the plow?' This she asked in silly child-fashion.

" 'Never,' They promised.

"So she persuaded my son, as a wife will. She told Their promises, she sighed and she moaned until at last he yielded and gave himself and his wife and children, his land and ox to the commune . . . Do you know, lady, what is a commune? It is something new."

"I have heard," Grace said.

"You cannot know all of what it is," Chou Ma replied, and she began a low moaning. "Ah me, ah me, how can I tell you?" She wiped her eyes again.

"What my silly daughter-in-law did not know was that in the commune husband and wife are kept apart. Once in

89

fourteen days they may come together. Then in a small room, with only a bed, they—"

Chou Ma coughed decently behind her hand and paused.

"I understand," Grace said. "Tell on, good mother."

"One narrow bed," Chou Ma repeated, her eyes now fixed earnestly upon the young face on the silken pillow. "And not so much as a door to the small room but instead a hanging curtain of blue cotton, swaying in the wind, and there, outside, a female comrade seated on a stool by a square table, she with paper and pencil, marking off what pair to what room, and shouting that each pair could be together but one half hour, when they must part to make room for another pair. Yet there is worse to tell."

Chou Ma let her voice fall.

"Tell on," Grace said. Was this not the voice of the people, those people who are three-fourths of the nation, whom They had come to save from tyranny?

Chou Ma glanced at the closed door, leaned forward and said in a whisper, "On the wooden wall of each room there hangs a big picture of Chairman Mao, two feet square, and so taken that his great eyes seem to move and see all that husband and wife do. Yes, my son told me. 'M-ma,' he told me, 'how could I so much as touch my wife's hand when he watched me with such eyes?' "

Grace could not laugh and yet was seized by the desire to laugh aloud.

"Of course he could not," she said.

"And so," Chou Ma went on, her voice a hoarse whisper, "and so all his desire festered in him. He felt himself grow quarrelsome and restless, and though each fourteen days he met his wife for the half hour, each time he could not take her, until at last he said to her, but softly, for the female could hear, 'Let us return to our village, let us go back to our own home.' But she said, 'I like working with the women, for as we hoe and plant we talk, and I am not lonely, and our sons are learning to read.' So quarrelsome did my son now become that at last she said it would be better if she asked to be sent to another commune and he could find another woman. At this my son would have beaten her, but he dared not with those eyes on the wall and the female comrade outside. Instead he thought quickly of what he could do. 'I will get a small boat,' he told his woman. 'We will cross the river into foreign country. To-morrow at midnight meet me by the big willow tree by the river. Bring our sons with you. We will go together, and across the river I will find work.' "

"A clever plan," Grace said, observing that Chou Ma expected a reply.

"A clever plan," Chou Ma agreed, "but hear what happened. Those two, my grandsons, had come by now to believe all they were taught in school. When their mother led them in the night to the willow tree, having told them before what their father planned, the elder of the two, and he but seven years old, cried out loudly when he saw his father, 'Here is the traitor!' At this, comrades swarmed out from the bamboos and they seized my poor son, my only son, and they tied him with ropes and carried him away, to what end I do not know. I have no letter, but he cannot write, nor can I read, alas!"

"What of the boy, your grandson?" Grace asked, her heart wracked with pity.

"Oh, him they made into a big hero," Chou Ma said. "He who betrayed his own father!"

"And the wife?"

"She is still in the commune, but grieving. A good soul but stupid—and now perhaps a widow!"

Chou Ma sighed and wept silently for a space of time. Then she got to her feet, felt of the mosquito net and made apology.

"I have kept you from your sleep."

"I am glad you told me this tale, sad though it is," Grace replied. "I will remember it when others praise too much."

To this Chou Ma made no answer, but only stole away on silent feet.

"Mother," Grace said the next morning at breakfast. "Chou Ma told me her story last night. Can it be true?"

Madame Liang glanced over her shoulder at the door. It was closed, and she proceeded. "As she tells it, it is true for her. Another person could tell it differently. We have each been given two eyes; one eye sees to the right, the other to the left."

"Together we see the object as it is," her daughter suggested.

"Exactly," Madame Liang said. "Therefore you must hear the other side of it. Chou Ma's son was unwilling to join the new commune. He wished to remain an individual. But at this time it is not important to be an individual. It may even be impossible, or wrong."

Grace looked at her mother.

"That doesn't sound like you."

They were still using English, agreeing in mutual knowledge, unspoken, that this was wise, at least for a few days, Madame Liang told herself, at least until someone could be found who knew English, and would be recommended to her as a new waiter for the restaurant, or a helper in the kitchens, and whom she must accept.

"Since I decided to remain in my own country," she replied, "I try to be an acceptable citizen."

"Are you sorry for your decision, Mother?"

"Once I decide, I never waste time being sorry."

Madame Liang pressed her lips together, lips still fresh and delicately shaped. "No," she continued firmly, "I am not sorry. I love my country, whatever it is. I have a duty to my country, whatever it is. Moreover, I am old enough to know that all things pass. It is a matter of outliving what one does not like—that is, if one cannot change it."

"Do you dislike something, Mother?"

Their eyes met over the table, set with the lacquered dishes, the ivory chopsticks, the single yellow rose in a black onyx vase. Madame Liang did not reply at once. Then she shrugged her graceful shoulders.

"Whether I like or dislike counts for nothing. I am where I want to be. If something is to be suffered, I suffer it. This I can do because I am here where I belong. I don't wish to escape anything which my country cannot escape. Long ago, when I was a young revolutionist, I learned the true love of country."

Grace lifted her eyebrows. "A patriot—and you make me feel guilty!"

"You may not," her mother said quickly. "I sent you three abroad with a purpose. I saw our doors closing to the outer world. I saw the old haughty pride of my people reviving and I sent you out, knowing that when you returned you would bring the life of the world with you. Into this stale atmosphere you will bring freshness, a different point of view, a new spirit."

Grace leaned toward her mother. "Do you mean that what is here now is not new?"

Madame Liang's voice was low, her words a murmur upon her lips. "Nothing new—nothing new! How can there come anything new from an ancient soul?"

"Meaning?"

"Meaning that we have returned to our ancient pride and isolation. We are still the proudest people on earth, we Chinese."

"We've had much to be proud of—"

"Granted, but all in the past. For centuries our pride closed the doors against what other people were doing. We were superior in reality for many centuries, but blind with pride, we refused to see that other people were changing, growing and finally outgrowing us. That is why I joined the revolution—to make our people see."

"And they would not?"

Madame Liang made a small wry smile, entirely mirthless. "It was we who were wrong. We led them by destruction, not by building upon what we already had. We did not understand history—not even our own. We thought what we had was altogether evil. An old outworn government, that is what we thought we had. So we destroyed it; we destroyed the achievement of thousands of years. We thought what the West had was all good, and what we had was all useless. We did not understand that there are times in the history of any country when the government is weak and evil because the rulers are weak and evil, as they always become if the dynasty lasts too long. We did not understand that we had been born into such a period in our own country, when the end of the Tsing dynasty was near. We should have seized the government, not to destroy its very structure, as we did, but to change the rulers. We should have seized the throne to maintain it and make it at its best again, not to bring an end to it, so that for ten miserable years the people were in chaos, without rulers. And what did we know, we who were only children in wisdom, what did we know of how to make a new kind of government? No, we wanted to be rid of all that we had hated, our old relatives and their rule over us, our old magistrates and viceroys, our old empress and her corrupt eunuchs. We said—and we believed—that what we did was for the people, but it was for ourselves. We vented our own private hatreds, thinking they were the hatreds of all the people. Our people—"

She broke off and wiped the corner of each eye with her silk handkerchief fastened in the button of her black satin robe. "My people—how can they ever forgive me? When I knew how wrong I was, when I saw These, the ones who came rushing into the emptiness the revolutionists created —which I created because I was one of them—I knew I could never leave my country. What my people suffer, that I will suffer. If I continue to live while they die, it is only because I still hope and I want them to share my hope."

She fell silent, her lovely face suddenly aged.

"Then you didn't send us abroad to escape?" Grace said.

"No," her mother replied. "I sent you abroad to learn and to be strong. As for Chou Ma, and her story—yes, it is true. It is true as she sees it, but it is also true as others see it. The more our people suffer, the sooner they will learn what they do not want."

"Do they know what they want, Mother?"

"They will learn what they want first by learning what they do not want. We tried our way and it failed. Now These are trying another way. But is it the Eternal Way of which Lao Tzu spoke? It is a way, but is it the Eternal Way? That is what our people must discover for themselves."

"And you will not help them?"

"How can I help them when in my way I was wrong, too? I can only suffer with them."

Grace glanced about the richly furnished room. "Is this suffering?"

"It may bring the keenest suffering I can know," Madame Liang said. "Those who have never known beauty cannot suffer when they lack it. But I love beauty; it is the only private love I have. If, having had beauty, I lose it, as any day I may, then that is the sharpest suffering I can know."

Grace said no more. She knew well that every detail of her mother's life was performed in beauty. She could not imagine her mother living in poverty and ugliness. Thrust into such circumstance she would die. Knowing herself, her mother had been clever enough to make its maintenance possible by feeding the gourmet tastes of her powerful clients. She held them, if not by their hearts, then by their stomachs, and she was cynical enough, in her elegant fashion, to believe that hers was the sounder method. A man easily lost his taste for one woman or another, but he never lost his taste for a favorite food.

Chou Ma appeared at the door. "T'ai-t'ai, the Minister Chao is here."

She made the announcement in a loud voice, conveying that he was, in fact, immediately behind her in the hall.

Madame Liang rose. "Ask him into the drawing room," she told Chou Ma. Then she turned to her daughter. "Will you excuse us?"

"Of course, Mother," Grace said, and she left the room by a side door, which opened upon a veranda and a garden.

The minister rose as Madame Liang entered. She acknowledged his presence by a slight bow, and seating herself, she waited for him to begin. Long ago she had learned not to begin a conversation with an official. She had almost learned to think of this man only as an official, except that a memory now flashed into her mind, a moment on a sunlit day in Peking, when she was on her way to a class at the university, the moment when she first saw him and had recognized him in the strength and health of his youth as the handsomest man she had ever seen. Youth had passed and he was still handsome, still that man.

"Forgive me for coming too early," he began.

"You are not well," she said softly.

He smiled. "Do I so betray myself? But, no, I am not well."

"What is your illness?"

"Nothing—and everything. I have the burdens of Sisyphus."

"Sisyphus?"

He laughed. "You don't know him? It doesn't matter. He was merely an overburdened man."

"It is true you have many burdens," she agreed.

He drew down his heavy black brows and began abruptly to speak in French. "You have not forgotten your French, Madame? We studied it together, remember? Under Monsieur Paul Joriot, remember? In Paris."

"I forget nothing," she replied in the same language.

He continued. "The windows of our classroom looked out upon green lawns and a great old willow tree. There was a pond, also, was there not?"

"The goldfish were fat," she replied. "There was one which looked like our professor, with small whiskers sprouting from its snout."

"Ah, you do remember! Then I proceed. It is to say that your daughter must be warned."

"Of what?"

"Why do you ask me? You know very well."

"You prefer not to put the matter into words?"

"Naturally. How do I know which wall or door or even keyhole understands French?"

"You are reckless enough to protect her? Then tell me what I am to tell her."

He hesitated, glanced about the room and began to speak rapidly under his breath and still in French.

"At least warn her that she must listen—for a long time she must only listen. She has been in America for many years and she has learned to say what she thinks. I am not saying that she cannot do so here, but let her listen first to those about her. Then when she speaks she will know what to say and how to say it. There are certain passwords, shall we say? If they are spoken she will be safe. If she does not speak them, she will be judged. She is too valuable to lose through—a mistake. Help her not to make a mistake."

He spoke very rapidly and with a purpose, and she listened closely, fearful of losing a word.

"I understand," she said.

They looked at one another, each remembering. On a certain day long ago, when they had become friends, he had asked her to marry him, a daring request as they both knew, for he had been betrothed in childhood to the daughter of a family friend. Yet she might have married him in those dreamlike days in Paris had not Cheng appeared a few months before. Yes, she remembered very well when this man had asked her to marry him and how she had been drawn to him, though she knew that he came too late. He had held in his hand that day a magazine, an anarchist journal, as she saw. She had rejected him, and he left Paris abruptly to study in Japan, from where he returned when she was already in Peking, teaching in the university. When they met again, she had asked him many questions about those people of the Eastern Seas, who were already a threat. Had they not been given, after the world war, the German holdings in China? Upon Chinese soil they had set their feet, and her first cause for bitterness toward Americans had been that they had not spoken at the peace conference against giving Chinese land to Japanese imperialists.

Yes, she had rejected him—and yet she had liked it that he did not touch her hand, even when he asked her to marry him; nor her shoulder, they standing side by side under a chestnut tree, that day in a street in Paris, and he might easily have put out his hand and moved more closely to her.

She had been half sorry for a moment that she must refuse because of Cheng.

"You are my best friend," she had said, "but—"

There she had stopped, and looking at him, she had shaken her head. For a long moment they faced each other; then he had bowed his head and left her. When he returned to China two years after her own return, she was married to Cheng, and though in these latter years they met often, yet until now he had never spoken of that day in Paris. The memory of the past seemed for the moment a bridge between them, a bridge of cobwebs, yet indestructible. For she, a woman, had never forgotten that the man had loved her. Nor could she deny that he still attracted her, he with his energy, his sharp analytical mind, his grace of manner. Yet how implacable he was, how dangerous when he discovered a traitor! What of one surnamed Kao, who had decided to leave Them and had gone to the police in Hankow to give his secret information? While he was gone, this man who sat now in her presence, toward whom her heart could still soften, had himself led a band of his fellows and they had gone to the traitor's house and had killed every member they found there, strangling even servants and infant children. Must she, as warning, draw this tale out of the past and tell it to her daughter?

He rose. "We understand each other, you and I—we always have, I think. It is my concern that she is your daughter and I would not have you grieve or live in anxiety. Prepare her, comrade."

Here he paused and his black gaze penetrated her own eyes. "Am I still your best friend?" he demanded. So he, too, could not forget! And what could she say? She dared not have such a friend today and yet he must not be her enemy.

"Why should you not be such a friend?" she asked.

With this they parted.

That night, therefore, her last before her daughter must set forth upon her journey to Peking, Madame Liang prepared her daughter as she had been warned to do. She had chosen her private sitting room for this ordeal, the doors locked and Chou Ma outside on guard. Far in the distance she could hear the sounds of the restaurant—music, voices, the clatter of dishes. It was the hour when the dining rooms were busy with guests. She had led her daughter to the door and allowed her to see the crowded place.

"It is exactly as it used to be," Grace had whispered, amazed.

"It is not at all as it used to be," Madame Liang had retorted.

Now, enclosed in the room upstairs, where their own dinner had been served, eaten and the table removed, now behind locked doors, she began to prepare her daughter.

"You must be ready to accept change," she began, "and you will be able to do so if you remember there is no change."

Grace laughed. "M-ma, don't be cryptic!"

"I mean exactly what I say," Madame Liang replied. She lay outstretched upon a couch, her negligee of pale pink satin, and she wore high-heeled satin shoes of the same color. No one ever saw her feet except Chou Ma. Long ago, when she was five years old, her mother had bound her feet. In her father's absence at the imperial court, her mother had wound bands of strong white cotton about her tender feet, tightening them each day until she, the little child, had wept constantly with pain. Months passed; she ceased to run about; she grew thin and waxen pale, and then one day her father came home.

"Where is she?" he had shouted. "Where is my little one?"

He had searched for her and found her sitting on her bed, stroking her wounded feet to ease the pain. What anger then! What shouts and bellowings, what imprecations and fury! He had torn away the bandages himself, had wept when he saw the small mangled feet, and then carrying her in his arms, he had burst into her mother's rooms.

"Did I not tell you to leave this child's feet as they were?"

Her mother, terrified, had coaxed and begged. "But consider, my children's father, who will marry a girl with big feet? Who but some farmer's family will want her? I do it for the child's sake, for her future happiness."

This her father had utterly refused. "You who cannot, will not, see what is before your face! Our country is changing, I tell you! Even I have changed. I wish your feet were not tortured stumps! Look at yourself and see what I will not have my daughter become!"

Cruel words, for her mother had been proud of her own tiny feet, measuring no more than three inches from toes crowded against heel, and drawing her kerchief from her sleeve, she wiped tears from her eyes. But for her, the child, her father's words brought only joy, for she was freed. True, months had passed before she could run, and never again were her feet beautiful except as they were useful. Useful they had been in the days of revolution when she and Cheng, two among many, had been compelled to flee one city for another. To comfort herself now for her crooked feet she wore shoes always exquisite.

"I must speak with you of many matters," she went on.

"About what, dear Mother?" her daughter asked.

"To prepare you for this change that is no change," Madame Liang said.

"Yes, Mother?"

"It is change because there are many changes. You will be shocked by the changes. And you will be rebellious; you will be angry; you will be frightened, unless you remember, steadfastly, that there is no change."

"Teach me, Mother," Grace said.

She listened, then, while her mother spoke at length. "The change is this, my child. Those who were below are now above. We are a nation of peasants. Eighty-five out of one hundred of our people are peasants. True, it is the fifteen percent who carry on the nation's business and contain the ruling two percent, but these no longer rule. The Chairman has released the dragon of the peasant youth. Those who controlled them are no more—the landlords, the gentry, the literate; people such as you and I sprang from, are gone. Ah, what a dragon the Chairman has released! What cunning, what knowledge, what understanding of his own people! Alone he could never have risen to power. But he is the son of country gentry, those who are called peasants by the literate and landlords by the illiterate, a between-man, one belonging to neither side and to both. With cunning he has used the peasants to send him high. But he rides the dragon, my child—remember that! He rides the dragon, and someday the dragon will rid itself of the burden!"

"Then what will happen?" Grace asked.

"Who knows what a dragon will do when there is no one to ride him?" Madame Liang replied.

Far into the night these two, mother and daughter, sat in deep talk, the one questioning, the other replying, and Madame Liang unrolled for her daughter the scrolls of history.

"You remember the brooks that flow down the mountains of Lu?" she asked, as she reached for a cigarette from the silver box at her side.

"M-ma," her daughter inquired as she held the lighter for her mother, "tell me how it is that you smoke American cigarettes."

"I prefer them," Madame Liang replied.

"Are they not forbidden?"

"There is always a way to get what one wants," Madame Liang said and proceeded with her thoughts. "Those brooks, you remember, my child, flow together at the foot of the mountain range, and rushing across the plains, they join the Yangtse river. At the point of confluence they create a turmoil which terrifies me however often I see it. Even a large ship is shaken by those waters. Yet if it is well managed, the ship survives the turmoil and proceeds on its way. So it is with our country at this hour." She paused, and after a time began again.

"Turmoil," she murmured. "Turmoil and trouble, and yet I survive, because I know that there is no change beneath the turmoil. Under it all, our people remain what they have always been, the sons of Han, the superior people. Yes, though it is forbidden to speak the name of the great Confucius, I read his words in secret. I feed my spirit upon the ancient wisdom."

Her daughter had listened to all this with silence and with full attention. Now she spoke.

"Mother, how can you remain silent, how can you live as though you approve?"

For reply Madame Liang rose and opened a locked chest and drew from its recesses a book wrapped in a red silk cover, and she read:

"The superior person acts in accordance with the character that has become perfected in him. His is a way of life that can submit to scrutiny on any day. Being hidden means that he is still in concealment and not given recognition, that if he should act he would not yet accomplish anything. In this case the superior person does not act."

And turning the pages, she read again:

"The superior person is inexhaustible in his will to teach, and without limits in his toleration and protection of the people."

She closed the book, wrapped it in the red silk cover and locked it again in the chest.

"You will stay here until you find a place to live which pleases you more. On the other hand, if this room pleases you, then live here as long as you like," her new guide said.

Grace looked about the room. It was large and carpeted in a dull blue. A double bed, a Chinese desk and chair, two easy chairs, cushioned in dark blue satin, provided furniture.

"This looks very comfortable," she said. "Perhaps later I would like a small house of my own, in one of the *hutungs* in Peking—those charming alleys—"

Her guide smiled widely, showing three gold teeth among his others. "Here is your bath." He opened a door with a flourish. "In winter steam heat is provided. Now, since it is only late summer heat is not necessary."

"Very nice," she said, smiling.

"We wish you to be comfortable," the man said. He was young and confident, yet there was about him an air, too, of anxiety, as though he doubted himself.

She went to the wide window and put aside the curtain. It was evening and the lights were coming on. Even as she watched, she saw them appear, glittering here, there and everywhere, the larger buildings outlined with lights until the city lay before her in a glowing map.

"What is that high building?" she asked.

Her guide, standing at her shoulder, replied with a question.

"Do you mean the Ch'ien Men Tower or the Great Hall of the People?"

"I recognize the gate tower," she replied, "but when I was here last there was no Great Hall."

"Ah, you will see much that is new here," the guide said.

"Much that is old, too, I hope," she replied. She turned away and let the curtain fall.

"What is good is still here," he told her, "and now I will leave you. You are to report at the Medical Institute at ten o'clock tomorrow morning."

He felt the pockets of his blue cotton uniform. "I have the address. Ha—it is here. I have too many pockets."

He gave her a slip of paper, upon it an address.

She had chosen to come by train the better to see the people and the countryside, as she had explained to her escort, this young man in blue uniform, his round head cropped, speaking in Chinese as she did so, since he spoke no other language.

"I have been away for many years and now I am come home. But there have been many changes."

"Many," he had agreed. "All is made new. The imperialists are driven away. In what country were you, comrade?"

"In America," she had told him.

"Ah, a bad country, an evil people," he had said promptly.

She was firm. "I did not find it so, and to me the people were kind."

"Ah, you were brainwashed," he said with a superior air. "Here you will learn the truth."

Indeed it had seemed strange to see no Americans on the train. True, there were few Westerners of any kind—a French journalist, young, his narrow face too eager, and speaking no Chinese, he was fluent with his thin, expressive hands; and a sturdy blond Swedish businessman who did speak an illiterate Mandarin. Beyond brief looks, however, these had not interested her. Instead she had examined the Chinese passengers. There were few of them, too, several businessmen in Chinese garments; a half dozen young men in Western suits, chattering in French and Russian; a college professor, spectacled and aloof; and a group of girls, going perhaps to college in Peking. Among them she felt alien and not inclined to conversation. They had cast glances at her in her Western suit. She must, she thought, get into different garb. But what were women wearing nowadays beyond the drab uniform? Purposely she had waited to find out before she bought clothes.

The train itself, however, had been cause for pride. It was clean and kept clean, for between every station the floors were swept, the plush-cushioned seats brushed. At either end of the aisles pots of hardy ferns gave a garden air, and the polished tables shone. From the windows she could see the autumn countryside, the fields ploughed for the sowing of winter wheat. Those fields, once small, had been thrown together into large areas of production, and that was new. But willows still bent their drooping boughs over the roofs of villages, and fishnets hung over ponds. When the train stopped vendors clustered about the exits and cried their delicacies as they had used to do. Ah, well, she thought, as she looked now from a window of her room, in any event she would not be living here for long. A few weeks, she had been warned, must be spent in reorientation, this China being new, she was told, and totally different from the one she had known. Then, so she dreamed, gazing out over those unchanging palaces, looking, she imagined, slightly self-conscious under the refurbishing that had been given them in recent years, she would find somewhere among the low, tiled roofs of the ancient city a small old house, walled behind a gate and a spirit wall, a house with a flagged courtyard and a lily pond. There she would live, rooted in the past, to which she would return at night after her day in her laboratory. For her one condition had been that she be allowed her own laboratory—

"Comrade," her escort said, "where shall I put your bags?"

She turned, having forgotten him. "Leave them, please. I will unpack them."

She opened her purse, but the man frowned and put up a protesting hand.

"It is not our custom now," he declared and marched out of the room, closing the door behind him.

Late that evening, after her dinner in a bare, clean dining room on the first floor, after her unpacking was done, she sat down at the desk in her room to write the first of the letters she had promised in America to send to her research associate as soon as she had reached Peking. The desk faced the window and instinctively she began to write.

"Clem: I see no compromise. Outside my window here in Peking the Past stands as solidly existing as though it were not history. The great square of what was once the Forbidden City, where emperors lived with their imperial households, is exactly as it was, but restored to primitive form and color. When I was here before as a small girl, clinging to my mother's hand, these buildings were showing the doom of coming ruin. The painted eaves were crumbling, dust lay upon the marble approaches, and dead leaves were not swept away. The guards themselves were corrupt, for their duty was to keep passersby from stealing the yellow porcelain tiles from the palace roofs. In secret, however, they sold these very tiles for a dollar apiece. I remember because my mother indignantly refused the offer from a slouching guide and gave him a lecture that all but skinned him alive. Now no one could steal a tile and not be arrested. But no one would steal, I think.

"Does this pride in the past mean that the rest of the city is built in imitation? Judging from what I have seen,

I should say that while my people are proud of the past—we really were rather glorious, Clem—we take an equal pride in being completely modern. Tall buildings spring up here and there even in Peking—I shall have to learn their names—and the interesting fact is that they don't contradict the old buildings. I think this is because the ancient architecture has clean lines and noble size. . . ."

Here she paused. Could she describe her brief visit to her mother? There was no reason why she should not, no spoken reason, that is, and no secret direction. Yet somehow she hesitated. She was still new to her country. In the old days she had felt safe. But these were new days, and new men and women were here, stirred up from the depths by revolution. She drew her brows together and wrote.

"My mother makes me think of both past and present. In her own being she is herself; she belongs to the past, yet she is living in the present, accepting the new with faith because the past has been so worthy of faith."

And then, in sudden change of mood, she changed the scene in her mind. "At this hour, Clem, you are beginning another day, a day different from mine. I see you in the laboratory, working with microscope and notebooks. I wish I could have stayed to go to India with you, especially to St. Xavier's College in Bombay. Sixty-four plants out of a hundred and sixty-five deserving further study—it is a life's work in itself. What about the extract of mandrake poison? Can the report be authenticated that given to women they produce only male children? What would be useful to me here, however, would be your findings on the substance derived from seeds of the soapberry family. Is it or is it not true that taken orally it is sure control over fertility? Tell me everything, Clem! I love it here, but I'll be lonely—sometimes."

She slipped the sheets into an envelope, vaguely troubled. Why was she reluctant to tell Clem more of her mother— Clem, who had been her superior in the Institute but her closest friend? A barrier rose between them now, as faint as a mist, but it had not been between them when she was in America. Here in China she felt it, and pondering upon it, she perceived that it was a barrier of pride as a Chinese. She was too proud as a Chinese to tell even Clem that after her visit to her mother she was afraid, and, moreover, she did not know why she was afraid.

When I get to work, she thought, this strange mixture of past and present will clarify itself through action. The daily necessity of activity will drive away vague fears. Upon decision, she prepared herself resolutely for sleep and tomorrow, and was somehow heartened to discover that the water ran hot into the tub, a porcelain tub of a vintage only a decade or so older than the one she had used in America and that the electricity, after a half minute of wavering, settled into serviceable light. Perhaps life in this new old country of hers would prove pleasant, after all, or at least comfortable enough to allay fear.

Madame Liang woke with a sense of oppression. She was accustomed to such awakening and she lay quietly for a space of time, considering the mood, for she thought of it as a mood, lacking better description, and yet it came, she believed, from outside herself—unless perhaps it was natural as she grew older? Was it, or could it be, merely the preparation in a human frame of that day when it would cease to be more than a helpless body? In fact, there seemed to be no reason for the darkness of her spirit, and in patience she lay motionless, her eyes closed, while she inquired of herself the reason for her fear. Slowly her intuitions gathered into focus, and the center of this focus she now perceived was her daughter Endien, or Grace. She decided in this instant to use the Chinese name she had chosen when the child was laid in her arms an hour after birth.

"A girl," the midwife had sighed.

"I am glad," the mother replied. "It is good luck to begin a family with a daughter."

She had not regretted the births even of two more daughters, nor that she had borne no sons. A woman could evade the dangers of these times, if indeed there were dangers, but a son, had she a son, would be compelled to leadership—or exile. She considered the son who had never been born and then put him aside. No, it was better without him. Why then was she troubled with vague fears about her daughter? Had she failed to prepare her—but for what? She could not have put into words, even for her daughter, the way of life that now was hers, the security in which she lived that was perilously insecure, the safe routine of her days which at any moment, were she to take a false step or speak an unwise word, would cast her into an abyss of danger. She had refrained from explicit description of her situation because it was not to be described.

In such hours as these Madame Liang had one recourse, to which she now resorted. She rose from her bed and went to her locked chest, and from under a pile of embroidered satin robes, which once had been her daily garb, she drew forth *The Book of Changes*. As her American friend Mrs.

Brandon had been wont to revere the sacred book of the Christians, Madame Liang revered this book, a presently forbidden work of the great and wise Confucius, who himself was now an outcast in the new society. Forbidden though he now was, and even ridiculed, she did not doubt that one day he would be recalled by a wiser generation and order restored to the nation. Meanwhile, she consulted his *Book of Changes* and ordered her own life by its principles.

Thus she opened the pages, her eyes shut, and placed her forefinger on certain lines. Opening her eyes, she read these words:

> Forward and backward, abyss on abyss.
> In danger like this, pause at first and wait.
> Otherwise you will fall into a pit in the abyss.
> Do not act.

Do not act—it was the answer. The hexagram in which this answer was contained was twenty-nine, K'an, The Abysmal . . . She closed the book and returned to sleep.

"*Huang ch'ang-shen*," the old doctor intoned in the precise, beautiful Chinese of Peking, "is one of two cures for malaria. The infusion must be prepared from the root of the herb. It is an ancient and trustworthy cure."

Grace opened her medical dictionary and found the English translation—*Diochroa Febrifuyl.*

She knew the herb.

"Second," the old gentleman went on, "is *ma p'ien ts'ao.*"

Ah, yes, this she knew, the European verbena.

"Is it not also used as a vermifuge?" she inquired.

The old doctor looked surprised. His long fingernails, she noticed, were very dirty. "How do you know this?" he asked.

"I have heard of it," she replied.

She had already learned that it was a waste of time to try to convince a Chinese doctor of the old school that Western medicine was of any value. The old doctor scratched his sparsely bearded chin and proceeded.

"The name of the disease differs in various parts of our country. It is called 'coldness entering the body,' 'the chill disease,' 'the shivers,' 'catching small chickens,' 'disease of the five devils,' 'the true illness,' 'the venerable old gentleman,' 'the daily disease,' 'once-in-three days,' 'the fluctuating days,' 'the forever recurring,' 'heat enters body,' 'guilt over skin,' 'tingling in fingertips,' 'devil's disease,' 'fever-chill,' 'irresistible disease,' 'dumpling in belly,' 'three-day disease,' 'hundred-day disease,' 'three fevers in two days.' "

She listened, marveling at the discernment in each name for the complex illness of malaria, the varying time schedule of chill and fever, the short space and the long, even the swollen spleen in the last stages, which could be described as "dumpling."

"The cause of the disease," the old doctor was saying, "is well known to be eels. Eels should be destroyed in epidemics of the disease."

He scratched his head with the long black nail on his right little finger and stared at it. "Lice again," he muttered and sighed.

Eels? She was stunned by the accuracies and inaccuracies of the materia medica of her country. Eels live in muddy areas of earth and water, and there, too, the Anopheles mosquito hatches its eggs.

The old doctor suddenly became animated. He leaned forward and shook his long forefinger in her face.

"And do not trust foreign medicine for this disease," he said, emphasizing his words by shakes of the finger. "Too much of the foreign bitter powder causes heavy fever of another disease."

She was surprised again. Blackwater fever was indeed the result of too much quinine. How was she to combine these medical truths and falsehoods into some sort of relation to the science of the West? Her thought was disturbed by a loud yawn from the old doctor, and his breath blew a foul gust to her nostrils.

"Enough for this day," he declared, and gathering his gray robes, he bowed and left her.

It was indeed the end of a day, her first day in the laboratory that had been set aside for her in the great modern hospital that years ago had been built as the gift of wealthy Americans. It was maintained, as she saw at once, with scrupulous attention to modern Western medical practice. Doctors and interns and nurses moved briskly about their business, clad in spotless white uniforms. Yet the old physicians in their long robes were treated with deference as they came and went from the building that was set aside for their use. The most eminent physicians had been invited here to the capital from all over China.

"Your task," she had been told, "is to provide a synthesis of the two schools of medicine. There is truth and falsehood in each. In the past we trusted entirely to our own. Then we discarded our own and trusted entirely to the

Western school. Both were mistakes. You have a great responsibility placed upon you by the Chairman himself. He is watching you."

These words had been spoken by a young man in the uniform of the Party, a handsome man, she observed, tall, as the men of the north usually were. He had introduced himself on the morning after her arrival.

"I am Liu Peng," he told her. "Also a doctor—a surgeon. You will get instructions from me. If you have questions, be free to ask them of me. We appreciate your return to our country."

He had then introduced her to the old doctor—"Dr. Tseng, one of our most eminent physicians of the Chinese school." Then he had gone away.

Her notebooks in order for the next day's work, she walked through the building and out into the grounds. These, too, were scrupulously maintained. Autumn was at hand and in preparation for early frost gardeners were wrapping the more delicate shrubs in coats of straw; a faint haze hung over the city, and though the air was mild, there was a hint of chill beneath. She paused beside a goldfish pool. The fish were making ready to hide in the mud, where they sheltered in winter, and in a last fever of energy were darting here and there in the late afternoon sun like flashing splinters of gold. Contentment crept through her being. Autumn was a lovely season here in the ancient city. There was no reason for fear—no, not one. She had her work to do.

"Acupuncture," Dr. Tseng announced, "may be called the science of the ducts in the human body."

He coughed raucously, and fumbling in his garments, he produced a square of tissue paper, spat into it, folded the paper carefully and threw it under the desk. An instant later, remembering certain orders to the staff, he got down on his hands and knees, found the folded paper and put it in a zinc pail which served as a wastebasket.

Grace held back laughter. In the past, which now had all the remoteness of another country, buried in history, the sight of an old and scholarly man upon his hands and knees, searching for a bit of paper, would have been impossible.

"Everything was easier in the old days," she said in pity.

To her surprise, Dr. Tseng, seating himself, looked at her in distrust, tinged with alarm. "On the contrary," he said, "everything is easier now. Everything is better under the guidance of the Chairman."

To this she did not reply. She had spoken thoughtlessly and he had reproved her. She felt a slight resentment, which she suppressed.

"Let us return to the ducts for acupuncture—meridians, we call them," she suggested.

She had recovered her fluency in Chinese as weeks passed, and Dr. Tseng knew no English. He cleared his throat, breathing with difficulty after a lifetime in Peking dust. Nevertheless he pursued his duty, which was to teach this ignorant woman. Privately he disliked the emphasis the new rulers placed upon women, but he dared not protest it, especially since the cadre in charge of his home precinct in the city had explained that there was so much work to be done to establish the new order that women could no longer enjoy the luxury of working for only one family, but must work for the nation. As a consequence he himself suffered from disorder in his house and from meals cooked in a common kitchen. Since he had a delicate stomach and was accustomed to special dishes, he suffered, but in silence, lest he be accused of complaint against the Chairman. He continued the lesson.

"There are three hundred and sixty-five points in the body where the ducts rise to the skin. Skin, ducts and inner organs are one system and therefore subject to the changes of *yang* and *yin*. The physician must learn where these points are, by the piercing of the proper needle at the proper spot. The length of time for the needle to remain inserted is also important."

"What is the purpose of the insertion?" Grace asked.

The old doctor gave her a look of reproach.

"I will explain everything in order. The purpose is to increase or decrease a fluid—not so much a fluid as a substance that is nevertheless not a substance. The needle is not to be inserted carelessly or quickly. First the pulse must be taken, the coloring noted, and all other signs observed. When the situation is clear, the diagnosis stated, the patient is asked to cough. In the same instant, while the attention of the patient is diverted for an instant, the needle is inserted. You must learn by memory how long the needle is to remain inserted—five minutes, fifteen, an hour, or even longer. The needle, too, must be carefully chosen, for there are nine different needles. On another day I will show you these needles and you will learn how to fit the needle to the disease."

He had spoken too long and was breathless again. Grace took pity on him, and opening her handbag, she produced a small bottle of an antihistamine she had brought with her from America, remembering the dust storms of Peking.

"Try this, honored doctor," she said.

He shook his head. "The two schools of medicine, old and new, may not be mixed, else the body becomes confused and *yang* and *yin* are put out of order. Two ways of life cannot be mingled."

He was sufficiently uncomfortable, however, so that he closed his ancient book. "Acupuncture," he said, "cannot be taught in a day. It is a long and complex study involving the very life of a human body. Correctly used, it brings healing. Incorrectly used, it brings death. We will continue tomorrow."

He rose and was prepared to leave when Grace thought of a certain discontent she was beginning to develop. She rose, for he was her teacher, and put a question to him.

"I have a kindness to ask of you, sir."

"Ha?" His drooping eyelids lifted.

"Could you recommend a small house to me? I dislike living in a hostel, and I would enjoy a house. I remember the *hutung* houses in Peking are very pleasant, but being a stranger, I do not know where to inquire."

He was surprised, she could see, and he considered in silence for a moment before he spoke.

"The question is, what sort of house? New or old?"

"Oh, an old one, with a courtyard and a few trees."

She spoke impulsively, remembering the charm of ancient Peking houses, hidden away among narrow streets.

"No self-coming water, no heat except the *k'ang*," he said.

"Such things I can live without," she declared.

"Very unusual," he murmured. "The young, now-adays—"

He broke off to stroke his little beard. "The house next to mine by chance is empty. The owner died last week and the family has moved to a commune outside the city. The wife wished to move long ago, a lazy soul, disliking the daily household tasks. Let us hope he died a natural death."

She made no instant decision, hesitating after his last words.

"May I come with you and see it?" she asked at last.

"I will lead the way," he told her.

Down the main street they went, she at a distance lest he be embarrassed if she seemed to be with him, past the gates of the refurbished Forbidden City, now a tourist attraction, through the narrow streets, through alleyways, until at last he paused at a gate set in a gray brick wall.

"This is my home," he told her, his voice strangled behind the large kerchief he had held over his mouth and nostrils against the dust. "Come in. I will ask my wife to lead you next door. She always knows everything about the neighborhood."

She followed him through the gate and stood waiting while he shouted. Almost immediately a spry little woman in old-fashioned blue cotton trousers and jacket ran out of the house, her hands covered with flour.

"I was just making noodles—" she began. "As a surprise—"

He stopped her, his hand raised. "Wash your hands. This is my pupil. She wishes to rent the house next door."

Mrs. Tseng heard this, opened her eyes wide and shook her head.

"But there is a fox spirit in that house!"

"What is this ancient foolishness?" Dr. Tseng demanded. "We all know the Chairman has exorcised all fox spirits."

He gave her a fierce look and went his way into the house. Mrs. Tseng wiped her hands on her apron.

"At least the rent is very little," she said, and then, in a lowered voice, "because there *is* a fox spirit!"

Grace laughed. "I am not afraid!"

"Fox spirits are very cruel, very cunning," Mrs. Tseng insisted. "They can change themselves into wicked, beautiful women."

"I am not afraid of anything," Grace said.

Madame Tseng yielded. "In such case—" and she led the way to the next house.

Two days later she left the hostel in the late afternoon and in less than an hour was in her own house, her own, that is, by way of rent. She lingered for an instant before the gate, a red gate, its double leaves hung with two heavy iron rings. Set in the surrounding wall, this gate was not different from those set in the walls of both sides of the narrow street. Yet it seemed to have a special air, nevertheless, because it was the gate of a home in her own country. The small two rooms in a New York apartment house had been a place in which to live temporarily while she was in a foreign country. Now, at this moment of lingering, she felt the deep content of every Chinese who returns to his own.

She pushed the gate open and entered. Someone had

swept the courtyard and at the entrance to the house had set two blue and white porcelain jars, each containing a dwarf pine tree. Kind Mrs. Tseng, she thought, and how like an old-fashioned Chinese woman to make the welcoming gesture! Now she stepped over the high threshold into the central room. It was furnished with old Chinese furniture of good quality, and as she visited each room she was pleased. Two elderly servants, man and wife, were waiting for her.

"At Madame Tseng's command," the man murmured, bowing. "We are surnamed Wang."

"We can do everything," the woman said in a pleading voice.

"Lao Wang and Wang Ma," Grace began, using the old honorifics suitable to their station. At once she saw she was wrong, and by the look of fear upon their faces.

"Comrades," she amended.

They smiled. The woman said coaxingly, "We also know the proper way to speak, but now everything is changed."

"It is better for the willow to bend with the wind," the old man put in.

"I must learn to bend," Grace replied.

"It is hard to remember," the old woman said.

They disappeared then, and in a few minutes through an open door, she saw them in the kitchen, busy with small bundles of straw, heating water, probably for tea. She sat down then by the table, which stood in its proper place against the inner wall, and surveyed the room. She must buy a few good scrolls for the walls, a landscape or two, or fine calligraphy, a comfortable chair—the wooden one in which she sat was beautiful to look at, but she had been spoiled by American comfort. No curtains to be put on the windows, however, and these occupied the entire front wall, for their small panes were covered with fine rice paper. Here her thoughts were interrupted by a loud knock on the gate. Lao Wang ran across the courtyard to draw back the bar. She heard a strong voice, which at once she recognized as the voice of Liu Peng.

"Is there a woman doctor here by the surname of Liang?"

"She has only just arrived, comrade," Lao Wang replied.

"I will come in," Liu Peng announced.

She saw him stride across the courtyard ahead of Lao Wang.

"Please do come in," she said and rose. "You are my first guest."

He did so without reply and seated himself opposite her.

"Why have you moved away from the hostel without permission?" he demanded without greeting.

She opened her eyes wide.

"Must I have permission to move myself?"

"Certainly," he declared. "Otherwise how would we know where to find you?"

"I continue my work, wherever I live, and you know where I am each day."

"It is our business to know where you are at all times."

"Why?"

The simplicity of the question seemed for an instant to confound him. He drew down his unusually heavy brows. She had not noticed before how black they were.

"It is required," he said brusquely.

She considered this and decided to accept it with lightness.

"Here I am! When I am not working at the medical center, I am here."

Suddenly he was cheerful. She even saw the glimmer of a smile in his eyes, unusually large and black.

"Now that I have done my duty," he said, "let us proceed to conversation. I will begin by asking if the old doctor has given you the basic philosophy of our Chinese medicine?"

She shook her head. "Only concrete illnesses and their remedies. He is teaching me now about acupuncture."

"Ah," Liu Peng said, "then I will instruct you, philosophically."

"Please teach me," she said.

It was the traditional reply of the classical pupil to a teacher, and he glanced at her suspiciously. When she met his gaze frankly he looked away and cleared his throat.

"We no longer use the ancient forms. You have been away and do not know this. Therefore I will overlook your mistake. I will proceed historically to outline the basis of Chinese medical philosophy. You understand of course that while we reject the ancient mysteries, we continue to accept them as part of dead history. Specialists such as you and I in the field of modern medicine nevertheless must know the past even though it no longer lives. Ours is a superior history, the greatest, the most ancient, on human record. Let us proceed therefore with the classical work of the great sage Lao Tzu, a man most strangely modern in that he opposed thousands of years ago the formalism of his contempory, Confucius. He, Confucius, is truly dead and with him his works. We reject him. Within his rigidity he imprisoned our people. Lao Tzu, on the contrary, set forth the flexible principles of Tao. Western scholars, contemptible in their pretentious and shallow scholarship, have translated Tao as Way. How foolish! Tao is Spirit, the Spirit that permeates all heaven and all earth, even those far beyond ours. Tao includes all that is not, and all that is; Lao Tzu describes it in these words."

Here Liu Peng paused. He cleared his throat again, brushed back his short stiff black hair, placed his hands outspread on his knees, and lifting his head, he closed his eyes and began to chant, as scholars do, the ancient poem, *Tao Tê Ching:*

> Silent, aloof, alone,
> It changes not, nor fails, but touches all.
> I do not know its name,
> One name for it is Tao.
> Pressed for designation,
> I call it—Tao.
> Tao means Outgoing,
> Outgoing, Far-reaching,
> Far-reaching, Return.*

Here Liu Peng paused and opened his eyes to stare at her as if he had asked a question.

"Beautiful," she murmured, "but I do not understand it."

"You cannot understand it," he retorted. "And why can you not understand it? Because it contains all that exists. It includes endless time and endless space. Yet in endlessness each thing exists separately and within the harmony of balance. What is this harmony? It is contained within the correspondence. What are the correspondences? They are the relationships between the five elements. What are the

* Adapted from *The Way of Life*, by Lao Tzu, translated by R. B. Blakney. Copyright 1955 by Raymond B. Blakney. Published by arrangement with The New American Library, Inc.

five elements? They are wood, fire, earth, metal, water. These create, and also destroy, each other."

He paused, his eyes inquiring again, and promptly she replied.

"Explain, please."

He proceeded. "On the side of creation, wood creates fire; fire, as ash, creates earth. In earth there is metal; metal melts to become liquid. Water creates trees, or wood. On the side of destruction, wood consumes water through trees; earth can stop water; water destroys fire; fire destroys metal; but metal in an instrument destroys wood. These are correspondences, outgoing, far-reaching; and far-reaching, they return. Within this circle of creation and destruction man must live harmoniously, with ebb and flow, in tune with all that exists. This is the fundamental philosophy of the cosmos upon which is based our Chinese medical lore."

"Difficult to define diagnosis and prescription upon this," she murmured.

"Ah, but you must consider the five planets and their separate influences," he exclaimed. He held up his right hand, a finely shaped sensitive hand, she observed, and counted off its fingers with his left hand. "Jupiter, the planet of magnanimity and gentleness; Mars, the planet of adventure and imagination; Mercury, the planet of intelligence, of risk, of withdrawal; Saturn, the planet of grace and power; Venus, the planet of sensual pleasure, of belligerence and of authority."

"Interesting," she said, "and corresponding, in some ways, to the ideas in the West of the planets but without the contradictions—sensual pleasure and war, for example."

"Not contradiction," he said, thus contradicting her.

"Love leads to war. No war is so bitter as that between persons or peoples who once loved each other. Witness ourselves and the Americans!"

She laughed, and with a triumphant smile he proceeded. "There are also other correspondences, such as those of the emotions and rules for conduct, those of colors and climate. Within the human body there are the correspondences of the viscera, the tissues, the fluids, the orifices. Beyond these are the correspondences of time and season and direction. To live in health until old age a person must be in harmony with all the changing cycles of the cosmos."

At this moment Wang Ma appeared with teapot and bowls. She addressed Liu Peng thus:

"Honorable comrade, you have talked yourself dry. Please drink tea."

He frowned at her even as he accepted the bowl. "Leave off the 'honorable'! It is forbidden according to the new regulations."

Wang Ma looked frightened. "Forgive this old stupid! I forgot."

"Then remember," he said sharply.

So sharply indeed did he speak that Grace was moved to defend the old woman. "Is it a new correspondence that she has broken, perhaps? Certainly it is not an ancient one."

He caught the sarcasm and was angry, as she could see. Under the tan skin of his cheeks a flush rose to his eyelids. "The task of teaching peasants is endless, but it must be done. Everyone, however ignorant, must learn the New Way."

"But is it the Eternal Way?" she inquired slyly.

The question was so impudent, so mischievous, that for a while he did not deign to answer. He set the bowl upon a small two-tiered table at his side and sat frowning and dark in thought. Suddenly he rose and looked her straight in the eyes.

"All I have told you is nonsense," he said harshly, and without further word or gesture he stalked out of the room and across the courtyard. At the gate Lao Wang stood bowing, but Liu Peng looked beyond and went out, and Lao Wang barred the gate behind him.

In the room he had just left Wang Ma was muttering to herself as she collected teapot and bowls. The small coil of gray hair on the back of her head had loosened and a thin tail hung on her neck.

"What are you saying, good soul?" Grace asked, amused. She turned from the open door at which she had stood to watch Liu Peng depart.

Wang Ma, arranging the dishes on the tray, looked up at her mistress, standing straight and tall in the golden haze of evening light.

"I am saying, Elder Sister, that I know we are forbidden to call anyone Honorable nowadays. Yet what will happen to us, who are the old hundred names, if we have no one to look up to as Honorables? Alas, today where are the Honorables? They are forbidden spirits. No head stands higher now than any other. Life is tasteless; we are all alike. Where are the ones whom Heaven ordains to lead, so that we know whom to follow? Ai-ya, bitterness! When I consider how my old master and mistress died! They were Honorables in this house—"

The old woman set the tray on a table, and lifting the corners of her blue cotton jacket, she wiped one eye and the other.

"How did they die?" Grace asked.

The old woman drew near, and looking left and right, she spoke in a loud whisper.

"This was their house. Besides house, they owned land outside the city—not much land but enough to grow our own wheat for bread. It was the land that undid my old master. He was called a landowner. The people he paid to till the land seized the chance of the New Way and spoke against him to get the land. The young men who work for the comrades shot him in this very room. He sat at that table eating a roll of bread wrapped around a stick of garlic. He ate such food at night and drank a bowl of tea. He knew an old rhyme and he said it many times:

> Eat the first meal early.
> Eat the next meal full.
> Eat the night meal sparely,
> Better not to eat at all.

"Thus he would live to be very old, he said. Alas, poor man, he did not live to prove himself. There he sat at the table one night and the room was suddenly full of the men and women he paid to work on his land. They pointed their little fingers at him and shouted.

" 'There he sits—the old devil! Eating the food we worked to make for him!'

"Before he could ask what they meant, a comrade shot him, a young comrade, too near childhood to know what

129

he did. Alas, my old master had no time to finish the garlic roll! It dropped from his opening hand and so that it would not be wasted, I ate it myself later."

To this Grace listened in horror, for it was impossible to believe. Yet she felt it was true, for this old soul would not make such a lie, of that she was sure. Then she remembered that her mother had bidden her to be patient.

"I cannot understand why this should be done. But I will be patient."

So saying, she went to another room to escape the picture of the old gentleman killed as he ate his frugal night meal. If she allowed herself to think of him, his spirit would haunt this house.

When night had fallen, however, when the old servants had brought her food and she had eaten, when they bade her rest well and had gone to their own quarters, when the door was barred and she was alone, she felt a strange foreboding permeate her spirit. She went into her bedroom then, and barring the door against the other rooms, she sat at a table and wrote a letter to her sister Mercy, imagining that in such a way she could summon at least a pretense that the lively young presence was here beside her. Before she put pen to paper, she leaned her head on her hands, closed her eyes and saw in the darkness the lovely girl, singing her trills and warbles as she prepared for her next day's lesson. Thus she had often seen her, and it was not difficult to summon the memory. When she saw her clearly, the slim figure in the straight Chinese dress, the smooth black hair hanging to her shoulders, the vivid dark eyes, the fresh young coloring of her skin, when she saw her sister entire, she began to write.

"Dearest of Sisters: I am now living in a small old house of my own. It is the first night. It is also the first night of my life that I have been alone. True, there are two old servants in the gatehouse. But there is only I, myself, in the house. Do I like it? I cannot decide. Everything is too new—and too old. These two, new and old, are not yet in balance. They oppose, and therefore are not in harmony. You will not understand what I am writing. I can see you puzzle. 'What is my elder sister trying to tell me?' And I can only reply that I do not even know what I am trying to tell you."

She wrote on for an hour and then brought the letter to an end. She put it in its envelope and sealed and addressed it. San Francisco—how far away that city, how far away was she! Then she called upon her common sense. I am being foolish, she told herself. I have not been here long enough. When I get answers to my letters, when Clem writes to me—and she saw Clem in her memory, peering through a microscope in the laboratory, the sun glinting on his red hair. She heard his loud young voice. "It's still not the right hydrangea, Liang! Or else this sample we've smuggled out by a refugee from your Red China has got the wrong plant. This has no antimalarial content."

They had discovered in an ancient medical treatise, *The Book of Herbs*, assembled by the Chinese Emperor Shen Nung, about 2700 B.C., that a certain hydrangea had a cure for malaria—*ch'ang shan*, the drug was named—and they had tried to secure a specimen of the plant, forbidden to export. His last words to her had been, "Try to get a root of the hydrangea, Liang! You can experiment on your own. God, I envy you all you can find out over there!"

O Clem, she prayed silently, write to me! I am so far away—

The sun was setting in the western sky beyond the Golden Gate Bridge in San Francisco. Mercy Liang leaned upon the railing, watching the last rim of gold, now about to disappear. At her side, so close that their shoulders touched, John Sung was talking. She did not hear him, her mind concentrating upon the sun slipping over the horizon.

"Hush," she exclaimed. "This is the moment. When the sun rises in just a short while, it will rise over our own country."

He was obediently silent, respectful of her mood, and together they saw the last glimmer of gold sink into the sea. Above the water the white clouds turned to rose. She sighed.

"John, we must go back to China!"

He did not reply at once. It was an old argument, yet one upon which in essence they agreed. Each of them felt a strong demand of duty. They were Chinese, and China, their country, had need of educated young Chinese, especially scientists, and he was a scientist in nuclear physics. Until now he had not been permitted to go to China.

"I've been talking again to my senior at the installation, but he gives no hope. . . . We had better speak in Chinese. These people passing—"

He spoke in a low voice, yet glanced over his shoulder at the few people passing. Mercy obeyed.

"I had a letter from my sister today. She is in Peking. All goes well with her. She saw our mother in Shanghai. She is living quite comfortably in spite of—everything. I want to go home, John. I want our children to be born in our own country. It will not be good for them to have been born American citizens if we go back to China."

He smiled at her. A lovely face, he thought, the evening wind blowing about it the tendrils of soft black hair. And he loved her. He loved her impulsive heart, her quick speech, her slender body.

"First we must marry," he reminded her, teasingly.

She responded with vigor. "John, you find every time we meet a new way to make me change our wedding date. On the tenth of next May we marry. I have told Mr. and Mrs. Brandon. They will prepare for our wedding on that day."

"Months to wait," he sighed.

"It will give you time to be released from your contract."

"I may not be able to get a release, remember."

"Then I have a thought. We could go to England—and not come back!"

She looked at him with sparkling black eyes, but he was shocked. "Is that honorable? After all, I have promised."

She interrupted. "They have no right to say you may not return to your own people!"

"They don't say that. They are simply working on my clearance before I go into secret areas of nuclear physics."

"You told me yourself that they were making an excuse of the clearance to hold you here. They don't want you to go back to your own country and work there in nuclear physics!"

"I said I *suspected* that was the reason."

"You know it *is* the reason!"

Passersby glanced at them curiously, not understanding their language but comprehending very well the half-angry argument, and these glances quieted the two. They turned away from sea and sky and walked back to the street where his car was parked. Almost in silence he drove her to the Brandons' house on a hillside, where she was visiting, and helped her out. For a moment their hands clung.

"Tomorrow?" he asked.

"Tomorrow," she said.

They parted, and she went into the house. Mrs. Brandon was in the living room arranging a bowl of roses on a low table in front of a long mirror.

"John isn't staying for dinner?" she asked as Mercy entered the room.

"I didn't ask him," Mercy replied.

"He knows he's always welcome." Mrs. Brandon saw the girl in the mirror. Was there a shadow upon that pretty Asian face?

Mercy sat down on the edge of a white velvet chair. "We had a—we had something of a small quarrel."

"Did you now," Mrs. Brandon murmured. She waited, but the girl did not go on. Instead she rose and went toward the door.

"Wait," Mrs. Brandon said in her direct American fashion. "You can't say that much and not tell me what you quarreled about. I take your mother's place, you know."

Mercy sat down again. "I want to go back to China, Mrs. Brandon."

"Doesn't he?"

"He says he won't be allowed."

"Probably not, a top young scientist!"

"Then he should go anyway."

"Against the government?"

"It's not our government!"

Mrs. Brandon left the roses and turned toward the girl. "My dear, that's not very gracious of you. Your mother would never speak like that."

"My mother is an old-fashioned Chinese. I am not." Mrs. Brandon stared at the defiant girl. She returned to her roses without reply, and Mercy rose and left the room.

That night after dinner when Mercy had excused herself to write letters, alone with her husband, Mrs. Brandon recounted the conversation.

"It's really not like Mercy to speak so—so belligerently," she said.

Mr. Brandon had listened without interrupting her. "John is a fine man," he said now. "He will do what he thinks is right. I wouldn't worry if I were you. And he'll never be allowed to go back to China—not under present circumstances."

"She's determined, Howard."

"She's not the government, in spite of all she says."

To such conclusion Mrs. Brandon had nothing to say. The affairs of men and governments were beyond her concern. She fell to thinking about the wedding she had promised to give the young Chinese couple. It would be a big wedding, for they had many friends.

"Where will you go on your honeymoon, dear?" she asked Mercy the next morning. They had lingered over breakfast in the pleasant morning room, whose windows overlooked the Bay.

The girl, looking as pretty as a half-opened rosebud this

morning, Mrs. Brandon thought, replied in innocence.

"I would like to go to England, Mrs. Brandon. And John wants to visit some great English scientists also." She paused to laugh sweetly. "Even on honeymoon, I think he will first be scientist! I must expect it."

"So long as you understand," Mrs. Brandon replied comfortably. "To understand each other is so important, so basic, so entirely—necessary."

"Yes, Mrs. Brandon. It is what my mother always said also. Now, excuse me. I will go for a walk and mail my letters."

"The child seemed herself today," Mrs. Brandon reported to her husband that night, "and they're going to England for their honeymoon."

Mr. Brandon looked up from his magazine. They were sitting in the library as usual when they were alone and she was playing solitaire at the card table.

"Hm," he grunted, "that's odd."

"What's odd?" Mrs. Brandon demanded, putting down a card.

"London—England—"

"Why?"

"The Communist Chinese have their embassy there."

"Oh, you like to put two and two together," Mrs. Brandon said tolerantly.

"Well, I usually make four, don't I?"

"I suppose so," she said absently, and searching her hand, she forgot to ask what four was, in this addition.

Six months and some days later, Mercy and her husband, John Sung, were received into an ornate private office in the Chinese embassy in London. The day was fair but the late spring sunshine did not penetrate the heavy draperies that covered the floor-length windows. Instead, the light of a crystal chandelier hanging from the middle of the ceiling fell upon the carved furniture and the blue and white Peking carpet. It fell, too, upon the handsome face of a Chinese man in a severe, dark uniform who sat behind a vast desk at one end of the immense room.

"You will need nothing in the way of official documents," he said in a meticulously accented Chinese. "I have already communicated with the authorities in our capital. A special plane will convey you, Dr. and Mrs. Sung, to Peking. There you will be welcomed suitably as patriotic persons and assigned to your posts."

"I, also?" Mercy inquired.

"You also," the official said gravely. "You will not be excused because you are a woman. We need good brains, wherever they are. I suggest that you consider the founding of a new school of music in Peking. We have many new folk songs, created by our young people. They should be compiled and written down, in order to be preserved. I make this a mere suggestion to you, Madame. To you, Dr. Sung, I say that you return to our country at an opportune time. Our scientists are devising a new type of hydrogen bomb, of a force superior to any yet known."

"A bomb?" John Sung repeated. "My own field is industrial rather than military."

"Industry is useless if it is at the mercy of a voracious Western power such as the United States, a country obviously determined to set up a new empire in Asia."

If he noticed that his guests did not reply he made no

sign. He stamped some papers with a large red seal, and taking the receiver from a telephone on his desk, he gave a curt order. Almost immediately the door opened, and a young man in a dark blue uniform entered. The man behind the desk looked up.

"Conduct Dr. and Mrs. Sung to the door. In two hours see that they are at the airport."

They rose. The man behind the desk nodded curtly, and Mercy and John left with the young man.

In the jet aircraft that night, when the lights were dimmed for sleep, Mercy reached for her husband's hand.

"Your hand is icy cold," he exclaimed when her small hand folded itself into his palm.

"I'm excited," she said. "Or perhaps afraid."

"Afraid?"

"Well, I know it won't be the same old easygoing country in which I grew up."

"How do you know?"

"My mother's letters are so—strange."

"Strange?"

"So much alike—and once every year or two a few lines tucked into a gift saying that I am to stay where I am—in America, that is. Did you think that man in the embassy this morning seemed guarded, stiff—or something? He didn't smile."

"He was just being official."

"You think so? Oh, what will the Brandons think when we don't come back? We'll write letters and explain . . . John!"

"Yes?"

"Wouldn't it be wonderful if we could explain Americans to our people? Just as we've tried to explain Chinese to Amercians. It's our duty, I think."

"Why not?" he agreed.

Now that the decision had been made, the step taken, now that they were beyond return, he felt a chill in his heart that he could not understand. He had left China as a little boy with his father, the younger brother of a merchant in San Francisco's Chinatown, and there he had grown up, dependent upon his uncle after his father died. He had not told even his uncle that, instead of a honeymoon announced for Niagara Falls, they were going home to China. For wherever its people wandered the earth, in spite of accumulating wealth and rising success, China was forever home. He searched his mind for childish memories and it seemed to him that he could remember a village, which must have been in the southern province of Kwangtung, near Canton, and in the village a peasant home but a comfortable one, and in that house an old couple who made much of him and a gentle woman who cried when his father led him away to go to America. His grandparents could scarcely be living but he would find his mother.

He fell into sleep, more weary than he knew from the wedding and the hidden excitement of immediate departure from the country where he had lived so long, and seeing his eyes close in the dim light, Mercy slipped her hand from his. Let him sleep, though she could not! There had been no time since the wedding—a beautiful wedding, she thought tenderly, remembering the flower-filled rooms alive with warmhearted generous people. It was impossible to believe that friendship was dead between such people and her own. Surely after a century of kindliness and esteem,

Americans could not be enemies to the Chinese. Mr. and Mrs. Brandon and their children were her American family. She even called Mrs. Brandon "Mother"—"American Mother." But love filled her heart for everyone now that she was going home to her own country. She glanced tenderly at John, asleep in the seat beside her. His handsome, relaxed face looked younger than his twenty-seven years.

"The most brilliant of our young scientists," his employer had said at the wedding. "I predict a great future for him, Mrs. Sung."

The jet craft trembled slightly, and she clutched the arms of her seat. She was always afraid so far above the earth, and yet it was the only way to reach China from the United States. The tremor sharpened to a motion more violent and the pilot's voice came over the transmitter.

"Ladies and gentlemen, please fasten your seat belts. We are in for a period of turbulence."

Should she wake John? No, for he had awakened, and they fastened their seat belts at the same moment. Then in the silence of terror they sat helpless, their hands clasped, as the aircraft floundered across the dark sky, but always eastward.

Madame Liang was in the main dining hall of her restaurant when her business manager and most trusted employee conveyed to her by a sign agreed upon between them that he had a matter of importance for her attention. She did not hasten her graceful progress among her guests, but in less than half an hour she had drifted out of the hall after greeting all her more important guests. Freed of this obligation, she entered the small private elevator which Mr. Brandon had ordered installed years ago when his mother, crippled by arthritis, had come to live with her son and his family in Shanghai, where servants had been plentiful and cheap. Now of course she was long dead—her grave was in the cemetery of what had once been the British Concession—and servants were neither plentiful nor cheap because of the new unions.

Her business manager, Chu San, was already in the elevator, waiting for her. He touched a button and the elevator stopped midway between the first and second floors. This was usual when he wished to speak to his employer without possibility of being overheard.

"What have you to say now?" Madame Liang demanded.

"Word has come that the eminent young Chinese scientist, Dr. John Sung, has escaped from the United States."

"Well?"

"His wife is with him, Madame."

"Well?"

"She is Madame's second daughter."

"No!"

"Madame did not know?"

"Not that they were married!"

"Madame's letters are being intercepted."

"All letters are intercepted," she said impatiently.

"But Madame's, especially."

"Why do you say that?"

"Madame has three beautiful daughters, educated in enemy country."

Madame Liang looked into his rugged peasant face. He was the son of peasants and had run away from the two-acre farm which had been the sole existence of his family.

In the city of Shanghai he had lived from one job to another, had gone to school and learned to read and write and at sixteen had been discovered by Madame Liang feeding himself from the slops of her kitchens. Something in his bony looks had impressed her with a conviction of his innate strength, and under her care he had advanced to his present position.

"Why do you mention my daughters?" she demanded now.

"*They* will not rest until all are here," he said.

"And when they are here?"

"We wait and see."

She made a swift decision. "I must leave at once for Peking. You will go with me." She paused and then added, with effort, "By air."

"Madame!" he cried in pity.

"No, it is necessary," she insisted. "I must go to my eldest daughter at once. She has not told me that my second daughter has left the United States. I must know why. I have been told nothing."

A flash of anger crossed her beautiful, aging face. "If I am not told everything, how can I act wisely?"

"I have told Madame what I overheard not an hour ago, at a table in one of the private dining rooms," he said.

"Release this conveyance," she ordered. "There is a flight in an hour and a half. Send Chou Ma to pack my bags and arrange for us to be driven to the airport. You will accompany me."

"Yes, Madame."

He touched a button and the elevator went smoothly to the next floor.

* * *

Madame Liang went at once to her eldest daughter. She knew the city of Peking well, for she and Cheng had lived there in the first years of their marriage—difficult now to believe that those years had ever been! Could she have foreseen, she and all those other young men and women who had learned in Western schools of a Western world, that what they had dreamed of, had been taught to dream of, that life, that freedom to pursue their own happiness, would she, would they, have overthrown the security of the ancient throne, the traditional past? She was troubled by the constant presence of the unanswered question with its aura of guilt. Guilt had kept her from flight to Paris or New York, with others who had found refuge—guilt accompanied by a deep love for her country and her people.

Guilt became heavy indeed when she realized, as she stood before the barred gate of her daughter's house, that she was responsible for the return of her own children to the present turmoil. By now it was night, and city gates were barred. On the streets the shops, open all day, were closed until morning.

"Beat the gate again," she bade Chu San, who had accompanied her as usual when she left her house. He was a good bodyguard, for he knew tricks of striking a blow with his fist or sending a kick with his flying foot if anyone threatened attack. There was always the possibility of such attack from some unknown enemy in the times in which they were living.

He beat the gate now with his two fists and it opened a crack. An eye peered out.

"Who is there?" a voice demanded.

"Open the gate or I will kick it open," Chu San shouted. "It is Madame Liang, of Shanghai."

Madame Liang also called. "I am the mother of Dr. Liang!"

Immediately the gate opened. She came down from her pedicab and walked across the court and entered the house. The doors were open, for the evening was mild. They were there, Grace and Mercy and her husband. Yes, the tall young man must be her son-in-law of whom she had only been told and had never seen. No one expected her, for she had wanted to arrive privately, if possible. Grace was the first to cry out.

"M-ma! How did you come here?"

"I flew," Madame Liang said with her usual calm.

She was enveloped now by embraces, and she felt her right hand in the strong clasp of her son-in-law.

"Have done," she commanded. "I came here to find out everything."

"First, have you eaten?" Grace asked.

"I have, and I want nothing except to know how it is that you are here together and I not told."

"I was not told, either, until an hour before these two were here," Grace said.

They seated themselves, Madame Liang in the place of honor by the central table and next to the inner wall. Western though her daughters might be, and though she thought of herself as a modern woman, instinctively she seated herself in the traditional manner of the elders.

"My daughter," Madame Liang began, addressing herself to Grace, "can you trust your servants?"

"They speak no English, at least," Grace replied.

"Then we will speak in English," Madame Liang replied. She turned next to her second daughter. "Explain to me why I was not informed."

Mercy answered, half apologetic. "M-ma, we were not sure whether we should come home or remain in America. John had a good job. Then suddenly one day we realized that after our marriage, when we had children, if they were born there, they would be Americans. It was confusing to me to think I might have to give birth to American citizens. I said to John, 'Our children must be born in our own country. They must be Chinese. Let us marry soon and immediately go home.'"

Here John Sung interrupted. "Moreover, ma'am, I felt that I should contribute to our own country. We need scientists. So we returned."

"How was this permitted?" Madame Liang inquired shrewdly. "I know the Americans will not release nuclear scientists."

Her daughters exchanged glances. Then Mercy laughed. "M-ma, how is it that you know everything? We went to England—and just kept traveling eastward."

"Under the protection of our own authorities?" Madame Liang asked.

"Yes," John Sung said bluntly.

She surveyed this first son-in-law. What she saw did not displease her. Tall, handsome enough but not too handsome —she distrusted a man too handsome, as her own husband had been—an open, honest look, direct speech, these were all acceptable to her.

"I appreciate your patriotism," she said, "but you must also have patience, now that you are here. Much has been done, but much remains to be done."

Before she could continue, they heard the sound of marching feet, of singing, of exploding firecrackers beyond the wall.

"May the thirtieth," Grace explained.

"I had forgotten," John Sung exclaimed.

They listened for a few minutes as the sounds came nearer.

"M-ma, how did May the thirtieth really happen?" Mercy asked.

Madame Liang was surprised. "Can it be you don't know?"

"I've heard—but so long ago."

"True," her mother said. "It does not seem long to me, but it was years before you were even born. I was in Shanghai, waiting for your father, who was working with Chiang Kai-shek and preparing for the expedition to the north to put down the warlords, who were against the revolution and were fighting among themselves to restore the old government. We needed the impetus of some dramatic incident to set the moment of beginning the expedition and win the support of the peasants. Without knowing what they did, the Westerners gave this incident to us. I was staying with friends in a house on Nanking Road. Suddenly on that day, May the thirtieth, in the year 1925, as I was reading a letter from your father, I heard angry voices in the street beneath the open window. I went to the window and then I saw a crowd of students on the street below, shouting and waving sticks at the policemen who were hired by the International Settlement in Shanghai. These policemen then threatened the students to shoot into the crowd if they did not leave at once."

"Which of course they did not," Mercy interposed.

"And I knew they would not," Madame Liang continued. "The students swarmed about and the police shot into the air above their heads. Again the police warned, and when the students refused to move away the police shot their guns into the crowd. Several students were killed."

She looked about her at the listening faces. "It gave us the incident we needed. The whole country burst into flame —violence against British and Japanese, boycotts, anger everywhere, newspapers attacking all Westerners. Early the next year, the expedition against the north began— a success, a triumph, scholars and peasants working together, invincible, when they unite."

She spoke eloquently, her English free of accent and forceful, and then she paused to shake her head.

"What is it, Mother?" Grace inquired. Her mother seemed suddenly weary.

"This incident was also the proof of something else."

Madame Liang spoke thoughtfully but indeed wearily. She brushed her cheeks with both hands and let those hands fall into her lap. They waited, and at last John Sung spoke.

"You mean—"

"I mean," she said, summoning strength, "this incident was proof of the lack of understanding between the Chinese and the Westerners. To the Westerners the police had acted legally—they had given fair warning to the students, who chose to disobey the law and therefore must take the punishment. To the Chinese, no law could excuse the killing of students, who were members of our educated elite. We believe that laws are only for the control of criminals. These were students, not criminals. It meant nothing to us that legally, according to Westerners, the police were within their rights in the International Settlement. The deeper soil was still Chinese. Only the skin of the earth belonged to the foreigners and even that was intolerable to us."

She closed her eyes and fell silent. Outside the walls, beyond the gate, the noise of marching feet, the shouts and songs of the marching swelled into the room.

"Let's go and see them," Mercy cried, clapping her hands. She jumped to her feet. "Let's open the gate!"

She was halfway across the room, but Madame Liang was already at the door.

"N-no," she stammered. "N-no, the gate must not be opened!"

"But why not?" Grace asked, amazed.

They were gathering about Madame Liang, and she looked at one face and another. Their surprise seemed to calm her and when she spoke again it was with her usual quietness.

"Stay apart from the crowd. Let them march and shout. It is a way but it is not the Eternal Way."

She did not move from the door and outside the house, across the courtyard, Chu San stood braced against the barred gate.

The next few days passed in hours of curious contrast. In the evenings the family took their evening meal, waited upon by the servants as safely as they had in earlier times, before the Great Change, as they called the coming in of the new rulers. In the daytime, however, Grace went to the hospital, where Chinese and Western medicines were taught and practiced, and continued her studies with the old doctor, while Madame Liang discussed many subjects with Mercy and John. She was especially curious about the Americans nowadays and put many questions to the young pair, so newly arrived.

"Is it possible," she said at last when her questions were asked and answered, "that the Americans do not know the injustice they have done us?"

"What injustice, M-ma?" Mercy asked.

Now that she was in her own country everything seemed good to her and she was in a bloom of happiness. What she had told no one was that already it was possible that she had conceived. It was too soon, to be sure, yet she could only rejoice that she and John had left America immediately after marriage. She had accomplished her purpose. Her child would be born here in his own country, the land of his ancestors, it was true, but now also the land of the future.

"I mean," her mother was saying, "that the Americans, in breaking off communication between our two countries after the Great Change, have violated the law of friendship. For a century Americans were our only friends in the West. They alone seized no territory of ours, nor did they ever make war against us, nor demand indemnities. True, to enrich themselves, they insisted upon the same privileges we were forced to give other foreign nations so that their citizens, too, walked our streets without fear of arrest or judgment. But they did not make demands upon us otherwise—indeed, they modified the demands of others. Yet it seems they do not realize the ancient bond of friendship."

She turned to her son-in-law. "Do you understand what I am saying or have you lived too long among Americans?"

"I have lived too long among Americans," John Sung said honestly.

"Then I will explain to you," Madame Liang replied, and after a moment's thought she continued thus:

"Friendship between two persons, or two nations, is an unbreakable bond, a tie which cannot be cut. An honorable heart does not cast aside a friend because he is in trouble, nor even if he changes his nature and becomes a criminal. Between two nations friendship must also be eternal, else the friend is false and being false in one event was always false. And what was our crime against the Americans? The Great Change? But is it a crime to change a government? By whose law can it be called a crime? It is of no more importance, between friends, than for one to change his garment! For this lack of reason our love for Americans is changed to hate. I fear for the future! A generation is growing up here in our country which has never seen an American face or heard an American voice. What do they know of Americans except to hate them as they are taught to do? There is no hate so dangerous as that which once was love."

John Sung listened to all this with utmost attention, and when Madame Liang had finished he made no reply for a space of time. Then he said, "To the Americans, Communism is a crime. They will have none of it."

"But why, when it is ours, not theirs?" Madame Liang asked with true wonder.

John Sung considered and replied thoughtfully. "I suppose this American concern with a form of government springs from their own history. Their ancestors fled from Europe to escape tyranny from their ancient rulers. Freedom was their dream. To them, therefore, tyranny is endemic in Communism. They will have none of it. It is not we who are Chinese whom they hate. It is the tyranny they imagine."

"Imagine!" Madame Liang repeated.

She shook her head. She looked east and west, and then she changed the subject. Three days later she returned to her home in Shanghai.

Spring passed gently again into summer and Grace, under a year's tutelage of the old Chinese physician, progressed from listening to practice. She attended clinic several times a week and observed Dr. Tseng's methods. On a certain morning in early June, however, the fifth month of the Chinese lunar year, at an hour so early that the clinic had not yet opened, an hour which she spent in taking notes from the old doctor as he expounded on some aspect of ancient medicine, the minister Chao Chung entered the doctor's office. He was dressed in his usual somber uniform of dark blue cloth, and though he looked somewhat pale, he gave his customary smile.

"Ah, Dr. Liang," he said. "I offer myself as a patient this morning."

The old doctor rose, but Chao Chung motioned to him to be seated. He himself sat down and addressed himself to the doctor.

"Dr. Tseng, I come to you to report that I have felt unusually tired for several days and I have not wanted to eat."

"I observe that the whites of your eyes are yellowish and your voice is somewhat hoarse," Dr. Tseng replied.

Chao Chung smiled again. "I put myself in your hands," he said.

"Allow me to see your tongue," Dr. Tseng requested.

Chao Chung put out his tongue and the doctor gazed at it for a long minute. Then he spoke.

"Now let me feel the pulse in your left hand."

Chao Chung put out his left hand and pulled up his sleeve. Dr. Tseng took the wrist in his right hand, while he turned to Grace.

"Observe how I take the pulse in the left hand. I press my fourth finger here where the palm parts from the wrist, placing my first and third fingers next to it. I examine the three pulses here, first pressing lightly, then with medium force, then very deeply."

So saying, the old doctor, his lips pursed, took the pulses of Chao Chung's left hand. This consumed almost half an hour. Then he spoke again.

"Comrade Chao, please extend your right hand." The minister did so and Dr. Tseng examined the pulses of the right wrist with the same care, except that now he placed his forefinger on the spot where wrist and palm met, and his third and fourth finger next to it. His thumb was on the ball of the palm. Altogether his examination consumed almost an hour. Then he gave his diagnosis.

"You have slowed the rhythm of your heart by fatigue. You must rest for three days, and do not use your eyes. I will give you a light treatment of acupuncture and you will be toned and feel better."

He proceeded then by helping Chao Chung to lower his jacket from his shoulders and when the flesh was bared he thrust a needle of medium length into two points, one to the left, the other to the right of his patient's nape.

"I feel better already," Chao Chung declared and he buttoned his jacket.

"It is because the balance between *yang* and *yin* is restored," Dr. Tseng told him. He turned to Grace. "I will discourse this morning upon the subject of *yang* and *yin*."

"Please do," Grace said.

Chao Chung was on his feet now and about to depart. At the door he paused.

"By the way, Dr. Liang," he said. "I am reminded— your brother-in-law."

"What of him?" Grace asked.

"Have you influence with him?"

Grace smiled. "No, but my sister has."

Chao Chung hesitated. "We are having some difficulty with him, now that his period of tutelage is over."

"Can it be true?" Grace asked, wondering. "Yet he seems very happy, they both do."

"Ah, yes, but he is individualistic."

"What do you mean by that?"

"He is reluctant to carry out certain instructions."

"I know nothing about this."

"Naturally! Since he is working in areas where secrecy is essential, you would hear nothing."

"What do you wish me to do?"

"Simply tell your sister that he must not be too individualistic."

"But will she understand?"

"*He* will understand," Chao Chung said, lifting his heavy dark eyebrows. With this he raised his right hand in a gesture of farewell and left the room.

She, however, did not understand, and so was not able to forget what he had said. She felt his words echoing in her brain even while she listened to Dr. Tseng's droning voice as he expounded upon *yang* and *yin*.

"Five thousand years ago in the Chou dynasty, in this ancient book, which the Chairman has ordered to be reprinted, in this book which I hold in my hands and which you are to study with care, you will learn that there are two kinds of blood in the human body. One kind is controlled by *yin*, the principle of darkness, the other by *yang*, the principle of light. These two work together, in balance—"

Then she began to listen after a time, even forgetting what Chao Chung had said. For what was this double blood in the human body but the discovery, centuries ago, of the blood in the veins and the blood in the arteries? Thus, long ago her people knew what others discovered only centuries later. No wonder hers was a proud people!

That afternoon before he left for his home, the old doctor placed on her desk the book which her mother kept always near, the *I-Ching*.

"It is necessary for you to understand these trigrams,"

Dr. Tseng told her. He was wrapping his instruments in the square of blue cloth he used as a bag. Now he placed his long forefinger on an open page of the book. "Observe here the eight *kua!* These are the changes of nature, flowing together, yet in opposition, the one coming in as the other goes out. This is the eternal motion of life, a duality of positive and negative, equally valuable and each indispensable to the other. Thus, there can be no light without the contrast of darkness, no day without night, no summer without winter, no autumn without spring, no strength without weakness, no male without female. Within each *yang* there is also *yin;* within each *yin* there must be *yang.* When the balance is disturbed, disease attacks."

When he was gone, she pondered the meaning of what he had said. As was becoming her habit, she reflected upon the possibility of a parallel in Western medicine to express the ancient Chinese wisdom. Was there not a likeness to *yin* in the parasympathetic nervous system? She was so engrossed that she forgot, when she reached home at dusk, to tell her sister Mercy what Chao Chung had said. But there was more to distract her, for as she entered the court, Mercy met her, and smiling with some secret happiness, she locked her fingers with her sister's right hand.

"I went to a doctor today," she confided as they walked to the door of the house, now open to the mild evening air.

"Are you ill?" Grace asked immediately.

"I have happiness within me!" Mercy said triumphantly, speaking in Chinese and using the old Chinese phrase.

"O fortunate sister!" Grace cried, embracing her.

In the excitement she forgot the morning's conversation and it was night before she thought of it. The evening meal was over, the servants had retired, and she and Mercy were alone in the central hall. John had excused himself. He had eaten less than usual and Mercy had been concerned when he left them.

"I wonder if he doesn't feel well," she had exclaimed as he left. These words reminded her sister.

"Ah, I'd forgotten," Grace cried.

So saying, she repeated Chao Chung's admonition. Mercy listened and was troubled.

"What does he mean by 'individualistic'?" Mercy asked. Her large dark eyes were so childlike that her sister was touched.

"He said my brother-in-law would understand," she replied.

In the night when she was alone with her husband, Mercy repeated the words, but in a question.

"Do you understand?" she asked him, after she had repeated what Grace had told her.

"Yes," John said bluntly.

Mercy waited and when he continued silent, she pressed him gently.

"Will you explain to me, darling?"

They spoke in English, as they did by habit when they were alone in the night. The Chinese language did not contain the words of love they needed for communication.

"There is nothing to explain," he retorted. In the darkness, when she could not see his face upon the pillow next to hers, she heard only the sharpness of his voice.

"Then why—"

He broke across her question. "I can explain it only by

saying that it is the difference between the mind of a scientist and the mind of a politician and a militant. I am a scientist and I have a conscience about my work. Chao Chung is a politician and he thinks of government and how to achieve its goals. We disagree, that is all."

He spoke firmly but with calm, and she did not know why suddenly she was afraid. She moved closer to him, she put her head on his shoulder.

"But, darling, we are so newly come. Do you think you should disagree so soon—and with so powerful a minister?"

He bit back the words that lay ready upon his tongue. Let her not be made unhappy on this day of her annunciation! For when he came home for his noon meal today, which they ate alone together, since Grace stayed all day at the hospital, she had come to him and had put her head on his breast. He was surprised, for she was not in the habit of showing her love for him by day. He had put his arms about her, had questioned her.

"Is something wrong?"

"Not wrong, only wonderfully right." And then she had for the first time used the old Chinese annunciation phrase: "I have happiness in me."

For an instant overcome, he had held her. Then, his voice husky with surprise, with joy, he had asked her if she were sure.

"Have you seen a doctor?"

"I have been to the gynecology clinic," she told him.

"It is confirmed?"

"It is sure."

Now, remembering, it occurred to him that he had no right to think of words such as "individualistic" that would

157

make her afraid. And was she perhaps right? Since a child would be born here in this their own country, should he put that new life into danger in order that he could maintain freedom for himself, a dedicated scientist?

"Let us be happy," he said at last. "We have so much to make us happy."

So saying, he put his arms about her, he held her close until she was comforted. But he lay for a long time awake. Chao Chung was right. He knew very well what the minister had meant when he had accused him of being "individualistic."

"Is it your right to question what use is made of your science?" Chao Chung had demanded.

They were in the minister's inner private office, a room within a room, the walls soundproof, the door, its only entrance, double in thickness. He had been summoned here early in the morning, and he had stepped from the bright summer sunshine into the dimness of this enclosed room. Behind a huge central desk of heavy blackwood Chao Chung sat, grim and without his smile. To the right sat Captain Li. It was the first time he, John Sung, had been summoned into the official presence, and in spite of himself and his accustomed self-confidence he had felt vaguely afraid.

"Sit down," Chao Chung had commanded.

He had seated himself in a side chair and had waited while his superior studied some papers. The light of the desk lamp fell with concentration upon Chao Chung's face—a cruel face, or was it only that at this moment it was without the smile? Perhaps it was the somewhat heavy mouth, or the thick dark eyebrows above the intensely black eyes—

"In reviewing the military possibilities of the future," Chao Chung began suddenly, lifting his head and fixing his eyes upon his subordinate, "it is a question of how we should be prepared to destroy the enemy in case of attack."

John Sung waited. What enemy? What attack? The questions formed in his mind, but he did not ask them, and Chao Chung continued.

"We have, it is true, the world's greatest expert in rocketry, who is in charge of our nuclear development—thanks to the foolishness of the American Senator McCarthy some years ago, he was not cleared as a scientist in the United States, though he waited five years for such clearance, and in disgust he returned to our country. I say thanks, for I do thank that McCarthy for thus compelling a great scientist to leave America—an act that we were not able to accomplish by any form of persuasion."

"I have not met Dr. Tsien," John Sung said.

"No? Well, someday," Chao Chung replied. "Meanwhile I will give your assignment. Let me explain it by telling you our military experts agree that pending the full development of our nuclear weapons we should protect ourselves by more subtle methods. Germs of some sort, or drugs, perhaps, something deadly that could be used imperceptibly but with deadly effect."

The heavy black eyebrows shot up above the questioning black eyes. John Sung stared steadily into those eyes while Chao Chung waited.

"Well?" he asked at last, impatiently.

"Please proceed," John Sung said.

The glimmer of a smile had appeared about the somber mouth.

"My own suggestion," Chao Chung said, "is a sort of liquid—or is it a gas?—which when it touches the skin results in paralysis and swift death. Or, if you prefer a simpler technique, it could be a radioactive poison, poured secretly into the sources of water supply. I have here a map —very accurate—"

He drew out from under the papers before him a large map, which he unfolded. He beckoned, and John Sung rose and walked to his side. Chao Chung continued, his long forefinger moving across the map.

"See, here are the sources of the water supply west of the Continental Divide. Observe how concentrated they are. Now we move across the States. The Tennessee Valley centers here—though eastward of course it becomes more complicated, but the population is more dense. It could be done so easily; beautiful, isn't it?" He looked up at John Sung, his face brightening.

"It could be done, of course," John Sung said.

He returned to his seat and became aware of his own heartbeat, tripled in speed and thumping in his breast. Was it possible that the minister was about to suggest—or worse, to command—that he continue so dastardly a means to— to—he pushed away the thought as impossible.

"I trust such an effort will remain unnecessary," he said at last.

"We must be prepared," Chao Chung retorted.

There was a pause which it seemed neither of them wished to break. John Sung determined that he, at least, would not break it. Chao Chung was finally compelled to it.

"I ask you as a scientist which method would in your opinion be most effective."

"I hope," John Sung said, "that none of these will ever be necessary."

"Not even in war?" Chao Chung asked, in seeming surprise.

"There is honor even in war," John Sung replied.

To his astonishment, Chao Chung had instantly lost his temper. He pushed aside the papers; he slapped the desk loudly with both hands.

"You have been too long in the decadent West!" he shouted. "There war is a game, with rules for this, rules for that—romance, glory, pity for prisoners—all nonsense! War is for one purpose only—to kill the enemy, put him out of existence by any means. There is no justice, no honor, in war. He who kills first wins victory—the first and the most!"

He was so angry that he leaped from his chair and walked back and forth across the carpeted floor.

"We hate war! We Chinese are too civilized, too realistic, to imagine war is a game! Long ago we repudiated the making of explosive weapons because such weapons were inhuman and if used would destroy innocent people. Did not the ancient emperors forbid even gunpowder, an invention of our own, to be used in weapons? We used it for innocent pleasure in fireworks and firecrackers. Or rocketry. Centuries ago we understood the principles of rocketry, but an emperor forbade its development, lest weapons so devised kill innocent humanity! Did we create the first atomic bomb and drop it on a city of people? Did we devise poisonous gas and noxious germs to use in warfare? Why are we compelled to think today of making war? For self-defense! We who for centuries have believed war to be utterly despicable and soldiers to be the lowest of criminals and a dishonor to their families are now compelled—"

He broke off, choked by his own rage. Suddenly he turned, and stopping at John Sung's side, he leaned over him, his eyes burning, his voice hissing.

"Do you know how to make this radioactive poison for the water sources of an enemy?"

John Sung did not draw back or flinch. He gazed into those furious eyes. "Yes," he said. "I know how to make it."

Then quickly, to prevent the command, he added these words: "But I will not."

Chao Chung bit his lip, restraining command. It was too soon. This man was still new to his own country. Indoctrination must take place. He must be changed before he could be obedient.

"You are too individualistic," he declared abruptly, and he motioned Captain Li to lead John Sung from the room.

"Madame!" Chu San thus addressed Madame Liang in the elevator. "When you have rested after that perilous journey in the sky, I have a matter to talk of with you."

They were home again, she to proceed upstairs to her own room and Chu San to return to his place in the lower floors. She was about to step out of the vehicle when he spoke, but she lingered.

"Is it a matter for haste?" she inquired.

"No, no, Madame—only a plan, a good one, or I would not trouble you with it."

"Then let it rest in your head for a few hours," she said and went to her own rooms, there to be met by Chou Ma, who had prepared her bath and laid out fresh garments and now gave her the usual solicitous scolding.

"This climbing to heaven in a flying ship, this wandering among the clouds—it is to tempt the devils of the air, Madame! The old way was best, to ride in a comfortable chair borne on men's shoulders, to stop for rest and food and tea at some wayside inn, to move among human beings on the solid earth—is this not to prolong your life?"

"You know very well there is not a sedan chair left in our country, or so I daresay, and if there is one, who will carry it on his shoulders nowadays? Besides, I have no time for slow travel—a month to Peking instead of a few hours!"

Madame Liang was weary and she spoke with unusual impatience, the more because she hated the "wandering among the clouds," as Chou Ma put it, and she did indeed remember, and with regret, the slow pleasant hours when as a young girl she had traveled with her family to the mountains in Kiangsi province to escape the heat of summer. For the ascent into these mountains it had been necessary to hire sedan chairs, since there was no other mode possible on the narrow roadway that wound among the ever-steeper cliffs. To this day she remembered how cool had been the mountain air, how delightful the singing of birds and the rush of waterfalls. How different, indeed, how infinitely better, than being encased in a cylinder in the sky, from which there was no escape until the scheduled hour—unless destiny provided a hasty exit to the next incarnation!

She maintained a stubborn silence while she bathed and allowed Chou Ma to dress her in a soft gray silk long gown, a silence that Chou Ma broke at last by a placating question.

"Dare I ask Madame if the young ladies are in health?"

"They are well," Madame Liang said and laid herself down upon a couch but carefully that she might not disarrange her hair.

"And the honorable son-in-law, did Madame—"

"I like him very well."

With this curt conclusion she waved her old servant away and closed her eyes, wishing that she had not promised Chu San to talk business with him tonight. She had so promised, however, and when soon she heard his cough at the door she rose, for she would not receive even so lowly a man if she were reclining. She walked to a heavy carved chair and bade him enter. He did so, and she saw that in courtesy to her, or perhaps only to win him favor when he had business to talk of with her, he had washed his face and had put on a clean jacket of black cloth.

"Sit where you please," she commanded and he chose a somewhat distant chair, out of respect for her, sitting on the very edge and not presuming to seem to make himself comfortable. He waited for her to begin and she did so.

"Well, what is hiding in your mind now?" she inquired.

He coughed decently behind his hand and she gazed at him, a good, honest, ugly face, she thought, a true peasant, the best of his kind. At least the present rulers had given him some benefit, for he had been young enough to learn to read and write in their schools and so had become a businessman of a simple sort. In other days he would have remained an ignorant oaf upon two acres of land somewhere in a distant province. As it was, though he was peasant at heart, he watched over her business, weighing the fish and pork, feeling the breasts of fowl, testing the freshness of eggs in a pan of water and suspicious of money in any hands save his own. Over the years he had made himself into her bodyguard and on land or in the air she could sleep, knowing that he was there. She knew, too, being woman throughout her being, that in his own way, forever silent, he worshiped her.

She waited therefore until he began to speak, which he did after a few more coughs behind his hand and glances here and there about the room.

"Madame, our business brings you more money every year, in spite of the—"

Here he coughed again and then went on: "in spite of Them."

"This is true because of your tireless watchfulness," Madame Liang said with her usual grace.

"Not so," he demurred. "It is entirely due to nature."

"Nature?" Madame Liang was surprised.

"The nature of men," Chu San explained.

"What is this nature?" Madame Liang inquired.

"To fill our bellies full of good food," Chu San replied.

Madame Liang gave her silvery laughter, and Chu San was pleased with himself and proceeded, lowering his voice against possible listeners.

"Since Madame succeeds so well with one restaurant, why not with twenty? We could make inns at famous places throughout our great country, each with its own restaurant. Our people thirst for amusement and they hunger for fine food. We have been without pleasure for these many years and the food—" He made a face of disgust. "Even in Peking, except in a few old restaurants! Ah, yes, Madame, I see you shake your head, but it is true. Only in a few of those ancient restaurants, where Peking duck is prepared or roast mutton in a Muslim inn, can one eat as before. And think, Madame, of the foreigners who would come here by thousands to our inns to eat our good food! I have heard that Americans eat our food even in their own country, but surely it cannot be properly cooked there since they have no such good water or vegetables or meats as we have on our soil. Americans are very rich, money drops from their hands. What do you say, Madame?"

He leaned forward, his voice urgent, his face intent, all eagerness to hear her agreement.

She was about to agree with him but prudence had now become a habit. Chu San she could surely trust—or could she? Was this reference to the Americans a clever trick to test her loyalty to those now in power? A cloud of depression stole over her spirit. She felt alone in her house, and even, for the moment, in her own country. There was not one in whom she could wholly put her trust; even her children were blinded for the moment by their joy in being in their own country again. As for Chu San, waiting to hear what she would say, better not to agree or disagree! Was this perhaps the Eternal Way, after all?

"Chu San," she said, "you are always thinking of my welfare. How could I carry on my business without you? I thank you for this good thought you have presented to me, although it cannot immediately be carried out. I fear it is impossible to think we can be friends with the Americans again. This present generation of our people will not forgive them."

Chu San looked stubborn. His small black eyes fastened upon an ivory Buddha that stood on a carved table across the room, and the lower lip of his big mouth protruded.

"Madame," he said, "we sons of Han are a people who know what is big business and what is small business. Americans are big business. We will forgive them, I swear to you, after this present dynasty is gone, because they are so rich."

"Pray do not call ours a dynasty," Madame Liang said. "Should one overhear you, he will think you a follower of the old government."

"Then what shall I call Them?" Chu San demanded.

"We must wait and see," she replied. "If their way is not the Eternal Way, it will be only an interlude in our history. Now leave me, good soul, I am very tired."

He rose, bowed and turned to depart. At the door she stopped him. "Chu San, kind soul! Truly your plan is a good one. In other times I would have considered it. If the present is indeed only an interlude, I will consider it in the future."

He nodded his head, bowed once more and left the room.

"Fresh tadpoles coming out in the spring should be washed clean in cold well water, and swallowed whole three or four days after menstruation. If a woman swallows fourteen live tadpoles on the first day and ten more on the following day, she will not conceive for five years. If contraception is still required after that, she can repeat the formula twice, and be forever sterile. . . . This formula is good in that it is effective, safe and not expensive. The defect is that it can be used only in the spring."

Grace put down the notes she was studying and laughed.

"Why do you laugh?" Mercy inquired.

It was spring again in Peking, after a long cold winter. The sisters were sitting in the shadow under a spreading date tree in the courtyard. Mercy was sewing on a small red satin jacket which she was making for her coming child.

"I am reading a formula for birth control," Grace replied and she read the paragraph aloud. Mercy listened, unbelieving.

"But it's nonsense, isn't it?" she exclaimed.

"It's disconcerting, but it may not be nonsense," her sister said. "That is the amazing fact about our ancient medicines. One thinks them absurd, but more often than not there's an element of truth, which a scientific method could develop. I wonder why our people did not develop science? We had a brilliant beginning, the invention of gunpowder, of printing, the knowledge of astronomy—"

She perceived that her sister was not listening.

"Anyway, tadpoles!" Mercy made a grimace of disgust. "And I prefer to follow the Chairman's direction. He said he hoped our people would take a wide view and realize that it is true our people number seven hundred million people and that this is an asset. A large population is a good thing, he said."

"And you proceed to add to it," Grace said, teasing.

"I'm proud of it," her sister retorted. She held up the

tiny jacket. "I hope it is a boy. I want to be a good Chinese wife. And I don't believe in birth control! It's a means of killing the Chinese people without shedding blood."

"You've been reading my old file of *The People's Daily*," Grace said.

"Well, so I have," Mercy retorted. "I'm anxious to know about everything here. I've been away so long, as though I'd been on another planet. There was no way of finding out anything while we were in America. Why don't the Americans want to know about us now?"

She looked at her sister, her lovely eyes wondering.

"They are afraid of us," Grace said.

"But why? We've always been friends."

"On their terms," Grace said. She considered, her mind absent. It was late afternoon. The heat of midday had subsided and an evening coolness was stealing in upon the wings of a slight breeze. In the round pool the fish, hidden under lotus leaves to protect themselves from the sun, came darting out to feed upon the minute insects floating upon the surface of the water.

"I can't imagine the Americans I knew wanting to act like imperialists," Mercy said. She put down her sewing and leaned back in her rattan chair.

"They wouldn't, of course, but here in China they were shielded under the umbrella of the empire of others. They have not yet created a way for themselves—the Eternal Way that our mother speaks of so often."

"Is ours the Eternal Way?" her sister asked.

"I don't know," Grace replied slowly. "I just don't know."

"Because, if it isn't," Mercy went on, "then we are lost, John and I. We have staked our lives on the faith that ours is the Eternal Way."

"And staked also the life of your child," Grace reminded her.

Mercy did not reply. She folded and refolded the small red jacket, while Grace was silent as twilight stole over the courtyard.

"He could have been born in America," Grace reminded her after a moment.

"We chose to have him born here," Mercy said firmly. "Come, let us go into the house. It is growing dark."

She would not say more as she rose to enter the house. John would soon be home and she wanted every comfort ready for his coming. For she had discerned, some weeks ago, a darkness of mood. The enthusiasm of his return seemed fading. He was as resolute as ever, early to rise in the morning and after a quick breakfast to be off to his work. Of this work he never spoke, and if she questioned he gave vague answers. She supposed then that he must be working on secret projects. In America she had made friends among the wives of nuclear scientists and had learned from them that these were projects so necessary to national security that scientists could not tell even their wives what they worked upon.

"I never dreamed my husband was helping to make the atomic bomb," one older wife had exclaimed.

All that Mercy could do, therefore, she did. When John Sung came home that evening he found hot tea waiting, his bath ready and fresh easy clothes laid out.

"You are tired again," Mercy said reproachfully.

"A very tiring day," he agreed somberly.

He sat down in a low chair in their room and closed his eyes.

"Drink your tea, darling," Mercy said coaxingly, pouring as she spoke.

He lifted the bowl and drank it half empty and put it down. Mercy watched his pale face. He had closed his eyes again and she thought she saw a tremor on his lips. Suddenly she was afraid. He was troubled or in trouble. Then why would he not tell her at least that there was trouble even if he could tell no more? She resisted the impulse to demand explanation. Instead, she took up the little red jacket from the table beside her.

"See what I made for the baby today!"

He took the jacket from her and smoothed it on his knee. "Very nice," he said listlessly.

Now she was really alarmed and hurt, besides.

"John!" she cried. "Aren't you glad we're having a baby? It's—he's—one of the reasons we came home, isn't he?"

He shook his head and handed her the tiny jacket. "Whether it was a good reason—valid, you know—" He broke off. "I'm tired, Mercy. I'll have my bath and rest a bit before dinner."

He left the room and she sat holding the jacket. Sudden foreboding clouded her spirit.

The museum was almost empty. The day was hot, a July day in New York, a clear summer's day, the sky blue above the city, but the heat dancing in shimmering waves above the narrow streets. A few people moved languidly about the vast rooms of the museum, the men coatless and the women sleeveless. Only one man, Joy observed, was dressed neatly in a dark suit, white shirt and pale gray tie. He was a Chinese, she had noticed the moment she entered. Strange how the Chinese eye selected at once the figure of a Chinese! He was standing before a painting, a modern conglomeration of colors and shape, and gazing at it with complete absorption. She moved nearer him and recognized the celebrated face of the famous Chinese artist Hsuan Teng. Her heart made a double beat. She had wanted to meet him ever since she had decided to become an artist. Indeed it had been his watercolors, faultless in Chinese technique, but of skyscrapers, docks, billboards and all the crowded sights of the city, that had helped her to her own decision to become an artist. Modern in every thought of her facile brain, she had not, however, wanted to paint in oils. Yet how could she express her own emotions, so inexplicably violent, in a gentler medium? In this hesitation she had discovered the paintings of Hsuan Teng, who, with all the subtlety of ancient Chinese art, could nevertheless portray the violence and the tragedy of modern life in a great city, and with such sharpness that she had quailed. Surely life was not built upon tragedy? Her own joyous nature refused the concept while she accepted the technique. I shall paint joy, she had told herself.

That he lived in New York she knew, and the knowledge had influenced her, at least mildly, to leave the shelter of the Brandons' house in San Francisco and take a small room in New York only a month ago. Whether or not she returned to China, at least let her discover all that she could of art before she went.

She approached Hsuan Teng. He seemed to see no one and she was obliged to ignore her own shyness.

"Mr. Hsuan?" she asked softly.

He turned his head and she saw his kind round face.

"Yes, I am he."

"I have wanted to meet you for such a long time but I have not dared."

He smiled. "Am I so formidable?"

"So far above me!"

Now that they had met she did not know what to say.

"We have not met, I think," Hsuan Teng said; his voice, somewhat high, was pleasant.

"Of course I know you," she told him. "Everyone must know you—but of course you don't know me. There is no reason why you should. I am Joyce Liang. My family calls me Joy."

"Quite truthfully, I am sure."

He had an air of old Chinese courtesy, a grace which reminded her of her mother's friends. How old was he? An indeterminate age, the face young but there was a glimmer of white at his temples.

"You are an artist?" he asked.

"How did you know?" she replied.

"Paint under your fingernails," he said.

They laughed, and his small eyes shone.

"I cannot resist an artist," he said. "Let us sit down. Tell me what you paint."

They sat on a bench side by side, facing a massive mural of conflicting yet blending colors.

"I can't answer your question," she said. "I paint, searching, perhaps, for what I want to paint."

"It is not easy to find what one is born to paint."

"Is one so born?"

"Beyond doubt. Do you know my work?"

"Who doesn't?"

He ignored the intent to praise. "Do you perceive an essence?"

She considered, but not for long and so replied. "The human figure is always small—so small that often he is lost. Your painting 'Father and Son'—I had to search the snow-covered landscape before I found them—no bigger than this!" She measured her thumbnail.

"The human figure is always there, is he not?" Hsuan Teng's voice was gentle.

"Always," she said.

"Because he is the essence, however small."

She looked at him earnestly. "I would like to learn from you."

"Why not?" he replied. "We are both Chinese. I will teach you what I have learned."

She could not speak for a moment. Artists were not often so generous but this was a great man as well as an artist. She remembered at this moment something her mother had once said:

"Talent is great only when the artist is great enough for his own talent. Only a great soul can fulfill his own talent."

She looked Hsuan Teng straight in the eyes.

"You are a great soul," she said.

From this hour their friendship began, the loving friendship of an older man for a young woman, the adoration of a young woman for an older man, asexual, and yet conscious, each of them, that they were man and woman. And then, inevitably, China came between them. Two artists, they fell into argument as to whether they should return to their own country. She told him of her mother, of her sisters, and he listened carefully.

"But none of these is an artist," he exclaimed.

"My sister Mercy sings."

"But you say she went back so that her child might be born in his own country! This is not the reasoning of a pure artist. She is mother first."

She could not deny this, for Mercy's letters now were always of the child soon to be born, and how right she had been to come home.

"I am giving my greatest gift to my country," she had written, "for what greater gift is there to one's country than a child, especially now when everything is new? You would not know how beautiful it is here; the hills outside the city are green with spring, and the people working in the fields are happy. Everyone works now in the fields, together. We are all one family—a wonderful time to be born."

Joy showed the letter to Hsuan Teng when she went to his studios for a lesson. It was their second meeting, and being still shy and anyway awed by the huge rooms, three of them opening one upon another, all richly furnished and hung with his paintings, she had almost immediately showed him the letter. He read it carefully, his sharp but kindly small eyes intent upon the lines. It was written in English, and he commented upon this:

"How is it she is writing you in a foreign language?"

"We've grown up with both languages," she explained.

He folded the letter and gave it back to her, then sat in reflective silence for a short space, his gaze fixed upon an old scroll opposite. Suddenly he spoke.

"Can you read the Chinese characters on that scroll?"

She blushed and shook her head. "I am the youngest of my sisters. When my mother sent us here I had finished only four years of school. Now I have forgotten many characters. I think anyway I could not read that ancient writing—seal characters, aren't they?"

He nodded. "Four ancient seal characters. Exactly translated, they are, 'Heart Resembling Gold Rock.' The scroll was presented to me by a society of artists before I left our country. I do not deserve such words but I keep them there on the wall so that every day I see them. They are carved on my brain. Do you know why?"

She shook her head, her eyes upon his earnest face.

"Because," he continued, "they describe the heart of a true artist. Gold, the finest of metals, as firm as a rock! When I am tempted, I remember, I consider, I hear the voices of my dead comrades, whose hearts were gold, but not rock."

"What do you mean, please?" she asked.

"I mean they are dead," he said sternly.

"In our country?"

"Yes!"

"But why?"

"They were gifted. They were hearts of gold," he said with such bitterness that she did not press the next question hanging on her lips. He asked it himself.

"How did they die? By decapitation for rebellion, by

hard labor for daring to criticize the rulers. The Hundred Flowers—have you heard of that?"

She nodded. Who did not know the days of the Hundred Flowers, proclaimed by the Chairman, invitation and enticement to free thoughts, ending in banishment, hard labor, death?

"Then you know why I do not return to our country," he said. "I know what I am. I am an artist—no more, no less. I have one duty—it is to fulfill my art."

"But can you not fulfill your art in our country? By helping them to understand?"

"In my country, where my friends are all dead?"

He gazed at her with somber eyes and she was afraid to speak. She could only return his look, half apologetically, as though she were at fault. Seeing her great sorrowful eyes, her tender mouth, he was gentle again.

"No, my child, freedom is the only air we artists can breathe, and wherever in the world the air is still free, that is our country. Do you understand?"

"I understand your words," she said, "but not your meaning."

"Ah, you are very young," he retorted.

With this he returned the letter and dismissed further discussion. Instead he rose and led her about the studio to look at one painting and another, talking as he went.

"In these rooms is the record of my life as an artist. Why do I say as an artist? I have no other life. Here you see the best of the paintings I did before I left China. I grew up in a village outside Shanghai. My family was good, but we were poor, for my father smoked opium. I was the youngest child and the last at home. We had very little money and not always enough food. Every morning my mother went out to work and she would give me money when she came home at night. 'Take this,' she would say, 'buy something for our supper. Don't let your father know I have given you money.' I promised, but he always did know. He would be waiting for me at the gate. He asked for nothing, he said nothing, but his eyes begged me. He was kind and quiet. I loved him—and I always saved some of the money and bought him a little opium secretly. When I came home he was waiting at the gate. I gave him the small packet and he took it and said nothing. And I said nothing."

"Did your mother never know?" Joy asked.

"If she knew, she, too, said nothing," he replied, and went on to another picture as he talked.

"Notice, please, this painting. It is the last I made before coming to America. A misty morning in a street in the Chinese part of Shanghai—a ricksha man pulling his vehicle, his customer a fat old gentleman, going to the teashop."

"All the rickshas are gone now, my mother writes me."

"Ah," he replied. "I daresay there is still bitter labor, nevertheless! All my friends—the best painter of us all was sent to dig a tunnel through a mountain."

He did not wait for her to speak and so continued, moving to the next painting. "This one is an experiment. I made it on the ship crossing the Pacific Ocean. I woke one morning to blue sea and floating clouds of white mist—nothing more."

"Space," she murmured, "infinite space of sea and sky, all expressed through watercolor! I have so much to learn."

"But when I reached San Francisco," he went on, "I was enchanted by great buildings high above the sea and the rocks. I painted my way across this foreign country, almost as vast as our own, until I reached the opposite ocean, the eastern sea, this city. Here I live, painting continually, blending my colors to express the meaning of the city, the focus of Western life, so beautiful, so hideous, so rich, so dangerously poor—"

He broke off and shrugged his shoulders. "Enough," he said. "Tell me what you painted before we met. Did you bring your portfolio?"

"I didn't dare."

"Are you afraid of me?"

"Of course I am."

"I don't understand. I, too, am still searching."

"Ah, yes, but you have your technique, your style."

"I never have my technique, my style. Each new concept demands—and brings—its own technique, its own style. An artist is always in flux, always ready for new impressions."

"But how to begin!"

"Begin by mixing colors and brushing them on your drawing paper. Let me show you—"

He led her to the third room, his work place, as she could see. An unfinished painting of enormous size was fastened to the wall. A smaller one stood on a large easel. Both were unfinished and both were of a vast theater filled with people, their enchanted gaze fixed upon a brilliant stage where dancers moved in elegant ballet.

179

"How do you blend?" she asked, fascinated by the nuances of light and darkness, of glitter and shadow.

"I mediate the colors with clear water," he said, and choosing a brush from a crowded jar, he dipped it in a bowl of clear water and applied it to a bold streak of scarlet in a woman's cloak, then blotted the wetness with absorbent paper. The harsh outline softened, the scarlet faded into deep rose and melted into the shadows.

"I may do that several times," he told her, "until the shades are exactly what I know is right."

It was the first of many lessons. She came to realize at last that it was he who kept her from returning to her own country, her own people, her mother and sisters. She was beginning to live her life apart and he was her teacher. Nevertheless she could not be with him day and night. He was famous and sought after, and it was necessary for him to appear in one place and another. Sometimes he went to Europe. Then she waited alone in her own small apartment in an old brownstone house on Thirtieth Street, or she even waited in his studios if his return were not too late. Waiting, she studied his paintings and at last she began a painting of her own, but an abstract, a troubled reflection of her secret indecision. Should she return or should she stay?

Days passed into weeks and weeks into months and slowly the question answered itself. She began to love him. If he did not love her, she would return to her own country.

"If, as you say, your younger sister is about to give birth to her first child, I recommend broth made from an old hen, in which a root of ginseng has been brewed," Dr. Tseng said.

Summer was over in Peking and the season of typhoons was at its height. Great waves lashed the shores of the southern seas. Shanghai, her mother wrote, was drowning in stormy rain. Peking was inland and far north, but high winds swirled the dust of the streets into miniature cyclones, and people closed their doors and windows against the difficult air. Mercy expected her child at any hour, and Dr. Tseng, aware of the expectation by means of the constant chatter of his wife, was expounding this morning to Dr. Grace Liang.

"To gain the best results," he said pontifically, "the ginseng root must be dug at the season of the full moon and the hour must be midnight. The best ginseng is to be found in Korea, the worst in America. In case of surgery and the need for anesthesia, Hua T'o, who became the God of Surgery in the second century, performed the most arduous operations without pain to his patients by an excellent anesthetic made from an emulsion of wine and hemp. It is said that one day the famous warrior Kuan Yün suffered an arrow wound in his upper arm. He laughed at Hua T'o when the anesthetic was suggested but he was able to play chess while the arrow was dug out. Unfortunately Hua T'o lost his life later. The usurper Ts'ao Ts'ao came to him to be cured of cruel headaches. Hua T'o was about to cut open his skull when Ts'ao Ts'ao grew suspicious and ordered him beheaded. Sad to say, while he waited in prison his ignorant wife burned all his papers in her kitchen stove."

"I think my sister does not wish anesthetics," Grace told him.

"Ah, in that case I commend her. The hen's broth, then, and do not forget the ginseng root."

Privately, Grace decided she would examine *Panax* ginseng, available here in the city, and discover for herself its chemical qualities. When her lesson was over, therefore, she retired to the small laboratory which had been assigned to her and set about her tasks. It was late afternoon and the building was almost empty of doctors and students when she finished her analysis. She had found nothing to justify Dr. Tseng's recommendations and was about to conclude that ginseng was useless except as a superstition when the door opened and Liu Peng stood before her.

"Ah, here you are, Comrade!" he exclaimed. "I have searched halls and classrooms for you. Then I met old Dr. Tseng on his way home, and he said you had studied ginseng today, since he had recommended using it for your sister who is soon to begin childbirth. I thought of your doubting nature, guessed you might be making your own experiments, and here I find you."

She poured into a pan the remaining elixir and threw the root into the waste. "There is nothing here to help in childbirth," she declared. "Tannin, bitters, resin, starch and volatile oils—that's all."

She was about to empty the liquid finally into the sink to be drained away when he stayed her, his hand on her wrist.

"Wait, you have missed an element. There should be a little panacin—very little, but perhaps enough for healing. There is always something true in our materia medica."

He did not immediately remove his hand and she was conscious of its powerful weight, a big hand, finely formed. She had noticed his hands months ago, on a certain night, to be exact, when he had taken her to an old, small restaurant, where duck was prepared in traditional fashion. It had been a moonlit night in August, the seventh month of the moon year, and she had worn Chinese dress, a long slim gown with a stiff high collar and no sleeves. The gown was of cherry red brocade, one that she had had for several years and had not worn since her return, for few wore bright colors nowadays. She had even been uncertain about a long gown, for Liu Peng was politically strict, even stern. But that night he had seemed gentle, and as they lingered over wine, he had given her a long contemplating look and had then spoken almost softly.

"I had forgotten how a woman glows—a beautiful woman in a long red gown."

"You don't think it wrong of me?"

"Not when we dine alone in a small old restaurant and drink shao-hsing wine with roasted duck!"

From that night on she had surmised his heart and questioned her own. Was there to be something between them one day? He was overworked, always busy, a modern surgeon, fearless and original, she had observed when she had seen him operate, and he suffered monstrously when he lost a case. Yet he had never been abroad. All he had learned of Western medicine had been in the great modern hospital here in Peking, the gift of an American, half a century ago.

"Ginseng is bitter at first when it is brewed," he was saying now. "Then it grows sweet. It's the starch."

"I have never tasted it," she told him, withdrawing her hand.

"Be careful when you do—it's said to be an aphrodisiac."

He was teasing her and she made a grimace. "I don't believe in such things. Aphrodisiacs are taken only by people whose minds are on lovemaking anyway."

"So you don't believe in lovemaking?"

"I didn't say that—"

Before she could finish, she heard her name called.

"Dr. Liang, you are wanted in the office. Your sister has arrived at the hospital to give birth. Dr. Liang! Dr. Liang! You are wanted—"

"Oh," she gasped. "I must go—immediately."

She left him without another look and hastened on her way. Her nephew, the child of Mercy and John Sung, was born six hours later in the western wing of the hospital. He was a strong child, plump and lusty, and he shouted his anger when Grace administered a sharp slap on his buttocks. Later his mother, sipping hen's broth and ginseng, smiled.

"I have fulfilled the purpose of my life," she said. "I have presented a new citizen to my country."

Madame Liang had received the news of her grandson's birth with emotion. It had been her intention to travel to Peking to be present at the birth, but since the child belonged to his father's family she felt it might seem presumptuous if she were present. She resolved to content herself with seeing him when he was brought to visit her after his first month. Nevertheless she celebrated in her own fashion by dispatching gifts to daughter and child and then by retiring to her own quarters for the rest of the day.

Here she allowed herself a mood of reflection and memory. For the day was not all joy. To balance the birth of the child was the fact that this same day was the anniversary of the death of her old friend, the famous female impersonator Mei Lan Fang. She remembered the afternoon, many years ago, when she had first called upon Mei Lan Fang, after seeing him perform the night before in his famous role of *Mulan, the Warrior Maid*. That one in history was thought by all to be a man, until, after twelve years of superb military service, the emperor offered his daughter in marriage and she was compelled to acknowledge that she was a woman.

There were certain experiences in Madame Liang's life which she kept as treasures in her memory and her friendship with Mei Lan Fang was one of the most precious, although she felt nothing romantic in their relationship, for to her he was neither male nor female, only an exquisite human being. He had made visible to her the beauty of pure art, and his gentle movements, like "wind over weeping willow trees," his beautiful high voice, his "asparagus-tip" fingers, all combined to make him the greatest female impersonator of Chinese opera. She had visited him several times in his palace, had drunk delicate tea there and had eaten the small cream-filled sweetmeats his Tibetan cook prepared, which he loved and which kept his figure always slightly too plump. Then she had ceased to meet him and had confined her acquaintance to his opera performances.

"In the flesh you confuse me," she had explained.

He had laughed but had understood. "It is true I am not myself except on the stage. But, if you are in the audience, stand for a moment when I enter. To know your presence will inspire me to my best."

His best was perfection. The sleeve movements, more than fifty, by which he could express every shade of emotion, the hand gestures which signified action—opening a door from inside, from outside, swimming rivers, mounting a horse, drinking, stepping into a vehicle, the daily events of life in an opera, when there was no scenery except a city wall, no props—all he performed with such detail of grace and accuracy that the audience went mad with delight. True to his art, he had not yielded to the persuasions of politicians but had continued to perform as usual, ignoring the clamor of propagandists. Indeed, when Japanese conquerors occupied Peking he had refused to perform and in protest he grew a beard, which his barber shaved off when they departed and the country was returned to the people again.

In his last years she had gone more and more often to see him in the ancient operas which portrayed the heroes and heroines of history, for in this strange and turbulent present it became essential to keep alive the past. And the day he died she in her heart had been chief mourner at the great state funeral which the new government had decreed.

So upon this anniversary which she would have spent in silent memory of a friend who was also a great artist and traditionalist, Fate had sent her a grandson, a portent of tomorrow, and none knew what he would become, surrounded as he was by great heaving forces whose influence none could foretell, except that they came out of the past. It occurred to her now that with the death of Mei Lan Fang that past had come to an end even on the stage and in story.

If this were true, then what powers would shape the newborn child?

*   *   *

The large bare room, the minister's private office, was chill with coming winter. A brazier of charcoal glowed in the center but its heat could not be felt a foot away, and John Sung sat far from it and near the door, though facing Chao Chung behind the wooden desk.

"You still refuse to develop the secret weapon for use in the United States?" Chao Chung demanded.

"I ask to be relieved of working on weaponry," John Sung replied.

His honest dark eyes, enlarged by the thick lenses of his spectacles, were unblinkingly fixed upon the handsome face opposite him. The minister took up a paper and appeared to be studying it in silence. Without lifting his eyes he began after a moment to speak, half absorbed, apparently, in what he was reading.

"You understand you have no right to refuse a command?"

John Sung did not reply. He sat motionless and waiting. The minister put down the paper and appeared to be searching for another among the pile on his desk. Meanwhile he continued talking.

"All scientific effort must now be concentrated in the area of defense. We have learned our lesson. We, the most civilized of people, have been misled by our own sages through the last four thousand years. We are now over-civilized in a world of barbaric peoples. We were taught centuries ago that war is not the pastime of a civilized people. We stopped the development of explosive weapons a thousand years ago, on the ground that it was inhuman and monstrous to kill innocent people. Let warriors fight with broadswords and kill each other, we said, but others who are innocent must not die by accident. Therefore, though we understood the principles of rocketry, we did not allow it to be used. Even gunpowder was used only in fireworks. We felt secure in our place under heaven, the center of a protective ring of subject peoples, beyond whose borders we did not penetrate. Who could have imagined that those outer barbarians would themselves develop atomic bombs and rocket weapons and all manner of deadly chemicals? You, a scientist, know their secrets. Can you refuse to protect your own people?"

John Sung did not reply. He sat in stolid silence, gazing at the minister. Suddenly that minister slapped his desk with both palms. He shouted in loud short barks.

"I know why you refuse to create the secret weapon! You hide a traitorous love for Americans! They are our most dangerous enemies! The Russians are too stupid for us to fear! The Americans are not stupid! They surround us with their bases! They must be destroyed!" He paused for breath.

"They don't hate us," John Sung said in a mild voice.

"Does that matter, if we hate them?" the minister retorted.

"Why should we hate the American people?" John Sung asked.

He knew very well how dangerous it was to make such inquiry but his sense of justice compelled him. He had lived in America with his uncle's merchant family since childhood. When he thought of America he saw crowds of forthright, kindly folk, ignorant of the world, but curious, and liking to be amused. He could not, to save his life, create a weapon to destroy them. He was in grave danger, yet how could he tell his predicament even to his wife, rejoicing in the child for whose sake they had returned to their own country? The minister was shouting again.

"Why should we hate them? Because ours is the only true civilization! Even in science—consider that we invented the sternpost rudder twelve hundred years before the Europeans did! Fore-and-aft sails in the third century! Treadmill paddle wheel for boats five hundred years later! Warships with rams and twenty paddle wheels by the twelfth century—the British thought we had copied theirs, the fools! In the thirteenth century we had ships with fifty cabins for passengers, six-masts, double planking, watertight compartments! Only in the last century did the barbarians even have transverse bulkheads! Five hundred years ago we already had ships four hundred and fifty feet long, and we grew fresh vegetables aboard in tubs! We sailed the high seas to Sumatra and India, to Aden and Africa and even to Madagascar—sixty years before the Portuguese bit a piece from the thigh of India! I curse Confucius and all those mad saints who persuaded us against war! Did you ever hear of Sun Wa, who lived three thousand years ago? No? Read his *Art of War!* 'If you are not in danger, do not fight,' he wrote. Now we are in danger! You among all our scientists, you can provide our defense."

He paused, breathless, and saliva foamed on his lips.

"Do you still refuse?" he demanded as John Sung sat staring at him in silence.

"I still refuse," he said, but his voice came more faintly.

"Then you must be—compelled," the minister said gently, very gently.

John Sung rose. "Am I dismissed?"

"Temporarily," the minister replied with sudden indifference.

John Sung entered their bedroom, where his wife was suckling their child. She was in a low rattan chair, her feet propped on a footstool. A Western oil stove warmed the room, and he spread his hands over it. She looked up at him and smiled.

"Our son has gained nearly a pound since we came home," she said.

"I wish you could see the picture you make," he said.

They spoke in English, uncertain of listening ears, and he realized at this moment what he had not before, that imperceptibly and unconsciously everything they said was with the unspoken consciousness that someone was listening. Now, feeling, too, that they might be watched, he went to the window and drew the curtain across the panes. Then he sat down on the edge of the big Chinese bed. Should he tell her of the danger? He could not. And would it not be useless, since they could not escape? He would be watched wherever he was, wherever he went. Better merely to continue his work in his laboratories! They had been generous in allowing him space and he had now put aside nuclear physics, at least for the present, to explore the nature of chromosomes. Scientists in other parts of the world were making the same explorations and he longed to know of their progress but he had no source of information. His country had returned to its traditional isolation. He pondered the dangers in this isolation, for how could a modern people live in safety who did not know what happened elsewhere in the world? He remembered the minister's recounting of history, all true, and yet how useless when the people here were ignorant of what others were doing and so could build no defense!

"We are repeating the same old mistakes," he muttered.

"What did you say, John?" Mercy asked.

"Nothing," he said. "Nothing at all. I was just thinking."

She laughed. "Now I know you are happy. You can't forget your work even when you come home . . . Look at his little hands! Aren't they adorable? Feel how soft they are! Like rose petals—"

He rose obediently, forcing his mind to give up its fear and even its thoughts, and kneeling beside his wife, he took his son's small pink fist and held it on his own palm. Looking down at that minute human hand, he felt his first real impulse of fatherhood. He was responsible for this new life. Had he the right, then, to imperil it at the very beginning? Dare he indulge his personal conscience at such cost? He could not bring himself to decide—not now, not yet!

Summer passed, the new child thrived and grew as autumn turned to winter. The household in the *hutung* in Peking seemed tranquil enough. Each member fulfilled the days, absorbed, it seemed, in the present. Thus on a clear cold day before the end of the moon year, the sky as blue as the tiles on the ancient palaces, Dr. Grace Liang was skating on the frozen lake outside the ancient imperial palace. She was a graceful skater, but Liu Peng was more swift. They passed, he turned, they skated side by side until she stumbled. He caught her before she fell and they paused.

"I twisted my ankle," she gasped, breathless.

"Let us stop," he said. "Also, I am hungry."

They spoke in Chinese, his English being of the school-boy variety, its accent Irish, because, as he had explained, his teacher had been Irish. She had laughed—it was amusing to hear Irish brogue in a Chinese! "Oysters, not eyesters," she had told him.

"And plase not to desthroy intirely my poor English!" he had retorted.

After that, however, he had spoken only in Chinese and she perceived that he did not like to be laughed at.

"Let me see your ankle," he said now as she unstrapped her skates.

She thrust forward her left foot and he felt her ankle delicately.

"The ice is rough," she told him. "I stumbled on a bump."

"In the old days," he said, "the emperor—and latterly the empress—always sent out servants to smooth the ice with hot irons. Now of course there is no empress or emperor—"

"And no servants, really—only comrades."

He looked up at her sharply but did not reply to this. "Your ankle is not sprained, only twisted. Your Dr. Tseng will prescribe for you, perhaps the herb *t'ien men tung* how do you call it in English—shiny asparagus, I think."

"Do you really believe in our ancient medicines?"

"There is much truth in them."

They were walking now toward the restaurant nearest the lake and she was trying not to limp. He continued:

"Take *ai yen*, for example."

"Mugwort wormwood?"

"I don't know the English and it was forbidden in the

West, although I read somewhere that now, very recently, it has been approved again because it has been found to aid the flow of bile."

They entered the restaurant and seated themselves at a small table in the corner. The place was crowded, for it was the hour of the late afternoon meal, the second and last meal of the day.

"I never know what to believe," she said. "Yet I must say—"

"Say what?" he asked, for she had paused.

"Well, Dr. Tseng told me to take my sister's left pulse before her child was born, and if it was quick and did not slow itself, she would have a boy. If her right pulse had these symptoms, it would be a girl. Her left pulse had them and it was a boy."

"People cannot live for thousands of years and learn nothing," Liu Peng said. "We are the oldest people on earth and the wisest. We are superior to the West in everything except firearms. Even our great leader Sun Yat-sen said that only in science could the Chinese learn from the West but in the true principles of philosophy the West must learn from us."

He spoke with innocent conviction, as she was amazed to perceive, for his handsome face was calm with self-satisfaction. Reflecting upon it later that night alone in her own room, she was astounded to discover that this Liu Peng, being altogether Chinese, was thoroughly convinced of his superiority because he was a Chinese. It was many weeks before she understood the full measure of such conviction and then it was her mother who made the revelation.

Meanwhile, comfortably in bed, she recalled the day. Was it possible that she was beginning to be attracted to Liu Peng? She thought of his handsome frame, solid yet graceful, his square face—here she remembered that the heroes of Chinese stories always had square faces, bold eyes, and firm, full lips. This was also Liu Peng's face. She remembered another face, Clem's, and realized that for a long time, months, she had not thought of him. They had interchanged two or three letters and suddenly she received no more. Were the letters stopped upon some unknown order? She would never know, and the uncertainty made her write no more.

" 'Drive out the tiger by the front gate and let in the wolf by the back gate,' " Madame Liang quoted.

Her daughter Grace had arrived from Peking on a visit at the moment when the Russian scientists in anger were leaving China.

"Now we are beginning to discover what we did," she continued, "and therefore let us welcome the departure of the wolf also."

Grace lifted her eyebrows. "The tiger being?"

"The Japanese, the Western imperialists, and the Russians are the wolf, of course," Madame Liang replied. "But I knew the Russians were not here to stay—a barbarous people, as hairy as apes! We have tolerated them all these years —why, I do not know. They took Outer Mongolia and Manchuria, by domination, at least. Now let them go."

Grace protested. "But, M-ma, no one else will help us, certainly not the Americans!"

"Let us use our own talents," Madame Liang said firmly. "For this I approved the return of my son-in-law, John Sung, to our country. He did well to join our scientists. We will take the lead in science again as we once did, to the astonishment of the world."

"M-ma, I never heard you speak so—patriotically, shall I say?"

"I am Chinese," Madame Liang declared. "I believe in our destiny. I trust our fate. In my secret heart, I now regret the revolution which in my small way I helped to bring about. Our mistake? We overthrew our own imperial government, the best, the wisest, ever devised by mankind. Yes, in our young ignorance, we destroyed our national treasure. Now all is confusion. Where will it end? We can only trust to our own genius, which has brought us to order and prosperity again and again during our thousands of years."

"I do not know what to think," Grace murmured.

Madame Liang did not reply. She sat at her desk in her private office. A large window opened upon the west garden, and across its wide panes snowflakes drifted to the ground. Although it was the holiday of the Chinese New Year, the city was quiet and she expected no callers, since she made no calls. Except for her business she lived in total seclusion.

"I suppose," Grace mused, "that we Chinese were led to the conviction of our own superiority because we were surrounded by lesser peoples and did not travel beyond our own borders to Europe and America."

"We knew our own superiority before Europe and America existed," her mother retorted. "And do you think there is anything new under heaven? I trust all to our own people! In the ancient *Book of History*, upon which Confucius himself based his philosophy, it is said . . ."

Here Madame Liang composed herself to recite:

> The people must be cherished,
> The people must not be oppressed,
> The people are the root of the country
> If the root is firm, the country is tranquil.

"And you remember," she continued, "that, when asked which was most important to a state, food, weapons or the trust of the people, the sage replied that weapons could be given up, and even food be sacrificed, but the state itself would be destroyed if the people had no confidence in it."

"And have the people confidence now?" Grace asked.

Madame Liang gave her daughter a strange look. "Ah, it is a question—have they?"

"And the answer?" Grace persisted.

"It is what it was when the question was first asked, thousands of years ago. Though all seems changed, the people are not changed. Did not Mencius say, 'Heaven has no fixed will, but sees as the people see, and hears as the people hear'?"

Her daughter heard these words with a sense of confusion. Was it possible that she did not understand her mother? Or was her mother trying to convey a secret discontent? Upon reflection later that night alone in her room, she comprehended a curious similarity of spirit in her mother and in all other Chinese, and this spirit was the ancient and absolute confidence in the superiority of being Chinese. Differ though they might and did, Communist or not, her people, the Chinese, still believed themselves the center of the world, geographically of course, but also of the human race itself. She marveled that this could be true except through ignorance. Yet her mother, so wise, so cultivated, so gracious, could not be ignorant. And were not these the attributes of superiority?

Lying awake in her bed, the cold moonlight slanting across the floor, she laughed softly to herself. Could any force, human or natural, destroy a people who believed themselves indestructible, had so believed for thousands of years and would so believe, perhaps forever? Was this not the guarantee of life, the Eternal Way?

Liu Peng sought her out the day she returned to Peking. He ran after her down the long central corridor of the medical building and when she turned to find him at her side he drew her into an empty classroom.

"Great news," he cried. "The Russians are all gone! Like thieves, they have departed."

"Since they helped us, what if you rejoice too soon?" she replied.

"What is this 'too soon'?" he demanded. "There cannot be two suns in the sky. We cannot continue to bow down before Russians. The Chairman is right. The break must be clean. Coexistence is fantasy. One must always be above. We have always been that one."

"You too!" she exclaimed. "You and my mother!"

"How me too?" he inquired.

"You are using Communism as an instrument to express

your convictions as a Chinese—an instrument instead of an ideology! Emperors did the same in the old days when China was the center of the world—to us, at least."

"How do you mean, 'to us at least'?"

"Our country never was the center of the world—we only thought it was."

"What is this? You are for Khrushchev? Coexistence!"

"No, only for truth."

"But—but of course we have always been the center! None was ever equal to us. The whole world wanted our trade. Our influence spread around the four seas! The world still wants our trade, and once more the world fears us. One by one the surrounding countries will yield to our influence as they did before. Under Communism, too, all will look to our leadership!"

She scoffed. "The ancient concept—the Great Unity!"

"Why not?" he demanded.

She was suddenly angry with him; he was absurd, medieval, anything but the modern man he believed himself to be. Yet in the vortex of her anger she felt drawn to him with a new and irresistible attraction. His eyes were brilliant in blackness; his square mouth was firm; he was all earnestness and fire. What was this rising fever in her blood?

"You—you, too, are Chinese," Liu Peng was saying. "You understand our people very well. If you do not understand, then I will teach you. I will compel you. Yes, you are right. Communism is our present instrument but the meaning is the same, the power is there. What does the instrument matter if the power is there, if the meaning is the same? One by one what was ours will return to us. The tributary countries will pay tribute to us again. All will be harmony under our direction. Without war we will win now as we always have. The lesser peoples are our younger brothers. They will deliver themselves to our guidance. Then will come the Great Peace. You and I are not on opposite sides. We are together on the same side. I will not have you separate from me. We stand together, you and I. We are Chinese!"

She tried to laugh; she tried to say that what he meant was that she must stand at his side, wherever he was, and that she could not accept the subsidiary position. She had seen the world beyond. She had seen America. But she could not laugh, she could not speak. His face was coming near to hers. His eyes burned into hers. He took her hands in both his hands and crushed them against his breast.

"Do I speak the truth?" he demanded.

"Yes," she said, her voice a whisper.

They parted hurriedly to fulfill the duties of the day, and she reviewed her feelings as she worked. Yes, perhaps she was in love, but how little she knew of the man she loved, and how little he knew of her! Yes, she was Chinese, but a Chinese who had traveled far beyond the fringe of countries that had been tributaries to an ancient power. Liu Peng knew nothing of the world as it was today and desired to know nothing. She was troubled by the monstrous responsibility of love. Of course she must somehow inform him and bring him into reality. He was young; he was brilliantly intelligent; he would see the truth when she revealed it. As for her mother, since she was no longer young, let her keep the comforts of illusion.

Such were the conclusions she devised during the morning while old Dr. Tseng droned on with the day's lesson.

"In case of acupuncture, the time period must also be considered. On a fine day, the sun shining, blood in the human body flows smoothly, saliva is free, breathing is easy. On days of chill and cloud, blood flows thick and slow, breathing is heavy, saliva is viscous. When the moon is waxing, blood and breath are full. When the moon wanes, blood and breath wane. Therefore acupuncture should be used only on fair warm days, when the moon is waxing or, best of all, when the moon is full."

"Interesting," Grace said in comment, "in bioclimatic research in the West, coronary attacks increase in frequency on cold chilly days when the sun is under clouds."

Dr. Tseng turned the page of his blue cloth-covered book. "Ah, doubtless the barbarians across the four seas have heard of our learning," he observed without interest.

"You are condemned to hard labor on the land," the minister said.

John Sung stirred in his seat. The wooden chair upon which he sat was suddenly intolerably hard. He cleared his throat.

"I have another reason not to enter the area of science where you have asked me to go, Mr. Minister. I am working now in the field of genetics."

"You are a scientist, and all scientific principles are the same."

John Sung did not reply. To contradict the man would be useless; to argue with the minister would be dangerous. He would simply not yield. His silence enraged the minister.

"You scientists!" he shouted. "Your political attitudes! You deny the very principles the Chairman gives his life to establish!"

John Sung was patiently stubborn. "Science teaches the spirit of inquiry. We are taught to observe, to examine, to conclude only when results are tried and proved."

"There are things which must be accepted as they are announced!"

"Not for the scientist."

"Then we cannot accept the scientist!"

"Whether he is accepted does not change him. He pursues the immutable, unchanging truth."

"You are sentenced to hard labor in a distant field!"

The minister's voice now was a roar. John Sung rose.

"When do I leave?"

"Tomorrow morning!"

John Sung bowed and was about to leave. At the door he paused, and turning, he faced the minister.

"Each man has his own way of serving his country," he said.

He told his wife at once, as soon as they were alone in their room. Their child was on a mat on the floor playing with a clay toy. She had been holding him in her arms in the main room, but when John entered she saw at once that he had something to tell. Now it was told. She had placed the child on the floor, had turned to face her husband, and he told her.

"I am to be sent away for hard labor."

Her breath left her. He saw her face grow ashen pale, and her voice was tight and high.

"You are accused?"

"Because I refuse to work on poison weapons against Americans."

He described the plan to poison the sources of water in the United States, the rivers, the reservoirs, brooks where cattle fed. She was defenseless against such reasons for his refusal to obey the central powers.

"No, of course you can't. I see that you had to refuse—of course—of course! I am proud of you—but I feel guilty."

"Guilty?" he asked.

"It was I who insisted that we come here, for the child—"

She bit her lip; he put his right arm about her shoulders, and lifted her chin with his left hand.

"Each of us serves his country as he sees best. Don't regret."

They stood for a fraught moment, he gazing deep into her eyes. Then, unable to bear the thought of not seeing her, perhaps for years, he released her and sank into one of the rattan chairs.

"We must give up the idea of the modern apartment," he told her.

They wanted a place of their own, now that the child was here, and she had said then why not a really modern sort of place in one of the eight- or ten-story brick apartment houses newly built outside the city area? The old city walls had been torn down, trees had been planted, and she could almost imagine the suburb of an American city here in the ancient capital.

"You must stay with your sister," he was saying, now, "or else go to Shanghai with your mother."

"I will stay here," she said. "I will start my school of music at last. I must make the time pass somehow!"

Tears filled her eyes, and he tried to comfort her.

"It is a good way to serve your country," he told her.

It was too soon for comfort. His voice sounded hollow even to himself, and their eyes meeting, she suddenly sobbed aloud and flung herself into his arms.

"Prices are higher than one can pay, Madame," Chu San said.

Madame Liang sighed. "Heaven has put a curse on us."

The day seemed like any other day. Yet each day, by imperceptible degrees, was worse than the one before. The people, blind with faith and hope, had been led astray. The year before, great decisions had been made by those above. She had distrusted them and had even dared to make known her distrust to the Minister Chao Chung.

"We Chinese are not like the outer peoples," she had told him. "Those peoples trust to their inventions, but we trust to the land."

"We will trust to everything at once," Chao Chung had replied with his usual confidence. "Where the outer peoples trust to their inventions, we will trust our own inventions and our land also. We will make a double leap forward, in manufacturing and in agriculture, and this at the same instant."

She had replied with doubting silence. As the months passed she watched in deepening dismay as the heroic peasants and other lowly people strove to learn how to smelt iron ore in small ovens built in their backyards and on their threshing floors. She watched with alarm as the peasants were herded into communes.

"Old Li has come to beg a little food," Chu San continued.

She was eating her own breakfast at this moment, but she pushed the dishes aside.

"Bring him before me," she commanded.

Chu San went away, and she sat in despondent waiting. She knew now that within her own family a blow had been struck. Without a word to her, Chao Chung, whom alone she had trusted, had banished her daughter's husband to hard labor. What a waste. she mourned, to put to manual servitude a man with his brain! Did not heaven create many men, each different from the other? To each, therefore, his own labor! The ancients were right when they so valued their scholars that they refused to allow them to do manual labor, lest mind be wearied with body!

The door opened softly and Old Li, a peasant, stood there, blinking and smiling. He had aged very much in the years since she had last seen him on his own fragment of land outside the city. She had known him first when, in the days of Japanese occupation, she had gone with Chu San to the farms outside the city to search for eggs and fowl for the restaurant. At that time he had been a self-respecting farmer, complaining only that the Japanese soldiers had found his secret grain storage a few days before. Then a ruddy-faced man of middle age, now he appeared thin and ragged and old.

"Sit down," she said, and to Chu San, "Bid Chou Ma fetch another bowl and a pair of chopsticks."

"I dare not, I dare not," Old Li said with country courtesy, but his eyes were fastened on the hot rice gruel in its wooden bucket, and the dishes of salted eggs and fish and hot twisted crullers.

"How can I eat unless you eat with me?" Madame Liang replied with equal courtesy.

Then, seeing his yellow, lined face, his bleak eyes sunken in their sockets, she motioned to him imperiously to sit at the table with her, and when, abashed and shy, he did so, she leaned toward him and said in a low voice, "Tell me all you have suffered."

Trusting her, as everyone did, he began in a low voice. "You know me, lady. I am a common man, as were all my ancestors. Not one of our many generations could read a book, or thought of reading books. Heaven put us on the land and we have stayed there. Nevertheless, in our own way, we did well. In my great-grandfather's time we were able to buy a little land. Since then each generation bought more until, when my father died, we had seventeen acres and I dreamed of making it twenty in this generation. Because I am the only son, I hired a few men poorer than I to help me till the land until my own two sons were old enough to do more than take the water buffalo to pasture. Who would have thought such an age would come upon us that those I hired would turn against me and call me a land-owner, and to be despised therefore?"

He looked so piteous, his little gray beard trembling on his chin, that Madame Liang tried to comfort him.

"They turned against you because they had no land themselves. But what of your sons?"

"They too have deserted me," the old man said mournfully. "They went to school and now they wander everywhere preaching the wonders of this new day. They declare I am no longer their father—I, who begat them from these loins!"

He slapped the lean shanks under his faded blue cotton trousers and let his head droop. Chou Ma came in with bowl and chopsticks and she filled the bowl and went away.

"Eat," Madame Liang directed. "Hot food comforts also the soul."

To encourage him she took up her own chopsticks again. He ate for a brief space, trying not to show his hunger and, his bowl emptied, she filled it without calling Chou Ma. When he had thus downed three bowls and all but emptied the small dishes, she insisting, he put down his chopsticks and began talk.

"We cannot let down our hearts, not even for an hour, we people of the land, we old hundred names," he said. "In truth, we work our bodies to skin and bone, with bitter labor. By day we till the land; in common we plant, we reap the harvest, an army of men and women. At night we try to make iron. How can we make iron? It has not been our destiny. When people work beyond their destiny, all they do fails." He leaned forward to speak in a low voice that none but she could hear.

"There will be no harvest this year! Even as the iron we make is useless, the land will not produce its crops. Many work, but they are strangers to the land. They plant too deep or too shallow, and the earth refuses to nourish the seed and the seed dies. By next year, lady, all our people will suffer from hunger and lack. These rags I wear and must wear, for there is no cloth to be bought! Even thread and needles are lacking, and who spins and weaves? By two years from now, the people will be desperate, and what then will become of Those?"

"They will change," Madame Liang said. "They know in

their secret hearts that the will of the people is heaven's will."

"Storms will come," the old man went on, unheeding. "Rain will fall in some places and drought will last for many months elsewhere. Locusts will eat what we grow, and our fields will be bare. Heaven is angry. Many people will escape to Hong Kong. Among them will be this humble man. I have nothing now to sell, no eggs, no fowl, no pork, no cabbage. I was not so poor even under the Japanese tyrants. But what of you, lady?"

"I will stay. I have always stayed," Madame Liang replied.

John Sung was sleepless on his narrow bed of boards laid upon two wooden benches. He had become accustomed to a spring mattress, and in justice he knew that in American comfort his body had grown soft. Now his body was sore, every muscle aching as though torn from his bones. Yet at daybreak bells would ring and whistles would blow to summon to the fields the peasants among whom he was now stationed. Again in justice, rough though it be, he was compelled to acknowledge in the privacy of his own thoughts that there was an element of rightness in the policy of subjecting the intellectuals to hard manual labor. A waste for the time being, he reflected, but a necessity if a modern nation was to be welded out of this vast population of seven hundred million people, three-fourths of them peasants! He admitted, here in the predawn darkness, his hipbones pressing against the boards, that he himself had never so much as lifted a hoe until now, nor wielded a hammer to drive a nail. In his boyhood home in Chinatown, San Francisco, his old-fashioned Chinese aunt never let him work even in the small vegetable garden in their backyard, or help her in the house.

"Women will do such work," she insisted. "You are the son. You must study your books."

Such separation of intellectuals like himself from the peasants, and this for centuries here in his own country, had led inevitably to a dominating elite that had no concern for their own people and were consequently the chief obstacle to the building of a nation. The Chairman, himself the son of a peasant, had early decreed that the scholars and students must also learn to work with their hands. His own palms were already blistered. The long-handled hoe, certainly an improvement over the ancient short-handled hoe, had nevertheless worn through his too tender skin. On his right hand the blisters had broken and were festering.

"Comrade, you hold your hoe too tightly," the young peasant who worked next him had said yesterday. "Hold a hoe too hard and it fights you. Watch me—" He had swung his own hoe high, had let it strike into the earth as if by its own weight.

The light of coming day now crept through the cracks of the wooden walls. Men stirred and groaned in their sleep. Here and there a man sat up and stared about him, bewildered. They were all bewildered, John Sung thought, and none more than he. Changes bewildered them, vast upheaving changes, such as separation of parents and children, old from young, men from women, and they were all living apart, each from each, and they woke up, dazed, to this new day of hard work and promises. Such promises! He heard them shouted out by hoarse voices of ardent young cadres.

"The production brigade is the foundation of the People's Commune! Comrades, you will have your reward! No more famines! No more hunger! Everything for everyone!"

His reply was silent but steadfast. It was all doomed to fail. The premises were wrong. Human nature prevails, and human beings think, work and live for themselves. Rewards were essential, and today there were no rewards.

The sun rose to the horizon. Bells rang, whistles screamed, men leaped to their feet and pulled their clothes about them. In fifteen minutes, the time allotted, the peasants had lined up. The commanders of brigades and teams shouted and men began to march to the fields. The careless, comfortable old days were gone, the days when neighboring peasants, two or three together, chatting and laughing, smoking their short bamboo pipes, went each to his own fields. The days that had lasted for thousands of years were now ended. Five hundred million peasants, men and women, marched like soldiers to the fields that were no longer theirs and with them marched John Sung. But still it was all doomed to failure. Under the heavy sense of doom he took up his hoe, one in an endless line.

The clock in the central room of the house in Peking was near midnight when John Sung's day ended. All clocks in the entire land marked the same time, in order, the Chairman decreed, that the country and its citizens would be a single entity, living at the same tempo and under the same conditions. Yet Jen Yu-ti in the official book, *The Geography of China*, had written:

"The sun rises in the east of China four hours earlier than in the west. When the Ussuri, in the extreme eastern part of the country, is bathed in the golden rays of the morning sun, it is still night in T'ien Shan and in the Pamirs in the far West." *

Mercy, entering her room at the end of her day's work, glanced at the watch on her wrist. The true time was exactly twenty minutes past six. A door opened and an elderly woman, carrying the baby, came into the room.

"The little lord cried not once while you were gone," she said proudly.

The baby stretched out his arms to his mother and she took him and pressed him to her.

"Were there letters today?" she asked.

It was her daily question, although in five months only once had there been an affirmative reply.

"A letter from your honored mother in Shanghai," the old woman told her. "Here, I have kept it in my bosom."

She gave the letter to Mercy and busied herself with pouring tea from a pot always hot on the table, and handing the bowl to her mistress, she continued to talk.

"The price of food is now getting very high, mistress. Pork is four times what it was this time last year. If the drought keeps on, there will be nothing to eat. The land is drying up and blowing away."

Mercy did not answer. She was reading the letter avidly. Had her mother succeeded or failed? No one had the quiet power that her mother had. Was not her mother invincible? She was able to buy food when no one else knew where to look. The great restaurant was more crowded than ever. She followed down the pages of thin rice paper the perpendicular lines of her mother's exquisitely fine brush writing:

* Jen Yu-ti, *The Geography of China* (Peking, Ed. Langues Etrangins) and page 200, *China, The Other Communism*, by K. S. Karol (New York: Hill & Wang, revised 1968).

"As I promised, I spoke to one individual of another. He agreed to see what could be done to shorten the period or ameliorate the conditions. Nothing more definite could be exacted. He then commended your music school. It is his wish to make it a part of the national university, lest it be frowned upon as an individualistic effort. I need not tell you that it might be generally useful in your present situation to do what you can to comply with wishes from above."

She folded the sheet and put it into her pocket. When her elder sister came home she must not know that she had asked their mother to intervene on John's behalf. A deep division was growing between the sisters. Grace, in love with Liu Peng, could believe no evil of those above. She argued even against her sister's impatience to have her husband home again. Last night the quarrel had become so open that each had fallen silent without conclusion, determined to stop short of mutual recrimination. Grace, the elder, had cut it short, saying that as sisters they must not quarrel.

"If we, the daughters of our mother, cannot agree, then let us be silent on the matter," she had said.

Now at the end of the day, as Grace entered the room where Mercy waited, she was determined to be courteous. They were dependent, one upon the other, she and Mercy, and childhood memories bound them together. Yet both were conscious of divergence. For a few moments they united in mutual admiration of the healthy little boy who sat on his mother's lap, playing with her gold bracelet. It was the bracelet that provided the approach to dissension. Their mother had given them twin bracelets upon their graduations from middle school in Shanghai, before they went to America.

"Where is your bracelet, sister?" Mercy now asked.

"I have put it away," Grace replied.

"Why?"

"I felt it did not suit, somehow."

"Suit the times, I suppose?"

"Perhaps."

Mercy laughed. "Or suit Liu Peng!"

Grace did not laugh. "And does that matter to you?" she asked too quietly.

"Not in the least," Mercy said lightly, "only—" She broke off but Grace compelled her to go on.

"Only what?"

"Nothing—except you've changed since you've known him."

"I am not conscious of change—except for the better. I understand much more clearly than I did."

"What, for example?"

"Why our government does—what it does."

"Such as putting its best men to hard labor?"

"Yes, such as putting men like John Sung to hard labor, if that's what you mean! One man cannot be an exception. The system doesn't allow for it. Individualism spreads like a disease. If John is allowed to refuse an allotted task, who can be compelled to any task? We must work together as one gigantic national team, a single unit, to achieve our place in the modern world. Each man, each woman, fits into a given position. We can't see the entire pattern, but those above, the planners, can see."

Tears welled into Mercy's large dark eyes. "That doesn't bring my husband back to me!"

"We can't think of personal emotions—none of us can."

Mercy was suddenly angry. Her eyes dried. She snatched the baby and went swiftly to the door. There she paused.

"I wonder what Clem would think of you now," she cried. "I can't imagine his even liking you anymore!"

With this she left the room. Grace sat motionless. Clem? She had not thought of him for many months and she realized that Liu Peng had isolated her, was isolating her, from everyone. What had been attraction was now love, an emotion as personal as the one for which she had reproached Mercy. She reviewed the meetings she had had with him since the one evening when upon impulse they had embraced—three meetings but all in the presence of other persons. Had she only imagined tenderness in his voice, warmth in his eyes? His words had been few, mere directions for her work, but his inner force, the power of his repressed personality, had poured from him in electric waves. She was not accustomed to the extreme control of a Chinese man, and it added to the excitement of his presence. Unchecked by word or act on his part, her imagination flamed anew. How simple, how almost infantile, Clem seemed—Clem so innocently demonstrative, so ready to take her hand, to parade his adoration, to share his thoughts! She resolved to be more reserved, more quiet, more respectful to her superiors, more distant with her inferiors, and to be more worthy of Liu Peng, she decided that she would study the philosophy and the policies of the Chairman himself. What manner of man was he, this one upon whom the structure of seven hundred million people depended?

It was a full week later before she saw Liu Peng and then it was by chance in a hallway. He stopped as though surprised to see her, and she stopped also, not knowing whether he expected her to do so. Thus, fixed for a moment among the swiftly passing students and bewildered patients, they faced each other, both not knowing what to say. She bethought herself then of her purpose and seized upon it as a pretext—though genuine, surely—for delay.

"I want to learn more," she said earnestly.

"About what?" he demanded.

"About the principles of the Chairman," she replied, improvising as she spoke. "What his dreams are, and what he wants to achieve—"

"Read his books, his poems," Liu Peng said and, she thought, coldly.

She withdrew her spirit from him proudly.

"Thank you," she said, and was about to walk away from him when he caught her by the wrist.

"Stay," he said in a low voice. "When can we meet?"

"Where you will, when you will," she told him. "I live with my sister, as you know, in the *hutung* of the Three Foxes."

"At nine tonight, after work," he said, and let her go.

They parted and she hastened to her laboratory and was dismayed to find that she could not forget the firm grasp of his hand upon her wrist. The pulse in that wrist beat more swiftly than usual, she could have sworn, and the day dragged. Old Dr. Tseng droned on as usual while he chose, by some strange coincidence, to discuss the different pulses of the body.

"The pulse can foretell to the discerning physician even the approach of death," he declared.

Each day he arrived with his own thermos bottle of hot tea, and now he poured the cup full and supped it loudly.

Then he cleared his throat and blew his nose, one nostril and the other, with a square of tissue paper, which he deposited in the wastebasket. He continued:

"When the heart pulse weakens, when it begins to pop without ceasing, like the seeds of a water lily, the face of the patient turns a dark red, the hair of the body is brittle, and death is near.

"When the pulse of the lung ceases its light and feathery beat, the skin becomes a pale red, the hair of the body is brittle, and death is near.

"When the pulse of the kidney—"

"Stop, please," Grace said, imploringly. "Is there no unity in these many pulses?"

"Certainly there is unity throughout the human frame," the old doctor said in great dignity. "Within this unity, there are three main pulse groups. Each group is divided into two, the external and internal. These are again divided into seven and eight parts—"

That night, when Liu Peng arrived and had been introduced to Mercy and the little boy, the pulses provided conversation. Grace described with merriment the old doctor's explanations, but Liu Peng refused to be amused.

"In spite of your laughter," he said to her gravely, "there is much to be said for pulse diagnosis. Western physicians who have explored and used our pulse theory say that they are able to make exact diagnoses which are proved correct through clinical tests."

She waited for him to develop this further, but instead he reached over and took Mercy's child from her arms. The little boy gazed at him doubtfully and drew down his mouth to cry, but Liu Peng coaxed him with smiles and hush-

215

ing until the child accepted him. Then, holding the child on his knee, Liu Peng began abruptly to talk of the evils of birth control, gazing into the child's enchanting face while he spoke.

"Consider what loss to the nation if this child had not been born! What if his mother had restrained his birth in the mistaken idea that she could serve our country better by becoming a Party member or the head of a commune or a brigade? Instead she gave birth to this fine child. Observe his long ears—they prove his intelligence, as does the height of his skull above his ears. I could never approve the population theories of Ma Yin-chu and his urgent pleas for checking our population. Especially do I hate the fact that such control is being practiced by our intellectual workers, whose brains we need to propagate, not prevent. Our Chairman is right. We need more people, not fewer. People are our national treasure. I encourage childbearing among my patients. Planning, yes—for we need more healthy children—but children!"

His piercing black eyes softened as Grace had never seen them. This man could feel tenderness! He looked at Mercy and smiled. "May you bear many more children," he said gently.

But she seized the moment for herself. "It is not likely with my husband far away in a peasant commune."

"Can that be?" he asked Grace in surprise.

"It is true," she said.

He rose and placed the child in the mother's arms.

"Then it must not be," he said.

When Mercy had left them, the child growing fretful with hunger, he was restless. "Let us go into the courtyard," he said. "The moon is bright. There will be no rain for another month."

She followed him into the court, and there under a plum tree that was ripening its fruit, he asked her abruptly if she would marry him. She waited to be told he loved her, but he did not speak of love.

"Let us be married soon," he said. "Let us have children as fine as that one. Together we will produce heroic sons for our country."

Still she waited and still there was neither sign nor word of love. She felt a chill creep over her heart. If he would not speak of love, neither would she.

"Marriage?" she said at last. "I am not sure. Let me serve our people as I am—for a year, or two years, even more, perhaps!"

Not for any cause would she speak aloud the cry in her heart: "But do you love me?" The cry was there, nevertheless, unspoken and therefore without answer.

By now he was unwrapping a package he had brought with him, and talking while he did so.

"Here are books," he said. "Read them. They will tell you about the Chairman—his life, his nature. You will see why we follow him."

"Thank you," she said.

This then was the purpose of his visit.

"China can be conquered," she read, that night when she was alone, "only when all the people of Hunan province are dead."

This was a proverb which she had heard repeated often by her father in her childhood. He was a shadowy figure to her now, a handsome, fiery man, impetuous and passionate, as the pepper-loving Hunanese were said to be, and she recognized these ancestral qualities as her own, too, though restrained and controlled by her mother's tutelage. That the Chairman was born in Hunan made him understandable to her. Son of a landowning peasant, he had learned nevertheless to read, and his youth had been spent in the revolutionary times of Sun Yat-sen and his second-in-command, Huang Hsing. The province was a network of secret societies and Huang Hsing made alliance with their head, Ma Fu-i, to foster uprisings in the countryside among the peasants while Huang planned bomb assassinations of chief officials in the cities. Though their plans were discovered and prevented, the Chairman had grown up in the fomenting atmosphere of revolution. She read two poems he had written recently on his return to his native village:

Only because so many sacrificed themselves did our wills become strong,
So that we dared command the sun and moon to bring a new day.
I love to look at the multiple waves of rice and beans,
While on every side the heroes return through the evening haze.*

Years before, when he was a young man, he had written:

The lonely peaks soar abruptly beside the great river.
I leap toward the summit, winding four hundred times through the verdant nature.
Calmly and coldly I turn towards the sea and gaze at the world.*

* Stuart Schram, *Mao Tse-tung* (New York: Simon & Shuster, 1967), p. 277.

She read and reread his many poems while she studied his essays and autobiography. The poems, she imagined, were the most true revelation of his nature, and deeply drawn to this man she had never seen and would in probability never see, she dreamed that Liu Peng was his prototype and that by feeling the one she could know the other. Moreover, her reading and study could give her endless material for talk with Liu Peng. She found in the reserved young doctor a passionate devotion to the older man and a readiness to reveal his devotion in words he might not otherwise have spoken.

"Where did you first see the Chairman?" she asked one day.

Spring and summer had passed into autumn and in every courtyard in the city chrysanthemums were in full bloom. It was a holiday, and by agreement she and Liu Peng had met at the Gate of Heavenly Peace to walk along a tree-lined boulevard near the Great Square. To the north were the palaces of the past, the tile roofs of royal blue, the vermilion pillars, the pink walls and white marble bridges.

"Let's leave this modern boulevard," she said now. The autumn sun, shining out of a sky as blue as the palace roofs, fell glittering upon the ancient scene, and in a moment their feet were treading flagstones laid before the birth of Christ.

"But I prefer the boulevard," Liu Peng said doggedly.

"Why?" she demanded.

She felt blithe at this moment, a mood usual to her in America, but which had seldom been with her since her return. Too many changes had taken place while she had been away; it was another country, different from the one she had left as a young girl, its people more subdued in behavior, more serious, more intense than she remembered them. Now at this moment of high noon upon the eve of the Autumn Festival, walking with Liu Peng, she relaxed and allowed herself to be happy. She would have liked to slip her hand into his arm but she did not. One did not permit such familiarity here as one saw on American streets. It was strange enough to notice couples walking together as they were doing, not touching. Nevertheless the still, autumn air, the heat of the sun, the general satisfaction of her work combined today to create happiness.

She was working now under Dr. Tseng's direction with Azure Monkshood, *Aconitum fischeri—Fu-tse,* he called it —and Clambering Monkshood, *Aconitum uncinatum,* or *Ts'ao wut'ou,* each herb containing poisonous aconite; yet carefully measured, prepared and used, the first was beneficent in colds, coughs and fevers; the second, if mixed with raw white of egg, beneficent as a poultice. If the measuring were in the slightest degree inaccurate, however, the dosage was pure poison. But these were only part of the rich store of medicinal herbs which Dr. Tseng was explaining to her and demonstrating through his patients. Added to the joy of satisfying work, infusing life, was the deepest and most profound joy of knowing herself in love with Liu Peng. She was an explorer in all she did, and she must now explore love and through her love for this man who attracted her so profoundly. It was not easy, for he held himself apart even when they were together, even today, when her longing for his touch was so strong that he must feel its demand in the electricity she felt in her own frame. But he was only talking—talking—and she could scarcely hear him for the thunder in her ears of her blood, coursing through her veins in a fever of love and desire. Yet his voice went steadily on. They entered an ancient palace open to the public, wandered through the opulent rooms, he still talking, while fragments caught in her brain—"the unfortunate season— restless peasants—uprisings in Hunan"—drummed in her ears. And what if she clasped his hand, hanging there at his side, so near her own?—only she must not, lest he repulse her.

They had reached a small bare room in a remote wing of the palace and now she perceived that they were alone. She stopped involuntarily and turned to him upon impulse, unconscious pleading in her eyes. She saw his look upon her change and his face flushed. Without a word he reached for her and, both arms about her, in an instant her lips were upon his. Nor did he draw back quickly. She felt the warmth of his flesh through his cotton jacket; she smelled the clean soap smell of his body; she knew to the full the passionate joy of this moment. Then he drew back, his arms still about her, and gazed down upon her.

"I have never kissed a woman before," he said in a low voice. "A man reads of such things—and wonders. Now I know."

"Know?" she repeated.

"What it means," he said.

On the other side of the world in the city of New York the day was as fair. It was the day of the opening of Hsuan's exhibition of paintings in the city's leading gallery. His openings were always events, and today the galleries were crowded. Word had flashed through art circles that the famous artist had developed new techniques, and collectors and art lovers had come from all over the country. Mr. and Mrs. Brandon, newcomers as collectors of Chinese modern art, had flown in from San Francisco and were now entering the doors, their eyes roving over the packed rooms. They were a handsome pair in their late fifties, carrying with them an air of affluence and pleasant self-satisfaction.

"I don't see Hsuan or Joy," Mr. Brandon was saying.

"How could you see anyone in a crowd like this?" Mrs. Brandon inquired.

At this moment they were discovered by Joy herself. Though usually she wore Western dress, today she had put on the long, close fitting Chinese gown of apple-green brocade which months ago she had asked her aunt in Hong Kong to send to her for this occasion.

"You have come!"

She cried out in joy at sight of the Brandons and was enveloped in Mrs. Brandon's plump and warm embrace.

"We wouldn't have missed this for the world," she declared.

Mr. Brandon clasped Joy's hand in both his.

"How are you, Joy? As pretty as ever, I see! Where are Hsuan's new paintings? I hear he's gone abstract."

Joy laughed. "But in a Chinese sort of way!" She extricated herself and continued. "You know we Chinese artists have always been abstract in our own way. We never copy from life. We gaze and meditate, and then we go home and paint the result of our meditation. It's the essence of what we've seen as reality."

"How is your dear mother?" Mrs. Brandon asked, never interested in art talk.

Joy was instantly grave. "I don't hear from anyone anymore. I haven't heard for months. My aunt in Hong Kong doesn't hear, either."

"The gossip is that things are going badly in our beloved China," Mr. Brandon said.

Joy turned to him. "Oh, what have you heard, Mr. Brandon?"

"Crop failures, drought in some places and floods in others—and failure of the communes."

"Oh, *no!*"

It was at this moment that Hsuan saw them. He pushed his way gently but firmly through the moving crowd, smiling courteously, shaking hands held out to clasp his, reaching Joy's side at last, always urbane, always pleasant.

"How good of you to come so far," he murmured, his right hand extended to Mr. Brandon, his left to Mrs. Brandon. "I am so happy—so very happy. I particularly want you to see my new monochromes. Will you follow me, please? I have had them hung together in the west wing."

"Hsuan!" Joy exclaimed. "Uncle Brandon says affairs are very bad in our country—famines and floods and no harvests!"

"What else can be expected?" the artist said with composure. "Heaven is outraged." He thus put a stop to what she was saying and conveyed his disapproval of her mention of disasters upon such an occasion as a successful opening for his paintings. Now he turned with his delightful smile to Mrs. Brandon.

"I do not allow myself to be concerned in political matters. As our great *Book of Changes* puts it:

If the superior man undertakes something and
tries to lead,
He goes astray.
But if he follows, he finds guidance.*

"Therefore, dear friends, I follow. But let me finish these
wise words! The next two lines:

It is favorable to find friends in the West and South,
and quiet perseverance brings good fortune.

The delicacy of his Chinese courtesy was such that he
omitted the next-to-last line, which is, "To forego friends
in the East and South," although he knew that no Americans would miss it, and he doubted that his "little Joy," as
he called her, had ever read *The Book of Changes*. His
sense of what was appropriate, however, was so acute that
he maintained the same behavior at all times, whether alone
or in company.

"Come, please," he said now with quiet authority. "Let
us proceed to the west wing. I want you to see my abstracts
before too many are sold."

His English was grammatically correct, but his accent
was his own, the stress often upon the wrong syllable, so
that even when he had said to Joy last night, "Truly, I
*ad*ore you," she had not been sure of what he said, and
although she had smiled, it was only afterwards that she
had grasped the full import of his words. The verb itself
was commonplace enough, meaningless indeed when
spoken by Americans, who used it to signify a fondness

* Helmut Wilhelm, *Change: Eight Lectures on the I-Ching*, translated
by Cary F. Baynes (Princeton, N.J.: Princeton University Press, 1960),
p. 11.

for anything from dimples to diamonds. Hsuan was a purist, however, and she knew that he used the word as a substitute for the word "love," which he would consider unbecomingly intimate. She had been in a state of mind too complex for her own understanding ever since he had thus declared himself, for she realized the seriousness of his declaration, since every word he spoke at any time was always fraught with undertones and overtones, and was therefore in itself only the essence of what he wished to convey. They, master and pupil, had strictly maintained the formality of this relationship, and while she did not hide from herself the passionate nature of her own feeling for him, which was a compound of the love she might have had for the father whom she only dimly remembered and the romantic love she might otherwise have felt for a young man of her own age, she knew herself well enough, nevertheless, to realize that she could never be happy except with an artist and among artists. When, therefore, he had, last night, made the announcement, simple but profound, of his adoration, she had been grave but deeply stirred. They had, at that moment, been hanging his small abstract, entitled "Dawn," in a narrow space between door and wall in the west wing. It was his last painting, and he had at first decided not to hang it, lest the room seem overcrowded. But she had persuaded him.

"It is one of your best," she had urged. "It makes me think of sunrise over the mountains of Lu, in Kiangsi province. I always rose early when I was a child and alone I watched the sky diffused first by rose and then by gold. You have caught the changing color."

He had stared at her, his rather small black eyes surprised

and then softening into tenderness. Almost abruptly, except that his voice was gentle, he had said, "I *ad*ore you!"

Tonight, when the crowd was gone and they were alone, he would continue—would he not?

They were in the west wing now and moving from painting to painting. Not many people were here, the crowds preferring his more realistic work, and so, except for a few long-haired men students and three mini-skirted girl companions, they were alone with the Brandons, and Joy was silent, listening to Hsuan. He was earnest, almost self-defensive, in his explanation.

"I am trying to catch the world mood as I feel it," he was saying to Mr. Brandon. "Realism, believe me, is no longer in objects, not even in persons. It is in the electric waves, made up of those particles which are the feelings of separate human beings, surging around our globe and soaring into space. I am trying through color, in motion, to express that surging, that soaring."

"Ah, indeed," Mr. Brandon murmured. He put on his spectacles and gazed at the painting, a medley of interweaving colors, blending and contrasting, but certainly expressing motion.

"A splendid performance," he announced, "but above the heads of most people."

"You think so?" Hsuan asked, somewhat dashed.

"I am sure of it," Mr. Brandon said with decision. "Nevertheless, I want that painting. I want to live with it. Perhaps without knowing it, you have expressed the spirit of your own country."

That night, when everyone was gone, they went to a nearby Chinese restaurant, master and pupil, to discuss the day. The opening had been a great success but of the abstracts only a few beside the one Mr. Brandon had chosen, were sold. Young men and women had asked prices and, sighing, had moved on, but Hsuan, in addition to being a great artist, was also a good businessman and had ignored the sighs.

"The small painting hung by the door," Joy had coaxed. "May we not reduce the price even by a little? The young man with the beard stands before it for an hour. He can't leave it."

Hsuan replied stiffly. "I do not sell myself cheaply—especially to young men with beards!"

The painting had been sold later at full price to an elderly woman with diamonds on her fingers and in her ears.

Now, at peace and together in the Chinese restaurant, nearly empty because the hour was late, the two of them, Hsuan and Joy, smiled at each other across the table. Yes, the day had been a great success; many paintings had been sold; critics had been respectful to the point of cautious enthusiasm, and pleasant relaxation was now the atmosphere for master and pupil. Joy looked across the table at Hsuan's somewhat round face, and he put on his spectacles and gazed at her in return and with intensity.

"Is something wrong with me?" she asked innocently.

"On the contrary," he replied. "I am merely inspecting the young woman I intend to marry."

She was stupefied by his directness and could say nothing, her pretty mouth slightly ajar, whereupon he put his spectacles in their case and the case in his pocket and smiled at her again. Then he looked grave and cleared his throat loudly. After this he began to speak in a solemn voice.

"For many years I reproached myself because I refused the marriage my parents arranged for me when I was a boy in school. At that age I was in revolutionary mood and I demanded the independence to choose a wife for myself. My parents were sad, for they wished to see grandchildren. Besides, they felt the worst possible time to choose a wife was when I was young, since I was their only son. But I was hard of heart as only the young can be. Alas, how could I tell that one day the government of our country would be destroyed by people as young and foolish as I was, so that in consequence Communism would fasten its sharp teeth upon our people? Knowing myself to be an artist, at that time I put aside all thought of marriage and escaped to America, where an artist can still live in independent peace. But it takes much time to find a wife and I have had no time. First I must be a success for myself. I am a success. And now, too, by good fortune I have met, without wasting any of my own time, the wife I have wanted for so long. She is you!"

She wanted to laugh; she wanted to cry out, "Of course I will be your wife! I have been waiting, waiting all these months while we have been only master and pupil." She wanted to laugh because he was such a character, so unlike anyone she had ever known, so much himself at all times, in every circumstance. He would have been exactly himself had he never left his native town in the province of Shantung. America had not changed him in the least, except to give him the English language in which to express his completely Chinese thoughts. She wanted to put her hand across the table to him and have his hand meet hers. She restrained herself because so frank a gesture might offend, and she replied in grave and modest tones, "I am honored to be your wife."

To her astonishment it was his hand that now moved across the table, his right hand that lay there waiting, palm upward, and seeing it, she laid her own small right hand into his open palm and felt his fingers close about hers.

The meager harvest fell before the storms of autumn. The wrath of heaven had not slackened during that interminable year. The peasants, persuaded by promises or by force, had been herded into communes. In rows, thousands upon thousands, they had plowed the rice fields of the south, the wheat fields of the north; they had planted the seedlings of rice and they had sown the wheat in due season, but the harvests were scanty. When rains should have fallen there was only dry, glittering sunshine hardening the earth; when rain was catastrophe it fell in drenching sheets, flooding fields already soaked. Old peasants muttered to each other that Heaven was angry.

"It is because we have no emperor nowadays to worship for us at the Temple of Heaven," they muttered.

Now, when the fields of rice should be golden for harvest, the empty heads bent before untimely wind and rain. Frost came early and the skies were perpetually dark. Strange rumblings were heard underground and the earth trembled, now here, now there. None could explain the failure of crops, for the planting had been done with hope and zeal. Now hope was gone and zeal died into despair. In vain did the young men who were their leaders run everywhere, trying in this way and that to encourage the doubting peasants.

On a day in early winter of that dark year John Sung sat among the peasants with whom he lived under the thatched roof and between the mud walls of a farmhouse in a northern village. Rain fell from the eaves upon the threshing floor, which was the dooryard; rain seeped through the aging thatch and dripped upon the peasants sitting on benches or boards inside the farmhouse as they listened to a young man, so young that he was still thin and reedy, his voice cracking, now childish, now manly, so that the peasants laughed, hungry though they were.

"The plan is good," the young man urged. "You yourselves know, comrades, that there used to be those who did nothing and others who did all. Under the wise new plan of our Chairman, all must work and at all kinds of work. This is indeed equality for all. No more shall there be bitter labor for peasant and idleness for the city folk. Each commune will work for itself, feed itself, govern itself, town merged into country, and each of you sharing the work of farmer, student, factory worker, soldier."

A dream, John Sung thought, beautiful and impossible. Why impossible? Because it did not consider the nature of man, which in each human being stands separate and isolated, the self its chief concern. Only when the self is fed, is safe, is warm in winter and cool in summer, possessing its own and working for its own, can peace prevail. Yet, by some contradiction and although he disagreed altogether with what the young man was saying, he found himself pitying that young man, standing there talking in his high, unsteady voice, but earnestly and with all his heart. For, alas, the young man believed what he was saying. He had been taught to believe and he had lost the ability to doubt. What then would befall him when one day he was wakened by truth and reality? What refuge would there be then for his soul, now so committed to that in which he believed? Would he not relieve his final despair in extreme violence against those whom he had trusted wholly?

As for the peasants, they needed no pity. They were inured to hardship, they were deadened to pain. Suffering had been their lot. For generations none had paid them any heed and they had learned to care only for themselves. They listened to the young man, willing to try the new way, but they would follow it only if their bellies were filled, their bodies covered, and if now and then they could laugh. Loyalty went no further; their hearts could not be reached, and long ago they had lost the power of dreaming. No, John Sung told himself, he did not pity the peasants. They could and would care for themselves. They had given up their land but they could take it back again. And they had no wish to be students or soldiers or factory workers. They were peasants and the sons of peasants. So long as there was land they were safe.

Such were John Sung's thoughts as he sat at a narrow end of a bench in a farmhouse among others in a village as the rain fell and the wind howled. He looked no different from the others, his face brown and lined, his body worn with hard labor, his feet bare and gnarled. These many months among the peasants had, nevertheless, been good for him. Without other companionship he had listened to their talk and observed their ways and learned of his own country through them, who were most of its people. His silence, his good sense, his wisdom, above all his steady sharing of their labor had brought him their trust. By natural selection he had come to be their unspoken leader.

Now the young man was finished with his talk and they should have dispersed and marched to the fields. The rain made this impossible, however, and the young man was at a loss as to what to do next, how to command and what work to assign. He, too, had come to depend upon John Sung, and he turned to him in pleading silence. John Sung rose to his feet and addressed the young man.

"Comrade, since the fields are flooded, would it be well for us to twist the old straw remaining and make rope from it? In this way we would not waste our time."

"It would be well," the young man said gratefully.

The peasants rose then, albeit half-heartedly for the most part, and in scattered ranks they sauntered into a low shed at the end of the house which sheltered straw and animals. John Sung did not go with them. Instead he lingered behind until he was alone with the young man. Then, drawing near him, he said, very low:

"Comrade, we have enough rice for only two days more."

The young man looked at him. "Supplies will come," he said, and when John Sung did not answer, he went on. "Do you doubt?"

"I doubt," John Sung said.

"I swear—" the young man began, but John Sung raised his hand to cut him short.

"You swore that eleven days ago, comrade. You said 'within three days,' but no supplies have come. The cooks in the common kitchen are frightened. What shall they do?

They ask me. I can but reply that it is not my responsibility. I am only the head of a work team."

The young man's lips trembled. His eyes filled with tears. "Is it my fault that the rains fall at the wrong time?"

"It is not yours nor mine nor any man's," John Sung said. "Nevertheless there should be a plan. Surely there must be reserves, grain stored against the possibility of famine—"

The young man's eyes flashed and his tears dried. "How dare you say that word? Can you doubt the Chairman? Is he not our father and mother? Be sure he has thought of everything. He plans for everyone!"

John Sung bowed his head and was silent. Though he was a full ten years older than this lad, he had learned by now that age had no meaning anymore. Youth was in power.

Youth was in power and famine fell upon the country in all its bitterness and fury. For the people were angry, having been promised that never again would they suffer famine. Yet famine was here with the old familiar pains of starvation and shortage, the old despair of not knowing where to turn. Silently and with fierce devotion to these humble men and women among whom he had worked for many months, John Sung went from one to another in the hierarchy above him. Quietly, contriving advice from one level to the next, he found himself by the end of the moon year at his own gate in the middle of a certain snowy night near the end of winter. He beat on the gate, but cautiously, having learned to move always without drawing the attention of others even to his presence. It was a night of deep cold, without wind, and a crust of ice covered the snow. He waited, shivering, and gathered his thin garments about him. Clothing had been short in the commune and had it not been for a cape made of straw he would have frozen. Today, however, he had been compelled to discard it, for the straw had disintegrated and gave him no more protection. He beat the gate again with half-frozen hands. The gate opened and Old Wang stood there, peering into the darkness.

"Let me in," John said.

"Who are you?" the old man asked.

"I am Sung, the father of the child here."

So saying, he pushed the old man aside gently and came in. The old man lifted the paper lantern he held so that the light fell on John Sung's face. Now he recognized him.

"But how thin you are, master," he exclaimed.

"Many are thin these days," John Sung said. "And do not call me 'master.' I am master of no one—not even myself."

So saying, he walked to the silent house, the old man preceding him with the key to unlock the door and then lock it again. Inside the house the air seemed as warm as summer. A small iron stove stood in one corner, and John Sung leaned over it for a moment to feel its warmth. Then softly, not to waken those who slept, he crossed the room and opened the door to the bedroom where his wife and son lay sleeping. A night lamp shed its dim light on the bed and he saw Mercy there, asleep, her dark hair loose on the pillow. In the curve of her arm, his face against her breast, lay the child.

For a moment he was reluctant to wake them. They were so beautiful, these who belonged to him and to whom he belonged! Tears came into his eyes. The tears he had not shed for misery and sadness now welled into his eyes for joy. These who were his own were safe. They did not even look starved. Somehow they had been fed. As though impelled by his presence Mercy opened her eyes. She looked at him for a moment.

"I keep dreaming of you," she murmured.

He knelt beside the bed.

"I am here," he said.

She realized it now, and putting the child aside, she turned herself and was in his arms for a long embrace.

"Oh, how does this happen?" she cried softly at last, drawing away to look at him. "And, oh, how thin you are —so changed, not like yourself! You've been ill!"

"Only starved," he said, getting to his feet.

Then he saw that the child was awake and was looking at him with wide, startled eyes. He drew down his little mouth and prepared to weep, but Mercy took him into her arms and began her mother talk.

"It's your *dieh-dieh*, little one! Don't cry."

She spoke in Chinese, and this meant, John Sung supposed, that she wished the child to know only that tongue.

She smiled up at him and spoke in English. "Forgive him, darling! He'll know you very soon."

And she held the child in her arms while they talked, she leaning against the pillows and gazing at him while he tried to explain to her why he was here.

"I've been passed on from one level to the next," he told her, "until here I am in Peking, with authority to appeal to the highest level."

She was instantly anxious. "But it's dangerous!"

"I can't think of myself," he replied.

"Then think of your son!"

He shook his head. "People are starving."

He told her then of what was happening, of angers and disaffection, of hopelessness and rebellion.

"But why are the communes failing?" she asked, bewildered.

"There are many reasons," he replied, "but the main reason is that too much has been taken from the peasant and too little has been given him in return."

She covered his lips with her hand and looked fearfully about the room.

"Hush, be careful what you say," she exclaimed.

Her words told him what he did not want to know. Even here in his own home there was fear.

He was received immediately in Chao Chung's office the next morning at ten o'clock. The sky had cleared during the night, and it was a day of glittering white under a cloudless blue sky. A hot bath, food and his own clothes had restored him somewhat to himself, although the clothes hung as loosely on his frame as though they belonged to another man. In many ways he knew himself changed in far more than those of the body. He was aware of a new interest in his own country. He was enmeshed in its problems and conscious of its power, and while he waited to be ushered into Chao Chung's office, he pondered both problems and power. Was he disenchanted with his country? No, on the contrary, he was enchanted by its landscape and by its people.

This morning he and Mercy had watched their son at play. The little boy had accepted his father very soon and the purest joy John Sung had ever felt was in that moment when unexpectedly the child had held out his arms to him and he had taken his son into his own arms and held him. Mercy had looked upon them with misting eyes.

"Should we have stayed in America?" she asked.

He had shaken his head. "No! We are where we belong."

The door opened now and a young man in the usual gray-blue garb entered.

"The minister is ready to receive you, comrade," he said, omitting the bow to which John Sung had been accustomed by his parents and which he himself now performed, although the young man turned away abruptly. He followed the man into the inner room. There Chao Chung sat behind the great desk. It was clean of every object except pens and papers.

"You've come, have you, Dr. Sung? I am glad to see you. Sit down," Chao Chung said cheerfully.

He wore a dark suit of fine English cloth, the collar buttoned to the throat. John Sung sat down and waited for his superior to begin the conversation.

"I have good reports of you," Chao Chung continued in his urbane fashion, his deep voice resonant as usual. "You have risen in your status and now are at the head of a brigade, although I daresay you have discovered that the work team is the basic unit in our agricultural policy. But I suppose you have come to ask to be released from hard labor."

"On the contrary," John Sung said promptly. "I have come first of all to thank you for sending me into the ranks of the peasants. I have learned a great deal I would never have known otherwise. Second, I have come to ask for food for our peasants and, more even than food, for a policy which will prevent famine forever. Other nations have solved the problem. So can we."

Chao Chung's heavy eyebrows drew down over his flashing eyes. He was easily angry these days and intolerant of criticism. He did not hide his anger.

"The Chairman has thought of everything. How dare you say there is no policy? For the last four decades the Chairman has most skillfully planned and carried out his policy concerning the use of the land. First the large landowners, then the rich peasants and finally the moderately rich peasants were eliminated. The Japanese war, too, proved to the poorer peasants that the Chairman was their protector. He has been able as a consequence to be the leader in every peasant movement. The peasants are his children and he is their father. When the first stage was ended, the blows struck at the landlord, the second stage was the equal distribution of land. The individual lots were then pooled into the final stage, which is the commune. Now cadres and Party members are in control of all rural areas and affairs. The peasants are in accord—or were, until these natural disasters befell the nation. And can we prevent flood and drought?"

"Yes," John Sung said stoutly.

"How dare you say that?" Chao Chung exclaimed.

"Other nations have done so," John Sung maintained.

He had gone too far. Chao Chung rose from his chair; he leaned across the desk and shouted.

"You have not yet known hard labor! You will prepare to go to the mines!"

John Sung could no longer be frightened. The peasants had made him tough and hard. He paid no heed to the minister's anger and frowns.

"If the Chairman is our father, then who are you, comrade?" he inquired.

Chao Chung could not but admire him. His eyes shone with unwilling amusement.

"I am the eldest son," he said, "and it is I who send you to the mines."

He had now to prepare Mercy for this new exile, but he resolved that he would not do so today. Let her for a few hours enjoy husband and son! When he was told the day of departure he would tell her and help her to bear. These sober thoughts filled his mind as he plodded through the snow, melting now beneath the unclouded sun. When he reached home Grace was there. She had heard of his return and delayed going to her work until she had seen him. When he entered she was waiting for him alone in the central room.

"Mercy is putting the child to sleep," she explained. "And she grieves because you are so thin. I have stayed at home to see for myself whether you are ill."

She spoke in Chinese now altogether, for Liu Peng did not like to hear her use a foreign tongue.

"I am well but hungry," he confessed. "We have been short of food, as you surely know. How is it that you and my wife and son look well fed?"

"We have not suffered," she replied. "Our mother has sent us food, and Joy sends us food from America. Our aunt even sends food from Hong Kong.

He was astonished. "How is it that they know of our suffering?"

She reproached him. "You use too heavy a word. None has truly suffered."

"We do suffer," he repeated. "It is to report our suffering that I went to the minister."

"And did he believe you?"

"He did not say. Instead he is sending me to labor in a mine. But I will not tell your sister today—not until I know when I must go."

He sat down, feeling suddenly weak, and leaning his arms on the table, he closed his eyes.

"You are ill," Grace exclaimed.

"Only exhausted," he replied. "I have no reserve. A long slow starvation—"

She felt his pulse. It wavered under her fingers, flickering and unsteady. "You must have food," she exclaimed, and leaving the room, she appeared again in a short time with a bowl of hot soup.

"Drink this," she commanded. "It is made with ginseng root. I keep it ready at all times."

He drank it, feeling grateful; the heat permeated his body.

"But how do they know?" he muttered.

"What do you mean?" Grace asked.

"The foreigners," he replied. "How do they know our secrets?"

Madame Liang was in retreat. From time to time in her life she entered into such retreats. They were periods, indefinite in length, when she reviewed life, herself and her family, assessing and reassessing, pondering and reflecting, until the immediate future appeared clear to her, emerging from the past. Such clarity came to her only when she shaped the present on the pattern of the past. Thus, the Chairman—whom she had seen once upon an occasion, when she was given an award, in his own handwriting, for her cooperation—she likened in her own mind to Chu-ko Liang, that great strategist of ancient times who "made a noise in the east, while attacking in the west." The Chairman kept as his Bible the great novel *Shui Hu Chuan*, and resembling those heroes therein depicted, she saw him as skillful and cunning. Although he believed in the doctrine of the foreigner Marx, yet this doctrine, too, contained a cosmic principle, as did the ancient book, a principle designed to order the universe, displacing all other orders. Though the Chairman disdained Confucius, yet like Confucius he gave commands on every detail of life from eating hot peppers to the correct use of scientific theory. The people worshiped him as a god-hero. When symbolically he lifted a pickax upon the occasion of the clearing of the Ming tombs outside the capital, the newspapers declared that "the great earth trembled." He could swim the mighty Yangtze in spite of old age, yet he also could write graceful poetry. In many ways he resembled the Emperor Ch'in, who, though he ruled as a tyrant, yet won the devotion of the people as a leader and ruler, following at all times those principles of a frugal life for his healthy body.

Only by seeing the Chairman's likeness to the ancients could Madame Liang accept him in the present. When she rebelled in secret, she counseled her own heart to have patience. The people had need of one whom they could worship. Without such a one they were frightened and lost between heaven and earth. They had no other gods now to worship, since gods were forbidden, and having no gods, they created a god of their own in their worship of the Chairman. Where the people have no gods, they create the image of a god. So it was, and so it always had been.

In her loneliness, for though she was surrounded, she was always lonely, she pondered often upon the nature of mankind as she had observed it through many changes, and she came to understand that throughout all such changes there is no change. She knew now that in all changes she could find the unchangeable. And who is the unchangeable except the people themselves? That ancient sage Lao Tzu pronounced the truth many hundreds of years past. "Throw eggs at a rock, and though one uses all the eggs in the world, the rock remains the same." Never was she more sure of the unchangeable than she was now when disasters created by man and nature fell upon the people. They were accustomed to suffering, but this present suffering was beyond the suffering of the past. The evils of Heaven were heaped upon the mistakes of men. Storm and cold in summer, thaw and rain in winter, drought when rice must be planted and hail at harvest combined with the unreasoning efforts of those zealot underlings, the cadres, who compelled peasants to ruin fertile topsoil by deep plowing, to waste fertilizers on rich fields and drain water from rice paddies, changing the age-old habits of the land because printed paper gave instructions unsuited to time and place, seed and soil. In ignorance they had led the bewildered peasants astray until half-starved people were leaving the country by the thousands to escape to Hong Kong.

News went abroad, to the disgrace of the nation, and this she knew because to her surprise she received packets of foods from her third daughter, Joy, who lived in New York. She herself needed no food, for she had her own ways of finding supplies for the restaurant, and she sent the packets to her daughters in Peking, where the markets were scanty. Nevertheless it was clear that the times were evil and she determined to fly to Peking and see for herself how her daughters and their household fared. The thought that her grandson might be in need of strengthening food was alarming. With every precaution and much admonition, therefore, to Chu San, whom she left in command, she took Chou Ma with her and flew to Peking, heart out of her body as usual when she was in the air. To divert her mind from this situation she conceived the plan to call upon the Minister Chao Chung and discuss with him the evil times and how they might be mended. In the old days propitiation of the gods by sacrifices and gifts to temples would have served, but since such superstitions were now forbidden, other means must be found.

She arrived without mishap at the capital city, and with Chou Ma, whose innards had been disarranged while in the air so that she was weak from much vomiting, she proceeded to the *hutung* of the Three Foxes. She had written to her daughter that she would come, but seeing that no one was at the airport to meet her, she concluded that slow mails had delayed her letter and she proceeded on her own way to her destination. When she arrived, all were surprised and properly overjoyed. It was evening; her daughters were at home, but her son-in-law was gone. Her grandson was waked from sleep, and after staring at her for a time, undecided whether to cry, he smiled instead and allowed himself to be taken into her arms. In this amiable atmosphere Madame Liang inquired into the details of their lives. Grace answered her questions first, as the eldest of her three daughters.

"We have enough to eat, my mother, never fear. You send us food, but Joy sends also. The child has milk made from the dried milk she sends, and she sends us other dried foods. Our servants find rice and chicken and eggs. We were able to buy pork a few days ago and dried bean vermicelli and flour."

"And the people?" Madame Liang inquired.

"It is here as it is elsewhere," Grace replied.

Madame Liang turned to her second daughter. "Have you anything to say?"

Here she saw a look of fire flash between her two daughters. Mercy took the child, now falling asleep, from her mother's arms.

"Grace has told you," she said, avoiding answer, and she gave the child to the old serving woman who stood waiting, who carried him away to his bed.

"Come now," Madame Liang said with authority. "What is between you two?"

Mercy put her handkerchief to her eyes and was silent, but Grace spoke with impatience.

"My sister keeps comparing our country unfavorably to others. Were she not my sister I should be compelled to report her unpatriotic attitude. As it is, I am put into a dangerous position. My duty points in one direction, my feeling in another. I find no peace, torn as I am."

Here Mercy took the handkerchief from her eyes, now

bright with tears and anger. "Tell what you like," she cried. "Don't think of me or my husband or my child! And it is not your country of which you are thinking but of that Liu Peng! You were not so patriotic until you began to love him!"

She turned to her mother with a piteous sob. "Oh, M-ma, can you help us? Can you speak to someone above and ask if John may come home? You should see him—a skeleton, his skin black and dried from the sun, and his poor hands blistered. He came all the way by foot to talk with someone above and for this was sent to the mines! And my sister blames me."

"Blames you? For what?" Madame Liang asked, looking from one daughter to the other.

They exchanged hostile looks and neither would speak, and what then could she do? These were new times and parents were no longer obeyed. She waited until she understood that she was not to be answered and then she withdrew gracefully, saying that she was tired and would rest for an hour.

Though she lay down on the bed she did not rest. Her active mind recalled the nuance of every look and word of her daughters and she resolved to do what she had never done. She would send word to the Minister Chao Chung that she was in the capital, and invite him to dinner at a famous restaurant. In his position he could not accept; therefore he would return an invitation to her. Such an invitation could not be refused and therefore she must accept. She knew his wife, and therefore the invitation would be for his home, since all were modern persons who behaved more freely than would otherwise be possible. She rose from her bed, then, wrote the letter of invitation and sent it by Chou Ma, who was pleased to be sent on such an errand since her sixth cousin was a servant in the minister's house.

When this was done, Madame Liang joined her daughters again and the evening was spent in pleasant talk and in reading the letters from her third daughter in New York. No mention was made of hardships or anger, and when Chou Ma returned before midnight with the invitation Madame Liang expected, she did not read it aloud nor mention it. She put it into her pocket and spoke of other matters until Grace was called out of the room by a servant. Then she leaned toward her second daughter and said in a low voice:

"Let your heart rest, my child. Tomorrow night I dine with the minister and his wife."

"Oh, M-ma," Mercy whispered, breathless. "You can do everything!"

Upheld by this faith, Madame Liang arrived at the home of Chao Chung the next evening at the hour between sunset and dusk, a time early enough to survey the garden before they entered the house. Chao Chung and his wife came to the gate to meet her. In spite of the chill of early spring they had been drinking tea in a small garden house which was only a roof set upon wooden pillars. This was Chao Chung's second wife, his first having been a Frenchwoman whom he had met while he was a student in Paris. She had returned to China with him, had stayed with him in the capital for some years during which they had built the French house in which he still lived. The Frenchwoman had returned to Paris when it was clear that the Communists would rule China, and Chao Chung had accepted her return gratefully since he was spared embarrassment thereby. In a year he had married a Chinese actress, a modern motion picture star of Shanghai, who was graceful, pretty and accommodating in her role of the wife of a minister. She knew of Chao Chung's early love for Madame Liang but, twenty years younger, she felt no jealousy. Therefore she greeted Madame Liang this evening with pleasure, and almost immediately excused herself, saying that she must supervise the cook in the final stages of a dish of fresh prawns, flown in today from the south.

Chao Chung now invited Madame to drink tea and then to walk through the gardens, which he himself had designed. The plum trees were in bloom and bamboo shoots were thrusting their pointed heads through the earth.

"It is far north for bamboo," Madame Liang observed.

"Too far," Chao Chung agreed, "but I have sheltered them, as you see, here in a corner. I must have bamboo."

Madame Liang smiled. "If you must, then you will. You were always like that."

"Except in one instance," Chao Chung replied with mischief.

Madame Liang laughed. "Will you never forget?"

"Never," Chao Chung said, his small eyes merry.

"Foolish," Madame Liang said, but gently, for a reminiscent mood at this moment was to be encouraged.

Her perception was delicate at all times and especially so now when she wished to speak to Chao Chung not only of her son-in-law, but also of national matters. It was too soon, however—better, perhaps, to wait until after the dinner. Yet, would he be drowsy then, or surfeited? No, he was a gourmet but no gourmand. She would wait. For this wisdom she was rewarded some three hours later by a moment when the last course of four dishes of meats had been served together with white steamed rice, Chao Chung leaned back in his carved blackwood chair and began to speak in French, a sign of intimate feeling between himself and old friends of Paris days, in this case Madame Liang. She had never lost her own proficiency in this foreign language, but after a courteous interchange in which she praised the feast, she returned to Chinese, and she asked pardon of Chao Chung's wife, to which the amiable young woman replied with a burst of laughter that she liked to hear French, of which she understood not one word, because it sounded like the cackling of fowls and made her laugh.

"Come, come," Chao Chung said, "believe her, my dear friend! She is a simple child who never lies, I assure you. She laughs for hours when she hears French. If she wearies, she will go away quietly and amuse herself in some other fashion. She is easily amused."

So saying, he changed into French again, himself leading the conversation. "I have felt for some time, Madame, my friend, that you do not entirely approve all that is now being done for our people. I speak in terms of the nation and government. This would not be dangerous except that we are in a period of national hardship and there is a central dislike of criticism, a stage which will pass as we become more secure. A secure government encourages faultfinding. Insecure, no criticism can be just because information is incomplete."

Madame Liang did not affirm or deny. "You believe,

then, that security will come? But security is based on success, is it not?"

"What you are saying," Chao Chung retorted, "is that we are not having complete success. I agree with you. We have made mistakes. But consider the cause! We were left without technical aid at the time when we needed it most. With heroic self-control we had put aside our distaste for Russians—"

"Hatred," Madame Liang put in. "Hatred, for centuries!"

Chao Chung waved a graceful hand. "Soon after the year 1950 of the Western calendar, we accepted Russian technical advisers in order to hasten our own industrialization. In 1956 we began disagreements. Two years later the archenemy Khrushchev withdrew his technicians, regardless of our need. Chiang Kai-shek made the most of the quarrel between Russia and ourselves, you remember. He flew his American jets against our Sidewinders over the streets of Taiwan because the Russians—why put it in the plural?—the Russian refused to equip our Migs with air-to-air missiles. We've been on our own industrially and technically, ever since. Most painfully we have had to educate ourselves in modern technology. That was why we took the Great Leap Forward in 1958. A failure? Yes and no. Technically, yes, but our people were awakened to the need for modern industry. And we've realized that our chief assets are the people and the land. Therefore the Chairman ordered the People's Communes. That is to say, he put the responsibility on the people."

"A failure, was this not?" Madame Liang said with deception.

Chao Chung sat upright and squared his shoulders. "All

has been for the best," he declared. "We are no longer subservient to a barbarian Russia. Remember our own old saying: 'There cannot be two suns in the sky.' We must be that one sun. I will tell you a secret—"

He leaned forward to speak so low that only she could hear. "The Chairman is the most Chinese among us all. He has never seen a foreign land—he has no wish to do so. He is not so much a Communist—oh, he believes in Communism, but it's an instrument, not a creed. Once more, through this instrument, China will become the center of Asia and therefore the central power in the world. That is his strategy. This is why we follow him and must follow him. He is thinking and planning within the framework of our history. We have only to follow him and under his guidance we shall see Chinese power pervading and reclaiming the whole of Asia—not through armies, mind you! We do not use the crude ways of the West. We will never send our military forces into one country and another. No, we will permeate! We will advise and aid the discontented, and they themselves will be our forces. We shall be what we have always been, an intellectual elite, in control of Asia. Why should we demean ourselves in the ignoble business of colonies? Why should we lower ourselves to sell our wares? There has always been a market for whatever we choose to sell. We need not buy from the outside, either—we can make whatever we need. We have the most ingenious people in the history of man."

Chao Chung paused to spit into a tissue, which he crumpled and threw into a porcelain jar under the table. Madame Liang said nothing but she felt her moment approaching and she was alert. Chao Chung continued:

"And what have these other nations that we have not? A hundred years before their Christ was born the capitalists of our nation were complaining that they, through private enterprise, could make iron implements more cheaply and of better quality than the foundries owned by the state could produce. Nearly two thousand years ago we tried communes. 'Exploitation of the masses?' Confucius and Mencius denounced it. And even the Nationalists, whom the stupid Americans are so heroically defending, declared themselves for nationalization policies. What has our Chairman done but return, by means of Communism, to our own ancient imperial ways?"

Her moment had come. Madame Liang had remained compliant and listening. Now she spoke.

"There is only one policy I question."

"What is it?" Chao Chung asked.

"Is it well," Madame Liang said, seeming to hesitate, "is it a wise use of the national treasure we have always revered, to send a man with an excellent brain, a scientist, learned in Western technology, to live underground in a mine?"

Chao Chung stared at her, then he gave a bellow of laughter.

"O woman," he exclaimed. "How deviously clever you are to boil down into a little pill no bigger than a pea the essence of all I have been saying! I stand convicted. No, it is not wise. It is a waste. I was angry. Moreover, he has been punished enough. He has learned to work with his hands. I will recall him at once."

"Thank you," Madame Liang said. "And now, shall we

not ask for the return of the pretty young Madame Minister?"

For Chao Chung's young wife had long since stolen
softly from the room. Before his hand touched a small table
bell now to summon a servant to invite his wife's return
he gave Madame Liang a look in which amusement was
mingled with a shadow of sadness.

"You never change, my friend."

"You are right," Madame Liang said. "It is true. I never
change."

"You are a Chinese," Chao Chung said, with admiration.

Madame Liang lingered on in the capital and for several
reasons. The dust storms which tortured the people in
spring, that fine sand blown by the northwest winds from
the Gobi desert, were now ended and the city was at its
most beautiful. The old imperial city with its palaces and
temples she knew well from the days of her youth, when
she was a student at the university before she went to Paris,
but this new city she did not know. Now, accompanied by
Chou Ma, she hired a vehicle and drove, one fine morning,
to the Gate of Heavenly Peace, a vast and ancient structure, from whose base she viewed the great new Square,
large enough to hold nearly a million people, and the
Hall of the People. From here she could see, too, the
soaring pillars of the Museum of the Revolution, and these
new buildings, mighty in size, were contained within the
space between two ancient city gates. New boulevards,
lined with trees, were busy with people traveling by foot
or pedicab, bicycle or bus, and now and again by car.
Policemen stood in glass-enclosed booths at every other

corner, wearing their uniforms, trousers of dark blue, jackets of white belted in red, caps of dark blue. They shouted orders through bullhorns, but the people were orderly and seldom needed reprimand.

Beyond the city limits in the surrounding countryside new houses were being built, five to eight stories high, with elevators and balconies, electricity and running water. She stopped to enter one such building and asked to see an apartment.

"You will not like it, comrade," the manager told her. "Young people rent these places, not ladies like you."

Nevertheless, Madame Liang entered one such place and looked about the small boxlike rooms, the little kitchen, the bathroom, the cage of a balcony, hung outside a door. Then she shook her head.

"You are right," she told the manager. "I could not live in this bird's nest, hanging against the sky."

When she returned to the house in the *hutung* that evening, she found that Chao Chung had kept his word. During the day, while she had been seeing the city, John Sung had come back to his family and by special plane. He had bathed and put on clean garments, but it would take many baths to wash his skin clean of the grime of his months in the coal mines. When she entered the gate he was working in the courtyard garden but he came to her at once and took her hand in his, in the American fashion.

"You have come!" she cried, proud that she had been able to bring him out of his banishment.

"I thank you that it is so," he replied.

Side by side they crossed the courtyard, while he told her that he had come in the morning soon after she left and had spent the day with his family, and now Mercy was putting their child to bed while he tended the garden.

"I do not regret my banishment," he told her when they had sat down inside the house in the central room. "I have learned very much. I am a good farmer now and acquainted with the earth's surface. I am also a miner, and I know the secrets that lie under the surface of the earth. But my most valuable knowledge is what I have learned of my own people."

She liked this son-in-law. She liked him very much, his large, finely shaped hands, worn with work, the nails broken and bruised, the earnest, almost somber dark eyes, the face too strong to be handsome in any usual way, and yet a manly, pleasant face it was. Here Grace came home from her work, and with her was a tall young man whom she introduced as Liu Peng, but being somewhat weary, Madame Liang excused herself and went to her room to rest, saying she would meet with them again at the evening meal.

The meal was over. The evening was warm with the first day of summer heat. Lao Wang had bought an early watermelon and had hung it in the well to cool it.

"Let us go into the courtyard and eat our melon," Grace suggested when their chopsticks were laid across their bowls to signify the end of the meal.

Into the courtyard they went, therefore, the younger ones standing back to let Madame Liang go first and following in order of their ages after they had persuaded Madame Liang to take the most comfortable seat.

She protested, laughing. "You are still old-fashioned," she said. "Who cares nowadays who sits where? All are equal."

"But we care for you," John Sung said, "and as for equality, are the fingers on one hand equal in length? Each has its place."

They sat down, and when there was no seat, the two young men sat on the stone doorstep, and Lao Wang cut the melon and each ate a slice, spitting the black seeds on the ground. A mood of happiness prevailed, first because John Sung was home again, and behind that and underneath all else was the hope that the third year, following upon the last two tragic years, was on its way to a better end. Crops in the south and in the central provinces were promising; the wheat harvest in the north was good, if not best, and food was coming back to the markets.

"We have been misled," John Sung said after discussion of such hopes, and then, laying aside his watermelon rind, he went on. "True, we have committed follies. One cannot laugh, and yet it is laughable that we did in fact even decimate the chickens on our farms and in our backyards in villages so that we might pluck enough feathers to make fans for our primitive forges when we were all ordered to make pig iron!"

Liu Peng would accept no criticism. "Say what you like," he declared, "but after a hundred years of confusion and unrest, we have achieved certain good ends. Work for every man and woman, schools for children, two meals a day— no feasts, but plain food—a just tax, soldiers who are not robbers. Ah, life is much better than it was in the old days!"

Madame Liang intervened mildly. "The sages have said, 'It is not poverty that is to be feared, but the lack of balance between riches and poverty.'"

"Which means," Mercy said somewhat sorely, "that we are all equally poor. What about the communes?"

Grace sided instantly against her sister and with Liu Peng. "A landless peasant may not know he has no land, but at least he doesn't have to sell a child in order to provide food for the rest of his family!"

Madame Liang listened, aware of hostile undercurrents and yet appreciating the freedom with which each spoke. Her daughters and John Sung had been in America, where freedom of speech was a habit, but Liu Peng also was free. She was proud of her family assembled about her here in the moonlight. They were young, they were handsome, and though Liu Peng was not yet one of them, she discerned that he might be one day not too far off. She spoke her proud content thus:

"I am grateful for all of you, my family, although, gods being out of fashion, I cannot thank the gods. My daughters will give me many grandsons. Although in my time when I was young I, too, was a rebel, now I no longer rebel, come what may. I have my family about me."

Lao Wang was gathering the watermelon rinds and Liu Peng began to help him, which distressed the old servant so that he complained.

"This is my duty, young sir, and why do you take it away from me?"

Mercy laughed and cried out in English, "Ah, you see? You have hurt his feelings with your equality!"

Liu Peng sat down again and looked somewhat hurt.

"Families are only a means of exploitation," he declared. "Parents treat children as capital assets and children wait for parents to die so that they will have an unearned income."

"So children spy on fathers," Mercy put in, "and sons are sent far from their parents—"

"That the young may not inherit the prejudices of the old," Liu Peng interrupted.

"And did not the sons leave their fathers in the old days and emigrate to many lands? Few families stayed together," Grace said, taking sides with Liu Peng. "And children were sold, and scholar-sons were sent to distant posts—"

"I shall keep my child with me," Mercy broke in.

Her sister turned on her. "You are only one. Many women are glad to put their children into a day nursery, and what woman wants to go back to having a baby every year and feet bound into stumps so that she cannot leave the house? Not I—and not you, either, if it comes to reality! No, young and old are glad to be rid of each other."

The evening, so benign in moonlight and quiet, broke thus into noisy fragments. The child wakened from his sleep and was brought out crying. Madame Liang made up her mind to return next day to her own house where, though lonely, she could live in peace. And John Sung, at his wife's command, next day went out and rented three rooms in a tall new concrete building on the far edge of the city.

To remove themselves, however, did not bring peace to John Sung and his little family. For the first few weeks all went well and they were happy. He resumed his work in genetics and was given a laboratory of his own, a small place in a large building dedicated to science, and Mercy busied herself with her child and her homemaking. Then they perceived that this period of peace was also, for those above them, a period of observation. One morning John Sung was visited in his laboratory by the tall young officer Captain Li. He presented his credentials, which included a letter from Chao Chung to John Sung. The minister declared therein that the Chairman wished to suggest that genetics, in the case of the scientist John Sung, should be related to the study of nuclear science and especially to the effects of atomic fission on the human frame, including chromosomes. It was necessary, the Chairman had declared, to relate all scientific study to some immediate and practical end. In the emergency of the present hour, when defenses must be strengthened against the imperialism of the West, neither time nor money could be allotted for the study of pure science. Reading this letter, John Sung saw that his banishment and hard labor had in no way changed the determination of those above. He would be compelled to yield or suffer some new punishment. A new caution crept into his mind and heart.

"Please sit down, Comrade Li," he said.

When both were seated, Captain Li began to speak thus:

"It is the wish of those above to consider the talents and the desires of valuable men like yourself, Comrade Sung. Only when these run counter to the welfare of the people or the plans made for their benefit, are citizens redirected."

"How am I to be redirected?" John Sung inquired.

Captain Li consulted a paper which he took from his inner pocket.

"You are to proceed to the province of Sinkiang," he said. "All instructions are written here plainly. Conveyance is provided, and you will be assigned living quarters upon arrival at your destination. Your work will be there for the next three years, and your superior will be our great expert in rocketry, who heads our nuclear scientific projects—"

John Sung interrupted. "Does my family accompany me?"

Captain Li appeared surprised. His black eyebrows lifted above his handsome black eyes.

"Your family?" he repeated.

"My wife and child," John Sung said impatiently.

Captain Li drew forth a second paper from another pocket, which he read to himself.

"I believe your wife has been assigned to a new school of music here in the capital," he said, folding the paper and putting it back in his pocket. "She was to have begun some months ago, but delay was permitted because of the birth of your child."

John Sung did not reply. Madame Liang had done her best, but it was not enough. He sat with head bowed, and only after a time did he speak.

"I must prepare myself," he said at last.

Captain Li rose. "You are allowed three days," he said, and with these words he wheeled smartly, clicked his heels together and marched from the room.

"I wish now that we had never left America!"

Mercy's cry pierced her husband's heart. It occurred to him for the first time that it was she who was compelled to

259

bear the brunt of their return. She sat on a low bamboo chair by the open window, the child on her lap. At the sound of her sob the child looked at her wonderingly, then, seeing her distorted face, he drew down the corners of his little mouth. John Sung lifted him into his own arms.

"Now, now," he said in English. "You are making our son afraid of you. Here—" He gave her his handkerchief and she wiped her eyes.

"Can we—is there any possible way that we can go back?" she asked.

He shook his head. "You know better than that. We will never be allowed to leave."

"But we could escape—get to Hong Kong, where my aunt would help us. Hundreds of people do!"

He returned the child to her knees and sat down at the table he used as a desk. "What would you think if I told you I don't want to go?"

"I'd say that I don't understand you!"

A flash of anger underlay the tone of her voice. He turned his chair to face her. The child slipped from her lap and walking to a patch of sunlight on the floor he tried to catch it in his hands. Both parents, diverted for the moment, joined in laughter.

"Poor baby," Mercy said. "He doesn't understand why he can't hold a sunbeam in his hands. Here, precious—" She reached for a string of wooden beads on the table and gave it to the child.

"To go back to what we were talking about," John Sung said, his eyes upon his child, "let us review the premises upon which we returned to our country. First, it was patriotism. We believed that our country needed us. Does that premise still hold?"

Mercy, accustomed to his logical mind, refused to reply, and he answered his own question.

"I am sure it does. In fact, the experience with the peasants reinforces my belief. Our people need us more than you or I can imagine. I had many hours in sleepless nights and I spent them in thinking about the future. Our country is coming to the end of an era, my wife. There is a deep struggle emerging at this very moment. It will rise to the surface the moment the Chairman dies of old age. Until that moment it will remain under the surface."

He had lowered his voice, though he still spoke in English. She lifted her head, suddenly interested.

"What struggle?" she asked, her voice as low as his.

"The struggle between the ideologists and the experts," he said.

"I don't understand."

"The old-line revolutionists, the fervent dreamers, the ideologists against the men of practical mind; the realists, the ones who can define our national problems and solve them—call them the nondreamers, the experts."

"I still don't understand," she said.

He was patient with her. After all, she had been absorbed in her individual task of pregnancy and childbirth, while he had been forced into the swarming life of the people and daily faced with the necessity for producing food for millions of human beings.

"Think, my heart, and you will understand that the people of any nation must be fed or they will rise up against their rulers. Not only must they eat but they must be given the means of earning a livelihood at honorable work. In short, our national problem is wrapped up in one word—production. But this production is divided into two parts, agriculture and industry. The theorists do not know how to organize for production. Witness the failure of what was called the Great Leap Forward! It was for industry, and it failed. Witness the communes! They were for agriculture and they failed. Our people all but starve even now, in comparison to industrialized peoples. True, the end is now in sight, for harvests will be good this year, but that is because we have had no untimely rain or drought—it is not because of better organization. In short, the theorists have failed. The experts are merely biding their time. They know they are needed, for without them there can be no national development. I am one of those experts. I bide my time, too. Now do you see why I want to stay, even if I could go?"

She was moved, but unwillingly. "But our son—"

John Sung interrupted her. "Ah, our son! By the time he grows up to be a young man, we will have had our chance, we practical ones. Ideology won't matter as it does now. Men will be chosen for what they can do, have been trained to do technically, not for what they think or dream. I want to be one of those who will create a modern nation here, because we know how to do it! Our son will enjoy his life. He will be proud of his people—as I am. But he will see the fruit of what men like me will plant."

He paused, remembering the weeks and months of bitter labor and scanty food and inadequate clothing. Yet what he really remembered was not those. He remembered the men and women among whom he worked, the peasants, the miners, so anxiously eager to do their best under strange, new direction, so respectful to the young men who were supposed to instruct them in better ways, so heroically brave when the new ways failed and they lost even their poor houses and bits of land. One by one he remembered them, each with a story, each with a hope, until the final disasters of nature and inexperienced management brought them to the brink of starvation.

"We have starved before," they told each other, this wan face looking at that one. Meantime they found weeds and wild fruits to eat and so saved their lives as they had done before.

"Our people are worth saving," John Sung told his wife. "I will stay with them. I am one of them, and I am proud to have my son grow up here."

Thus, word by word, he encouraged Mercy and she gained strength from him and was at last, she said, willing to do her share by setting up the school of music within the boundaries of the national university in the capital.

"But I will live here alone, I will not return to my sister," she told John Sung.

"Do not send more food," Madame Liang wrote to her daughter Joy. "The harvests are good this autumn. Rice is plenty; the wheat is sufficient for our needs, or nearly, much of it shipped from Canada and France. Next year we may grow enough of our own, but if not we can ship it in again. Both these countries can buy unlimited amounts from the United States and transship to us. It pays them to do so, and gives us the flour for bread and noodles."

She would not have been a true Chinese had she not felt a satisfaction, which amused her as she recognized it in herself, that the wheat which had kept her people from starving in the last bitter years, and which provided her restaurant with the delicate steamed breads her customers so enjoyed, had been grown on the broad fields of Kansas and Illinois. She believed in the inevitable success of trade. Whatever the ideologies proclaimed, life was based on necessity and trade. She had never yet failed to find what she needed to maintain her flourishing restaurant if she paid enough for what she wanted. And she was always willing to pay, in spite of Chu San's remonstrances.

"Madame, how can we afford such a price for a handful of eggs?"

"How can we afford not to have eggs?" she retorted. "Or flour, or fats, or meats, or fish, or sugar?"

She believed that before such necessities all ideologies failed in the end. One had only to wait in patience for the theorists to face hungry folk—or, for that matter, those rich enough to be gourmets. How well she knew her customers!

"I told you, my child, that we need not send food to our country," Hsuan said in New York when Joy read him Madame Liang's letter. He was only mildly interested in her letters, or indeed any letters from China, for he was engrossed in his work and it was entirely incidental to him that he happened to be born a Chinese. He was above all else an artist and could have been happy anywhere in any country where he was allowed to devote himself to his art. His closest friend was a German scientist, an expert in rocketry, engaged in Florida in the designing of spacecraft. This scientist, as Hsuan very well knew, would go to any country which provided him with the best means whereby he could pursue his science. Such men, Hsuan believed, as artists and scientists, were supranationals, consumed by the magnitude of their own talents. He dreamed occasionally of a society of such supranationals, who would dedicate themselves to mankind, regardless of the divisions of nations or races. Yet these were idle dreams, as he very well knew, dreams of men like himself who would never submit even to their own organization. Others must use their fruits, a still different breed—traders, perhaps, businessmen. What difference if the product were paintings or space vessels or meats and fruits and vegetables? There were those who created and those who distributed. As for the ideologists, he dismissed them as idlers who brought nothing to fruition. Next to his art, he valued science. Both art and science were based on logic and principle.

Meanwhile he had a series of exhibitions scheduled in the United States and later in Europe. He had long had a fancy, too, to paint in Greece. To see that ancient land through Chinese eyes might be interesting and new. He respected history, not so much for its own sake as for the pattern it provided for the future.

"Have you shipped those twenty paintings to San Antonio?" he now inquired of his young wife.

He maintained a half-fatherly attitude toward her, touched with magisterial dignity as a critic and teacher of her own painting, and this gave her the assurance that she needed, and the protection, now that she was alone in the vast landscape and conglomerate population of the United States.

"I shipped them yesterday," Joy said. "The porter helped me pack them and the van came at noon. They should reach San Antonio in good time before we arrive."

"Excellent, my little heart and liver! And now I am hungry and I would like a bowl of soup with noodles for my midday meal."

She hastened away to this fresh duty and he settled himself before his easel. With his penchant for large subjects expressed through the infinitesimally small, he was painting the Niagara Falls from the Canadian side. At the foot of the immensity, all but lost in the mists of the spray, he began to create, with his most delicate brush, two minute human figures, standing hand in hand. They were no one in particular and could have been any two, except that he and Joy had gone to Niagara Falls on their honeymoon and had stood there, hand in hand.

"I propose," said Liu Peng, "that we live together as comrades for some months before we marry officially."

Grace Liang drew herself from his arms. "Is that necessary?"

She put the question lightly, she hoped, so that he would not think she was conventional or bourgeois or in any of those classifications that he detested. For herself, however, she was deeply shocked, for she belonged to the generation later than that of her parents. In that earlier day the young, inspired by the Russian revolutionary, for example, had ostentatiously paraded their theories of free love. Her own mother, however, had suffered a revulsion after marriage, when her father began to take concubines.

"It seems that free love is not different from the enjoyment men have always allowed themselves," her mother had said one day to her daughters. "There is only one advantage in the old form of free love—advantage for the concubine, that is. A concubine is brought into her lover's house and family. Of course this is an annoyance to the wife unless she despises her husband, in which case she is glad to be relieved of her wifely duties."

These remarks, scarcely understood at the time by her young daughters, returned now to Grace's memory. And what indeed was Liu Peng asking of her except to be his concubine, but without the protection his father would have been compelled to provide for a concubine?

A question sprang into her mind, a question she had not thought to ask in the bemusement of love.

"Have you ever had a wife, Liu Peng?"

He looked at her, abstracted, his thoughts elsewhere. "Yes, of course. How could a man of my age escape a wife?"

"But you did escape?"

"Of course."

"How?"

"By never being where she was."

"Then you never saw her?"

"Never! I was engaged as a child by my parents and married by proxy. My parents thought they won by proceeding with the wedding, but I won by not being there. Thus they never had the grandson they wanted from me, which was the purpose of the wedding in the first place."

He spoke brusquely, carelessly, his dark square face unchanging. They were sitting in her courtyard on a September day, late in the afternoon. It was the autumn festival but they had taken no part in the popular festivities of the day. Instead they had worked all morning at the hospital, she upon refinement of a drug she was distilling, emodin, found in many plants as a glucoside, and he upon the analysis of a slide of a tumor that he had taken from the underarm of a patient the day before. They had met at midday for a modest meal in a small restaurant, had watched a parade and folk dances from a balcony at the hospital and then before sunset had come to her house. They were alone, for after serving tea the servant couple had asked leave to see the evening fireworks and were gone. Almost at once, but after a silence, Liu Peng had made his proposition and she had evaded it, slipping from his embrace as she did so. He had sat down then on the bamboo chair and leaned back, his hands clasped under his head. She, on the other hand, had knelt beside the small pool and was throwing bits of stone at a few goldfish darting about in the water. Each spoke apparently without passion, and yet each question, each answer, was pregnant. She proceeded.

"But you have had—lovers?"

"Three," he replied.

"And?"

He replied, gazing into the sky now golden with sunset. "You wish me to describe them?"

"Only if you wish," she said carelessly. She searched for the bits of stone, accumulating a tiny pile as he talked.

"I neither wish nor not wish. They came into my life at separate times, we shared life, more or less, and we parted."

"I thought you said—describe them."

"You said, if I wished."

"Since you are willing—then, yes, describe them to me."

"Why is it," he mused, "that women like to torture themselves? Now, I don't care how many lovers you've had."

"I have had no lovers," she said abruptly. For how could one call Clem a lover?

"Everyone in America has lovers," he said harshly. "It is well known."

"Not true," she declared.

"Ah, you are an American-worshiper!"

"Again not true!"

"Let us not argue about facts," he replied. "As for the three women I have known, the first was a girl I met when I was in school. She ran away from home to join me. I lived alone in a small room and there we lived together. She made excellent soups into which she threw dough strips. If we had a little extra cash we bought an egg for the soup. When we had eaten all we could—or perhaps only when we had eaten all the soup there was—we talked about anarchy. In those days I was an anarchist. I believed that anarchy was the happiest state for mankind. Although there were many secret societies in our school, I would not join even the Society of Anarchists. Later I came to understand that organization is necessary for national progress and I ceased to be an anarchist."

"What became of the girl?" she asked.

"She got pregnant and had an abortion and died. I think that was what made me want to be a surgeon. The old woman who did the abortion was filthy and clumsy."

"Why didn't you marry the girl and keep the child?"

"Marriage was against my principles—in those days, I thought it a form of slavery, especially for the woman.

Then, too, I was legally married, even though I'd never seen my wife. She was living in my parents' house, waiting on them like a servant in the feudalistic way."

"And again?"

"Again? Oh, the second woman! She was a good Communist. We worked together in a brigade. I was given hard labor for two years as an intellectual and was detailed to a cooperative that afterward became part of a commune. She was very pretty. I fell in love in the bourgeois fashion and we even talked of marriage. Then one day I found her behind a stack of rice straw with another man. That was the end of her. I lived without women for four years. Then I took up with a Russian girl. It was no good for either of us. Her father was a technical adviser. When all the technical advisers were sent back to Russia she went with her father. She was only eighteen. Since then—no one. Only you."

"But you still don't want marriage."

"I am not sure. Perhaps if our relationship is—good, you know—I'll want it."

"And if I want it now?"

"You'd be foolish. You don't know me well enough to marry me."

"But well enough to sleep with you?"

"I hope so."

"But just for sleeping—wouldn't someone else do as well?"

"No. I want to be serious."

She was silent for a moment, then with an effort she put her question,

"I thought you said—when we first kissed—that you had never kissed a woman before."

He laughed. "Nor had I! I never kissed any of them. The Chinese girls never thought of it in those days, and the Russian—well, kissing seemed disgusting to me then—a Western notion. But with you—suddenly I wanted to."

She considered this and then reminded him.

"Yet when you brought me the Chairman's book—remember the moonlit night in the courtyard? You said, 'Let us marry and have children—heroic sons for our country,' you said."

"And you said you were not ready!"

"Now it is you who are not ready!"

He did not reply at once and when at last he did, his voice was grave. "I have learned that marriage between two people such as we are cannot be only to have children. In the old days marriage was to make children for the family. Is it so much better to make citizens for the state? Now I know it is not enough. Marriage is first of all for the man and the woman. When we know from experience of love, not just from saying the words, then marriage, yes —and children, yes. We shall be fit for both, because we know ourselves."

He lay gazing into the sky, the sunset light golden upon his face. He did not look at her, but while he waited for her to speak she looked at him, dwelling upon every line, the strong bony structure, the large intensely black eyes, the heavy black brows, the surprisingly tender lines of his beautiful mouth. She loved him with deep physical passion. For the first time in her life, devoted to science and the acquiring and use of knowledge, she loved a man for his body. His mind she had not explored and did not want to explore, lest she find there something that might prove him less worthy of love than she wanted him to be. She wished he had not told her about the three women, even though she had demanded it. What did they matter, after all? Nothing mattered except this moment when they were alone together. She let herself gaze at the length of his sinewy frame, outstretched before her eyes. She felt the heat in her blood rise to a height uncontrollable because until now it had been so rigidly controlled by her inexorable brain.

He looked at her, startled, and she saw that he perfectly understood what was taking place within her. Without a word he rose from the chair. Slowly and with every sinuous grace he walked across the courtyard. The gate had been left unbarred against the return of the servant couple. He drew the iron bar across and set it in its hasp.

"Now we are alone," he said.

He clasped her right hand in his left hand, and together they walked silently into the house and into the room which was her bedroom. She had once bought a great old Chinese bed, carved and curtained, and he loosened the curtains from their silver hooks and let them fall together, enclosing the bed like a tent. In silence he took off her garments, one by one, and she let him do so. In this unimagined moment she felt no shame except that she was not ashamed, and while she stood, naked, he stripped himself, too. Then he held aside the curtain for her to enter the enclosed bed and he followed her and fastened the curtains together. Side by side they lay for a brief time. Then he turned to her and she let him, all the while in a stupor of wonder at herself because she let him do what she had allowed no man to do and because that which before had seemed wrong to her now seemed right.

Mercy sat at her pupil's side, listening to the faltering music which the young girl was trying to draw from the old piano in the classroom of the music school. She listened, her trained and acute ear hearing every discordant note while her thoughts pursued their separate way. Her life in these days was a distraction of fragments in which she could discover no theme of unity. It seemed to her nowadays that she was at least three separate persons— wife, mother, teacher—and which of these three was her real self, her primary being, she did not know. Months had passed since John Sung had gone to that remote spot in the distant province of Sinkiang, and his letters were few and dry. She sought to forgive him for what seemed coldness since he did not use words easily as communication, and she knew, too, that the meaning and purpose of his work he could not communicate even to her. She guessed that he was engaged somehow, not, she felt sure, in the making of a nuclear weapon, but in chemical defense against radiation or poison which an enemy might convey against the people. The enemy, she sorrowfully perceived, had become, in the minds of her young pupils, the Americans, and for her own safety, and her son's, she did not dare to speak what she felt. Again and again she longed to cry out, when she heard words of hatred against the Americans, "You do not know them as I do—they are not what you think!" But in prudence she kept silent and this silence, too, lay on her heart as a burden. In spite of her private longing, therefore, she felt she was very far from her husband, especially since she could not know the day of his return. There were times in the night when she was wakened by the sound of her own sobs, and then she felt she might never see him again.

Nor could she write him about their child, for she dared not put into words, which other eyes might see, her increasing fear for the child. On his third birthday he must enter a state school, as all children did, but what would he be taught there except that which she herself less and less believed? And how could she dare tell him, even at home and alone with him, that Americans were not their enemies, but a kindly, careless, generous folk whose nature was friendly? She could not teach him the truth, for he would then be taught that she was a traitor so to love the Americans, whom he would believe she ought to hate if she were a patriot.

In this confusion she did not know what to do and so she did nothing, and in doing nothing she became a lonely soul. She did not see even her elder sister, who, she heard, had accepted Liu Peng as her lover. And she did not trust her mother. Yes, to such an end she had come that she could not be sure her mother would not betray her, for how could this mother have lived so many years in seeming peace and moderate luxury when all about her the people of her class were reduced to poverty or else had lost their lives? What compromises had her mother made? And if she made them because she believed that the people would break free one day and take power into their own hands again, did this love not come first in her heart?

Living solitary, as Mercy now did, in the small three rooms in this huge new building where all were strangers, she had no one to whom she could confide such thoughts except her woman servant, who slept in the narrow entrance hall at night and cared for the child by day, and this simple soul would only have been frightened if she had heard such doubting words. And who could tell whether she also could not be trusted, but would run to someone above with what she had heard? With her heart locked and lonely, Mercy could only devote herself to her work.

As head of this new school of music, she was compelled to work, for she had business to do as well as pupils to teach. Her school had begun with eleven pupils, nine of them girls. Of the two boys one was a young man of twenty, who until now had little teaching. A Danish lady, wife of a businessman from Denmark, had begun to teach him the piano when he was five years old. He was the child of this lady's cook, a man from near Canton, and one day when she was upstairs the lady heard the boy downstairs touching the piano softly, fearful that he be forbidden. His father, the cook, forbade him the house, commanding him to stay in the servants' quarters in the back garden, but on this day he had seen his father take his market basket and go out the gate, and knowing that his mother was asleep, the boy stole into the drawing room of the big house, and seeing no one there, he went eagerly to the piano. He had never touched it or been in this room, but he had often listened to the Danish lady, who was a true musician, and he believed that he, too, could bring beautiful sounds from the great black box. He was trying his best, both hands on the keys, as he had seen hers, when suddenly she had entered the room. Terrified, he had tried to escape through the open glass doors, but she caught his arm. He had never seen her close before, and now he saw that she had strange eyes, the color of blue glass, and her hair was not white with age, as he had supposed, but the color of pale gold, and she was young, her skin white and pink.

"Stay," she said, her hand on his arm. "You must not be afraid. I will teach you how to play music."

She spoke his own language, not very well, but he understood enough so that he let himself be led back to the piano, and then, her voice kind and soft, she began to teach him the first of many lessons. When all foreign business houses were seized by those above, the Danish lady and her husband were compelled to return to their own country and the boy, with his father and mother and two sisters and three brothers, came to Peking, where his father became chef in a new hotel. And he, the son, continued his music from one teacher to another, until the new school of music was opened in the national university. Here he was content, for Mrs. Sung, as Mercy was called, taught him herself, and while she was a singer, she also knew the piano, and under her teaching he not only made great progress, but she showed him how to write down the music he composed and until now had been able to play only from his memory. He found her not only an excellent teacher and a good friend but to him she was also a very beautiful woman, and he wove his youthful dreams about her, fancies of how someday he would rescue her from unknown danger or even save her life.

Of such young man's dreams Mercy herself was altogether unaware. She knew only that here in her pupil was one who someday would be a great musician. And what, she often asked herself, would become of this strong talent? Would it, must it, be at the command of uncomprehending minds? Would he, must he, be denied the freedom to create the music which came from his own soul and must he be warped to suit some narrow chauvinist? She was deeply troubled by such questions, whose answers she could only fear, and so the questions led into further thoughts and new questions. What of her own son? She made this inquiry of her heart, her mind. Would he one day be like Chen, the young musician, gifted but with no power to achieve the heights to which his gifts entitled him?

Such questions had no answers, and at last she came to the conclusion, avoiding it and evading it as long as she could, that she had done her son an injustice in bringing him to be born here in his own country. For some, yes, it might be well enough, but not for this son of hers and John Sung's, for they were intellectuals, artists in music and science, and their son was born to be among those who create and command. Yet how would their son be taught and by whom, and would it be that in which she believed or would it be that in which less and less she could believe? Would he, too, be taught to hate Americans? She thought with love and remorse of Mr. and Mrs. Brandon and their children, how she and her sisters had spent free and glorious holidays in that big household, careless and happy, afraid of nothing and no one. And here in her own country she was always fearful, although she did not know why, for no one had molested her. Yet fear was in the air, in whispers and rumors of this one who had disappeared and that one who had died a strange death.

So much did her thoughts disturb her that at last she
wrote a letter to her mother, asking her to visit her, and
using as pretext the fact that her son, her mother's grandson, was growing into a boy almost ready for nursery
school, and she wanted him to know his grandmother from
his earliest memories. Madame Liang, receiving this letter,
discerned in it some inner, importunate meaning and she
made up her mind to fly to Peking at once, taking with her
only Chou Ma, and thus see for herself the outlook and how
nearly right she was in what she surmised.

"And when did you last hear from my son-in-law?"
Madame Liang inquired of her daughter Mercy.

She had asked no questions until this moment. It was now
the evening of the second day. She had arrived the day before in the late afternoon and had gone early to bed after
the evening meal and an hour spent in admiring her grandson, who was, she observed with satisfaction, an unusually
intelligent child. He did not cry when he saw her, and yet
he did not give her ready smiles. Now he sat himself on a
small bamboo stool and observed her carefully for some
time. She, on her part, made no overtures and even today
made none, but continued her quiet conversation with his
mother.

"I seldom hear from him," Mercy said in answer to
Madame Liang's question. "Perhaps once or twice a month,
and I know that not all his letters reach me, for he refers
now and again to something in a previous letter of which
I know nothing."

"He is in a highly classified area," Madame Liang said.

"But he is not working on the hydrogen bomb," Mercy replied.

Madame Liang lifted her beautiful eyebrows, inquiring.

"No, M-ma," Mercy insisted. "He will not work on explosive weapons which may be used against—"

Here Madame Liang looked hurriedly about the room, laying her forefinger on her lips as she did so. All doors were closed and since the season was late autumn, even nearing winter, the windows were shut, and since, too, the rooms were on the third floor, it was not likely that their voices could be heard. Nevertheless Mercy fell silent, startled by her mother's gesture. It was at this moment that the little boy left his stool and came to his grandmother. Approaching her, he placed his small hands on her knees and gazed into her face, whereupon she smiled at him and lifted him to her lap. Here at close range they looked at each other for a long moment. Then suddenly the child gave her his confidence. He leaned his head upon her shoulder and she, deeply moved, put her arms about him.

"He recognizes me," she told Mercy. "We have met in another incarnation."

Madame Liang, in her youth so rebellious, so revolutionary, had refused to go to the Buddhist temple even with her mother, but now, as she gently aged, she was returning to the teachings of her childhood. As a fiery young girl, perpetually angry with her elders, scornful of the history of her country, repudiating the teachings of its wise men, she had been without tenderness. Now as she entered upon her solitary old age she felt tenderness growing in her like a flower in the shade, and pondering often upon death and the survival of her spirit, she sought knowledge and wisdom from the sages of the past. With her daughters she had been patient and dutiful as a parent, but she had not been tender. Now, however, she felt deep, soft tenderness pervade her being as she gazed at her little grandson. She had never borne a son, and here was the child who was nearer to her, in his own fashion, than any child had ever been. For though Madame Liang had maintained heartily, in her youth, that woman was as valuable and as able as man, and therefore to a mother daughters were as welcome as sons, the old, inherited traditions were hidden in her, waiting until her young fevers subsided, to emerge again. At this moment it seemed to her that her grandson was the most precious child ever to be born, and she understood why her daughter was troubled because she had brought him here to be born in a country whose future was yet unknown.

"What are you thinking, M-ma?" Mercy asked.

"I am thinking," Madame Liang said slowly. "I am thinking of this child's future. Of the future of our country and its people I have no doubt, no fear, only confidence and peace. As they have done in the past for thousands of years, our people will one day right themselves, keeping what is good of our new life and restoring what is good of the old. But where, in the transition, will this child's lifetime be spent? In our vast and ancient nation, a hundred years is no more than a day. Yet this same hundred years is longer than his life-span. Will he suffer while we discover the wisdom of the past? Must there not be decades of struggle and bloodshed, and can he survive? Will tyrants oppress his mind and heart, and even martyr his human frame?"

At this Mercy leaned to whisper to her mother, "Ah, you see what I fear!"

Madame Liang considered while she continued to embrace the child, who rested in peace against her breast. Then she spoke in a low voice. "So long as his father lives, you need not fear. A scientist of his high learning is too valuable to kill."

The two women exchanged looks.

"Thank you, Mother," Mercy said and without knowing she did so, she spoke the words in English.

Unknown to the people all this while, unknown, too, to the world, a moment drew near in that lonely place in that distant province where John Sung lived among hundreds of young scientists, each with his own work to do upon the weapon. Even the scientists did not know if the moment would come to pass when the most powerful of modern weapons would be freed to soar into the sky and there release its fury. Yet without words some sort of communication was made so that on a certain day, in a certain year, months after Madame Liang had visited her second daughter in Peking, the young scientists, three hundred or so, most of them trained in the country they were now urged to hate, found ways of being near the remote spot where the mighty creature was to be released. It was the first of its kind and all felt it to be a pride and glory. Even John Sung, hesitating to leave his own work, had done so at the last moment in order, he told himself, to salve his conscience, that he could see for himself the stage of sophistication at which the other scientists of his country had arrived. If all went as they had planned, if the firing were a success, then they had reached a level, scientifically, that made them the equal of any. Theirs would be the honor and the glory.

He, therefore, was among those who waited that day as near the site as possible, a desert spot surrounded by high and barren mountains. Meanwhile, delay was announced and then another and another. The sun rose over the crest of the eastern range, it mounted toward zenith and changed the morning chill to noonday heat. A third delay was announced, while impatience appeared among those who waited. John Sung also began to doubt in his heart whether the weapon were ready to be fired, and he was about to return to his own laboratory when suddenly it was announced over the loudspeaker that the countdown was surely about to begin. He stayed then, pressing among others who pushed forward as the fateful seconds passed.

Alas, that final second never came. Without warning, the huge object, trembling with impatient inner energy, burst of itself into a roar so mighty that the earth shook and the whole sky turned into flame. A rain of fire fell upon the desert for miles around, and in that deadly rain all perished.

Captain Li mounted the stairs of the wing in the National University which was devoted to the school of music. In his hand he carried a white envelope stamped with the seal of the offices of the Minister Chao Chung.

"Put this into her own hand," Chao Chung had commanded. "Then turn yourself so your back is to her face. Let her be as though she were alone. Until she speaks, stand there."

Captain Li had saluted, wheeled and left the room. The newspapers had made no report of the desert blast. There had been no announcement, no one spoke even in whispers, no mourning was allowed, yet rumor went from mouth to ear that a catastrophe had taken place in that distant place, although its nature remained unknown, for none dared to speak of it as truth. Captain Li surmised that this white envelope concealed secret news, yet so loyal was he that he did not think of opening it to see what the news could be. Instead, sturdy and dogged, he pursued his duty and at sunset he found the one he sought as she was about to leave the small room that was her office. When he knocked and when upon her reply he had entered, she was putting some books into a cloth bag on her desk. He clicked his heels and saluted.

"Comrade Sung," he said, "I have a message. From the minister, Comrade Chao Chung."

He offered her the envelope with both hands. She took it, sat down in the chair behind the desk and slit open the envelope with a narrow brass knife. He turned his back as she drew out the paper within. She read it once, twice, three times, and then he heard a low long moan.

"Are you ill, comrade?" he called, not turning himself.

She did not answer, only gave the strange moan, as though her breath were caught in her throat. He could but wait, and when at last she did not speak, he felt compelled to look over his shoulder and see if she had fainted or even had died. No, she was neither faint nor dead. She sat there holding the paper, her face green, it was so pale, and out of it her eyes were black and staring. When she saw him looking at her, she spoke, her voice strangling in her throat.

"Do you—do you know what news you have brought me?" she asked.

He shook his head. "No, comrade. I do only what I am told."

"Then go away," she said.

And he, accustomed to obedience, opened the door and went away.

When he was gone, Mercy sat for a long time, the white paper crushed in her hand. Her pupils were leaving for the day. There were nearly a hundred of them now. She had done her duty; she had built a good school. Waiting for her husband to come home, she had done her work. Now he would never come home and her work, too, was finished. She would take her son and together they would leave their country forever. She was not as brave as her mother, or perhaps it was only that she had not her mother's faith in her own people. Yet how could she get away alone, with the child? She would be watched; she would be caught. Nor would she ask her mother's help. No, no, she must not let even her mother know. If it were discovered that her mother had let her go, what bitter punishment would ensue? She must do the best she could alone. Stay—if she asked permission to visit her aunt in Hong Kong? Better to ask nothing—better simply to go, swiftly and in secret.

At this moment she heard a piano. Someone was playing Beethoven's "Tempest," playing it brilliantly, beautifully. Of course it was Chen, it could be only Chen, who often stayed to practice after the others were gone. Suddenly she knew what she must do. She put the crushed paper in her bosom and went in search of Chen, following the music as though it were a guiding light until she reached the room where he was playing. She opened the door softly and went to him. He saw her face and his hands crashed on the piano.

"What has happened?"

She could not reply except to draw the paper from her bosom and hand it to him. He read it twice and gave it to her again.

"How can I help you?" he asked, his heart tender with mingled pity and joy. This was the hour of which he had dreamed.

It was impossible for her to speak. Her lips were dry; her tongue seemed swollen in her mouth; her throat was tight.

"You must help me," she whispered at last.

"Only tell me how and I will do it," he said.

"I must get away—get to my aunt in Hong Kong. My son and I—we must get away. Go on playing—someone may be listening."

He began to play again, soft music that his hands remembered, while she talked under her breath.

"If you could get me to the border, my aunt could meet me. We could disguise ourselves—you could be my brother. No one would think of your helping me—you are only one of many here. We could put on old clothes, like peasants—tell everyone we're on our way to Canton, where we have relatives—no, not that—we can't speak Cantonese."

"I speak Cantonese," he said, and the music under his fingers slid into a minor key.

*   *   *

"I assure you I know nothing of my second daughter," Madame Liang said in Chinese.

Chao Chung stared at her. "I don't believe you," he said in French.

"Whether you believe the truth or not is beyond my control," Madame Liang said steadfastly in Chinese.

Chao Chung continued to stare at her and continued to speak in French. "It is absurd, Madame, that we argue in different languages. Only tell me the truth and I promise there will be no punishment for you."

"Why should I fear there might be punishment when I know nothing and have done nothing?"

Madame Liang's voice was tranquil and Chao Chung laughed. "Let us agree on English," he said.

Madame Liang smiled very slightly. "Very well, I will repeat in English. My daughter did not tell me she intended to visit her aunt in Hong Kong. I am happy that she decided to do so. She has suffered a great tragedy in the loss of her husband. He was a noble and distinguished man. We have all suffered a great loss, not only for the present but also for the future. That he was only one of many—"

Chao Chung interrupted her. "It is not to be told how many. This loss, in addition to recent catastrophes, is more than our people can bear. Let it be said that only several of our scientists—"

"I agree," Madame Liang said, also interrupting, "and I will never tell all I know, even to you, my friend. I will say only that I am glad my daughter is visiting my sister in Hong Kong, and I do not know why she did not tell me or why she did not follow the usual procedures and ask for the necessary permissions. For this I apologize to you. She is always the most impulsive, the most independent, of my daughters. When she returns, I will bid her come to you herself and ask for pardon. I pray you will overlook her mistake. She was too long in America."

When Madame Liang said these last few words Chao Chung's face changed and he looked at her sharply. She met this look with a gaze innocent and bland.

"Have you nothing more to say?" he asked.

"Nothing," she replied.

To reach the border might not be difficult, Mercy told herself, but to reach it as themselves would be impossible. Yet she dared tell no one what she planned and she continued her work for a day so that under cover of his music lesson she arranged with Chen to go with him to a certain place near the border, a village where his paternal grandmother lived. His father was a native of the southern province of Kwangtung and had left there in his early youth to find work in the city of Shanghai, returning to his childhood home only to attend his own father's funeral. This had taken place when Chen was eleven years old, and he remembered the village and his grandmother.

"We will fly to Canton," Chen said, his voice low under the music his fingers made upon the piano, "but we must make speed before our absence is discovered. Day after tomorrow is a summer holiday. Let us leave tomorrow by night flight, though separately. That brings us to Canton by day. I know how to get to my grandmother's village. It is a short ride on the railroad. If any asks, I will say we are brother and sister and we are visiting our old grandmother. In the village we will change our clothes to poor ones and return to the city immediately. Early in the morning, but not too early, for we must be lost in the crowd, we will press across the border, with baskets of vegetables and fruits to sell."

After further talk, always with music hiding their voices, they arranged details, and they were able to do what they had planned. The holiday, the speed with which they made ready, Mercy telling her woman servant that she went south and would not return for four days, made all easy enough, it seemed, until that moment when she crossed the border, a basket of late peaches on one arm and holding the child in the other. Among the crowd she passed easily into the territory of Hong Kong. When she knew herself safe, she turned to see if Chen had followed. For she had persuaded him to continue with her, assuring him that in America he would have great success in music and make riches which he could keep, for the most part, for himself, whereas in his own country who knew what his fate would be? Young and gifted and devoted to her, he believed all she told him and he promised to follow close behind her as she stepped from Chinese soil. So he had prepared to do, but even as he had one foot over the line, an officer seized him by the shoulder.

"You are no peasant," he said roughly. "What peasant has such hands as yours?" He snatched Chen's right hand and showed it to those about. "Is this the horny hand of a peasant? Even the handle of the basket makes a blister. Step back, you!"

Chen could only obey, and Mercy, watching, felt tears rush to her eyes. What had she done to this innocent and talented lad, and why had she asked him to help her? Yet without him she could not have escaped so easily, if at all. As for Chen, he did not turn his head to give her so much as a last look, for he would not have the officer know that he had anything to do with her, lest she, too, be stopped somehow.

But she was safe now on the other soil, and with her the child, and she went her way on foot to her aunt's house, allowing all she passed to think she was what she seemed to be, a young peasant woman in rough peasant garments, her face dusty and over her head a blue kerchief that hid her hair. Yet as she went she mourned over Chen. What was his fate? If he were not shot as a traitor or put in prison it must at very least be hard labor in some distant place where no music could be made. She could never know.

"Your sister is a defector," Liu Peng said sternly.

Grace did not reply. She waited for him to say more. The news of Mercy's escape had already come to her through the usual servant channels. The woman who had taken care of the small apartment and the child had come last night to the couple here at the houses in the *hutung*, the Three Foxes, and they had spent an hour together, exchanging loud whispers, so that before they parted they had pooled their knowledge of the Liang sisters. One had run away with her child; one had accepted as her unmarried husband the famous young surgeon Liu Peng; and the other had stayed in America. They disapproved of all three sisters, for old tradition lingered deep in the hearts of these ignorant folk. Such disapproval had nothing to do with their duty, however, and they continued as faithful to their new employers as they had been to their gambling, opium-smoking former masters and mistresses.

It was from Wang Ma, therefore, that Grace heard of her sister's departure. The old woman had come into Grace's bedroom, and closing the door behind her, she had begun in her loud hissing whisper:

"It was night before last, Elder Sister, your second sister packed a few garments for herself and the child and took the night flying-ship for the south. She did not say she went to visit your mother, but she did not say she did not. Putting this and that together, it can be seen she did not, for an officer, Li, came this afternoon to inquire if she were at home. This humble soul, who is her serving woman, told him her mistress had gone south to visit her honored mother. He said she had not, since she had told no one at the music school that she was leaving for a visit to her honored mother, as she would surely have done if such a visit was being made. The serving woman could say only that she knew nothing, since she had been told nothing by those above her. Putting this and that together, my old man, the serving woman and this humble one, who am I, we believe she has escaped."

"Escaped where?" Grace asked.

The old woman had shrugged her scraggy shoulders. "Who knows? Yet there are only two ways of escape, one to her husband, the other to Hong Kong. The truth is"— here the woman drew so near that Grace turned her head from that foul breath—"the truth is, Elder Sister, your Second Sister was never happy here. And she had some bad news the day before, for she sobbed all night."

"Did she say nothing?" Grace asked.

"That Second Sister said nothing, then or at any time."

Such talk Grace took as truth, for serving folk always know the truth about those they serve. She waited therefore until Liu Peng continued. It was the end of the day; they had taken their evening meal and were in the central room for a while before they went to bed.

"Your sister," Liu Peng now said, "has crossed the border. A pupil went with her, a young man named Chen, but he was caught before he crossed. The officer in charge was clever, and though Chen was dressed as a peasant, his hands betrayed him. His hands were soft and clean. He has been returned here to the capital for questioning and punishment. Already he has confessed."

"What does he confess?" Grace asked. It was a part of the misery of her love for Liu Peng that she was constantly aware of him physically. While he talked she could not forbear seeing his mouth, his eyes, his extraordinary, expressive hands, the set of his head upon the broad shoulders, the grace of his lithe body, with which now she was so familiar and yet which was imbued with a charm more powerful.

"Simply that he wished to go to America because he thinks there his talent will bring him money!"

Liu Peng's voice, resonant and strong, expressed his scorn as he spoke these words. Grace laughed.

"The cardinal sin, to want to go to America, to want money!" she observed lightly.

Liu Peng was not pleased. "You speak more truly than you know," he replied. "I cannot understand, for my part, how a young man in our country today can deviate so profoundly, after going through our school indoctrination. I begin to agree with the Chairman that the old revolutionary fire is dying out of our young men. True, he is speaking especially of our armed forces, where young soldiers are being inducted who know nothing of the evil times of the past and cannot share the bitterness of those days and therefore cannot taste the sweetness of the present. The reminiscences of our older revolutionists cannot stir them to feel that which they did not experience."

Grace was interested in spite of his physical charm. Her good brain could bestir itself. "Perhaps the young need a new idealism; perhaps nationalism rather than revolution would appeal to them."

Liu Peng pondered her reply. The charm of this woman for him was not primarily physical but intellectual. He had never known a woman with whom he could exchange ideas rather than embraces. True, their passion was mutual and profound, but his was aroused first through his growing admiration of her scholarly instincts, her professional skills. Thus, too, although he had never allowed himself to ask certain questions prompted by his secret curiosity, he felt the excitement of her strangeness, her knowledge of that great unknown enemy, the Americans, her personal experience in that forbidden country, the United States. His curiosity grew with his amazement at her skills. She had been highly trained; she had a perfection of technique which he, being an honest man, was compelled to recognize as superior to his own. There were times when he resented her superiority and then he was brusque with her and even cold toward her and he knew this hurt her, yet he could not explain it to her. But he was beginning to understand that she was the first woman who had ever roused his love. The others had been only flesh to his flesh.

She was speaking and he compelled himself to hear what she was saying. "I am not sure that we do well, moreover, to return at this late date to the early methods of the revolution. Nations grow as people grow."

"Of what are you thinking?" he asked.

"The recent decision to abolish professional differentiation in the army, for example," she said. "The decision to abolish officer titles and uniforms and insignia and address everyone as 'comrade,' whatever his position."

"But that is to eliminate the consciousness of rank and the hope of personal fame and financial reward," he declared.

"Yet these are necessary incentives—they are what men live by!" she insisted.

"Bourgeois thinking!" he cried.

"Old slogans!" she retorted, laughing.

He was always aroused by her laughter. How dared she laugh? The conflict of their minds spread its heat to his body. He wanted to subdue her, to force her to his will and way.

"You don't know what you are talking about," he shouted, slapping his knees with both hands.

"Then tell me what you are talking about," she said boldly.

He had no intention of telling her now or at any other time what he had learned only yesterday from his officer friend, who was Captain Li's superior, but Captain Li, who was now to be called only Comrade Li, while conveying an invitation for dinner, had been the first to hint important policies about to be put into effect.

"The comrade above me urgently invites you to dinner," he had said.

"Why urgently?" Liu Peng had inquired.

"New commands have come down from the summit," Comrade Li had replied in an importantly low tone.

Liu Peng had postponed an operation, though reluctantly, and had dined with his military friend, whom he had known since their school days together in Nanking, the southern capital of the Nationalist regime.

"The Chairman," his friend had told him over a superb dinner of Peking duck, "has decreed that a new way must be devised to continue the struggle against landlords, rich peasants and bad elements of all kind. If this revolutionary struggle is not maintained, he fears our people will slip into revisionism and even fascism."

"What is the new way?" Liu Peng had asked.

"You will see," the friend had said mysteriously.

"What will I see?" Liu Peng had persisted.

"The young will rise up," the friend had told him. "The Chairman will use our youth. Rebellion, which is the ancestor of revolution, is indigenous to the young."

They forgot to eat as the revelation continued, and it was dawn before Liu Peng parted from his friend.

"Tell no one," the officer bade him.

"No one," Liu Peng promised.

But the officer had caught him by the shoulder. "That comrade of yours—Liang, the woman doctor—she was educated in America."

"There could be no reason for me to tell her," Liu Peng protested.

And indeed there would have been no reason except that tonight her mood was to defy him with laughter, and when she dared so to do he used every weapon against her in order to subdue her. Now, in spite of his promises, he outlined to her the plans he had heard the night before. She listened, incredulous.

"But I am shocked, I am appalled," she exclaimed. "Do you mean—can you mean—that revolutionary talk and indoctrination is to take the place, even in the army, of teaching our men how to shoot accurately and how to master the techniques of modern warfare? Why, it's medieval! It is the folly of the past, the superstitions of the Boxers, who believed their ideas made them immune to Western guns! What punishment our people suffered for that folly, what disgrace! And is this now to be repeated? You know, I know, that no ideology can take the place of the hard disciplines of *learning*. This is true whatever the profession. We can't do without the 'experts'!"

"We can't do without the revolutionary spirit, either," Liu Peng said stubbornly.

"Then that means another purge!"

Her voice, her face, were grave. For the moment she had actually forgotten him and this he could not bear.

"Why do we grow angry with each other?"

His cry was demand and he rose abruptly. In two strides he had crossed the space between them and she was in his arms. She yielded immediately and utterly. She had taught him how to express his love in kiss, in embrace, and now, crushed against him, she felt the old sweet faintness creep into her blood. Every argument, every quarrel, ended in his arms, and she was happy that it was so. She could not face the essential difference in every part of their separate beings, except this, their physical love. Her aristocratic mother, gentle and firm, disciplined and independent, had shaped her daughters. His father, a quarrelsome, illiterate narrow-minded "rich" peasant, the "riches" comprising twenty acres of land tilled by tenant workers, had shaped his rebellious son. Now, in her lover's arms, she asked herself why she loved him and why he loved her, and her self could give no answer except that her heart said simply that they loved. In those moments, which she instinctively avoided, she knew that she could not and did not respect his mind, compressed and limited by narrow revolutionary doctrines. She knew that if she allowed it, she could pity him, but she would not allow it. She evaded every criticism of him by recalling, if he were not present, the strength and beauty of his body, the natural joy they took in making love, the lesson that he quickly learned from her of putting love into words and caresses.

When they had made love and he lay sleeping in her arms, it occurred to her that she had altogether forgotten Mercy, her sister!

Madame Liang was inspecting her kitchens, Chu San at her heels. She made comments and corrections in what she saw—the immense wooden chopping blocks were not scrubbed white; the cooking vats did not shine as she wished; the refuse was not cleaned away fast enough, nor the leftovers sorted quickly enough so that the hungry poor could make use of them.

The hungry poor? They were there at twilight, as they had always been, stealing to the back doors, holding out their empty bowls, mute and fearful as they looked left and right. It could be a crime to be hungry and beg. It was easy these days to commit a crime. One might not even know until it was done that it was a crime. In the old days there had been nothing criminal about hunger and begging, but nowadays there were many new ways of committing crimes.

Chu San nodded his head after each command as Madame Liang gave it. His memory was a recording machine. When she had finished her inspection also of her dining rooms, her waiters and cooks and their uniforms, she proceeded to her private rooms and reflected upon her situation. It was not good in that it was not clear. Ever since Mercy and her child, her grandson, had reached her sister's house in Hong Kong, Madame Liang had felt herself under surveillance. Outwardly all was the same. Her arrangements with those above had not changed. For ten years technically all that she once possessed privately had belonged to the state, and this made her, technically, the employee of the state, on salary. In fact, however, she operated her restaurant as she always had and no accounts were formally submitted, though she was ready and willing to submit them upon demand. She would, of course, have been extremely angry if the demand had ever been made, since this would have shown a distrust which she could not tolerate.

Her affairs in order, she sat down to a cup of green tea in her own sitting room and continued to reflect. Was her unease, perhaps, because of the disturbance obvious throughout the nation? The disturbance was taking the form of rebellion of youth which until recently she had not considered serious since the young are always rebellious. Moreover, their unrest here in her own country seemed far less grave than the reports she read in newspapers of the murderous assaults committed by the young in other countries, especially in the United States. True, her third daughter, Joy, had never mentioned in her letters the riots of the American young, but perhaps she, too, had to be careful of censors. Who could know what the outer world was today? Such curiosity was forbidden, for it might lead to communication and communication to influence.

She sighed and suddenly felt old and solitary. Yet she ought to be content. Her grandson was safe and two of her daughters were safe. Sooner or later a letter would come from her third daughter in New York, saying that Mercy and the little boy were there. Her sister's letters from Hong Kong had cleverly conveyed this news.

"Your second daughter is visiting me for a few days. After that she will return to her sister." The key was in the word "return." There would be no return to Grace, since those two were very far apart. Therefore it could mean only return to Joy, in America. Nor could it be in a few days. The Americans, too, were proud and they also guarded their borders. Many papers would have to be signed and exchanged, many guarantees given, before Mercy could enter an American port. Once there, however, Madame Liang could let down her heart and worry no more, although she might never see them again—nay, let her face the truth. She would never see her daughter Joy again, never see even once her son-in-law Hsuan, the great artist who resolutely refused to return to his own country. Nor would she see Mercy again—nor her grandson. Ah, there was the real stab in her heart! She would never see that beautiful boy again, not in this incarnation. He would grow up in another country, foreign to his own people. He would marry and have children, all of them foreign, for she knew his mother could not allow him to leave the safety over yonder. And it would be a very long time before there could be peace in this distraught country of hers—a very long time.

For who knew what was happening here? She had always believed she knew but now she could not even pretend to know. The ruthless young, instigated by secret permission, were destroying and killing and burning, all in the name of the aged Chairman. This could, of course, be stopped by withdrawing the secret permissions. But in the army there were other struggles, more profound, more hidden. The chief of the general staff—had he been purged? He had not been seen since the tenth month of last year. And if he were dead, how many more with him were purged also? It occurred to her that no military heads had appeared in her restaurant for several months. And now there was talk everywhere of another Great Leap Forward, this in spite of the failure of the last one. The quarrel between the ideologists and the technicians, the industrial and military experts, was reviving again. In his old age the Chairman was insisting that the revolutionary spirit would compensate for lack of technical knowledge, an idea so impractical that Madame Liang did not allow herself the luxury of anger, lest she betray herself and be lost in the chaos of those who dared to disapprove. She could only wait for the old Chairman to die, as many others were waiting, so that the people could prevail.

In the midst of such reflections the frightening thought came to her at this moment that she herself might die before that time and so never see the restoration of the wisdom of the past. She was now altogether alone, except for Grace, her eldest daughter, in Peking, and she avoided thought of her, dreading the moment of confrontation when she could not ignore the situation in which Grace was living. Now, however, there was no other soul to whom she could turn in case of her own illness—or possible arrest. It was always possible to be arrested for unconscious sins against the state. She had known that for years, but until now she had not been afraid because she had not felt so alone.

When she thought of loneliness she thought again of the child whom she would never see again—her grandson. Without her grandson she was truly alone, for she had no stake in the future. Her daughters—what were they but women? Where there was no son, no grandson, there was no future. This thought sprang into her mind with all the force of conviction. She laughed, a bitter laugh. The old superstitions were in her still, even as they were in all the people, and they would be in her until she died. She would never be free of them, and indeed it now occurred to her, she did not want to be free of them. But what would happen when she died? What would happen when all her generation died and only these ruthless and ignorant young were left? Who would there be then to restore the wisdom of the past? Thousands of years of wisdom and greatness destroyed in a handful of years!

She rose from her chair, impelled by the frightfulness of this possibility.

"Chou Ma," she called, "Chou Ma, come here!"

The old woman, never far from her mistress, ran into the room. "Here am I," she cried.

"I am going to my daughter in Peking," Madame Liang told her. "She is all I have left now."

The season in Peking was midsummer when Madame Liang arrived at her eldest daughter's house. She had delayed coming until her mood of depression was over and it had taken longer than she had expected. The reason for this was twofold; first, she wanted to know that her second daughter and her grandson had reached the United States safely. She had this assurance in a letter from her youngest daughter, Joy, who sent a letter to her aunt in Hong Kong, which letter this aunt, Madame Liang's sister, had cleverly hidden in a jar of candied coconut and sent on. The news there hidden was received by Madame Liang safely, and she read the letter three times and then once more before she burned it with a match and blew the ash out of the window. In a few words Joy was able to tell her happiness that Mercy and the child were safe, that this had happened only through the help of Mr. and Mrs. Brandon, that no one must worry anymore except for the mother herself.

"Oh, my mother," Joy wrote, "come here to us. You have never seen my husband. He is good to me. I am so happy. I am expecting my first child. Come and see your grandchildren. I think of you all the time. Mother, Hsuan is a great artist, but I am improving. I took a prize for my portrait of you. I had to do it from memory. Mother, come and stay with us the rest of your life. We will all live together."

Madame Liang had long ago ceased weeping, no matter what trouble befell her, but when she read these words of love, when she thought of grandchildren, the tears so long dried came welling to her eyes. Why should she not leave this country of turmoil? As long as she lived the turmoil would continue. So vast was her country, so countless the numbers of her people, that decades, perhaps even a hundred years, must pass before the old order could be restored, or a new order hewn. And now she had begun to doubt that order could ever be restored unless the order the people had built through five thousand years of their history could be rebuilt. For what house, once destroyed, can be built again in all its meaning? And how, until an age again had passed, could it be known what to salvage from this present age? No, however long her life, she could not hope to see peace. Why, therefore, should she stay to watch revolutions and antirevolutions that she could neither avoid nor end? She was sorely tempted, therefore, to find her way to the United States. Sitting alone here in her rooms, she imagined herself in that other country, in peace and surrounded by her grandchildren. Then she bethought herself of her eldest daughter, and how could she leave her not knowing where her mother had gone? Thus had she decided to leave at once for Peking, taking with her neither Chou Ma nor Chu San. She wished to be alone with her daughter.

Now it was the first evening in her daughter's house in

the *hutung* of the Three Foxes. She and Grace sat in the courtyard with palm-leaf fans in their hands and waited for Liu Peng to come home, Madame Liang, guarding herself against any reproof of her daughter, behaving as though Liu Peng were her true son-in-law and not an interloper in her daughter's house. While they waited, a small breeze sprang up and Madame Liang put down her fan.

"Perhaps Liu Peng can tell me if it is true that armies of our own people are fighting each other in the south," she said.

"What have you heard?" Grace asked.

"I hear that in the city of Wuchow on the border between Kwangtung and Kwangsi provinces there is war between those who are for and those who are against the Chairman. Two thousand homes have been destroyed or badly damaged and tens of thousands of people are homeless—so I hear."

"Liu Peng will know," Grace said.

At her mention of his name a silence fell between mother and daughter, which it seemed the daughter waited for the mother to break. Madame Liang, however, felt it was not the moment for her to speak against Liu Peng. She continued to talk of turmoil.

"Many people, I fear, use what is called 'the class struggle' to take revenge on old enemies while bandits and hoodlums use the disorder to loot and kill. In Nanning, the capital of Kwangsi province, as you know, people lock their doors at sunset. The streets are dark and only looters and contending groups are abroad. The schools were closed for a year and a half. They opened for a short time last spring but closed again on account of the disorder. And Nanning is only one of many such sorrowful cities. Alas, our country is torn and our people are distracted."

"M-ma," Grace said, "I wish you would not speak of such matters only because you do not wish to tell me what it is you want to talk about in reality. Say to me what you wish."

She had so long spoken no English that now at all times she spoke only Chinese. Madame Liang, though secretly astonished that her daughter could so cleverly discern her private thoughts, would not be thus coerced.

"Tell me about your work, my child," she said in a sweet and coaxing voice.

Her daughter gave a peal of clear laughter. "M-ma, you are so—delightful! Do you think I don't know why you came? But, well enough—we will proceed as you wish. What is my work? My work, Honorable One, is to study our Chinese folk medicine, analyze it chemically and see if it contains the elements necessary for healing the particular disease it is supposed to heal."

Madame Liang ignored the teasing affection in her daughter's laughter. Indeed she was diverted by the reply Grace had made.

"And do you find the elements are suitable?"

"Amazingly often they are so," Grace replied seriously. "And Dr. Tseng is amazingly a good physician. He knows the human body very well. He diagnoses with accuracy. Where he fails is in the crudity of the drugs he prescribes. Also he does not understand the existence of germs. Somewhere along the way, M-ma, our people refused or were forbidden to develop the techniques of modern science, based on freedom of thought and experimentation."

Madame Liang's quick mind seized upon the word "freedom."

"Ah, you have the kernel of truth," she remarked. "The ancient rulers did not allow freedom to the creator, but neither do the new rulers."

Before Grace could reply there was a thunderous knock upon the wooden gate; the old man servant ran out of the kitchen to draw back the bar, and Liu Peng entered. He was a man unusually tall, and darker than most men of the north. He appeared weary, his eyes shadowed under his black brows. There were spots of blood on his trousers below the knees and on his cloth shoes.

He bowed slightly to Madame Liang and turned to Grace. "Allow me to change my clothes. I had too many operations today. There was fighting in the outskirts of the city."

"By all means rest yourself. You must be very tired," Madame Liang said courteously.

In a very few minutes he was back, however, and Grace poured a bowl of tea and gave it to him. He took it in both hands, bowed slightly in the direction of Madame Liang, supped the tea and set the bowl down on a small bamboo side table.

"You were speaking of the new rulers when I entered, Madame Liang?"

Before Madame Liang could reply, her daughter replied for her. "My mother was speaking of science and why our people with their long history nevertheless did not develop modern techniques."

Madame Liang refused, however, to be thus protected. "And I was saying that it was because of repression from those above that these techniques could not develop."

To her surprise, Liu Peng agreed heartily. "You are right, Madame! The emperors, steeped in the rigidities of Confucianism, permitted no initiative or innovation. This was the death of science."

Madame Liang, thus encouraged, proceeded to finish what she had begun. "And I said next, and was saying when you entered the gate, young sir, that our present rulers also allow no freedom of thought."

Liu Peng gave her a piercing glance from those black eyes of his. "There must be order before there can be freedom," he declared.

This was the burden of the argument that continued for several days of Madame Liang's visit. Almost against her will she began to discern in this strong domineering young man a power which she could not analyze and yet was compelled, though reluctantly, to admire. She had long hours alone, for the two younger ones went to their work every day, but Grace came home before Liu Peng and mother and daughter had these hours together.

On one such day Madame Liang addressed her daughter thus: "Your sisters beseech me to leave our troubled country and to live out my old age with them where they are now."

It was a rainy evening; the air was cool after a thunderstorm, and they sat in the central room, while the rain dripped from the tiled roof and made a silvery curtain over the door open to the courtyard. The day had seemed long and quiet to Madame Liang and yet she knew from distant sounds rising over the walls of the courtyard that there was unrest in the city. Cries and shouts, loud weeping and complaints she had heard, but she asked no questions of the servant couple. Whatever took place was beyond their comprehension and they were already fearful enough. Once, at noon, when she herself went to the gate to open it and see what was beyond, they had laid hold of both her arms and had besought her not to open the gate.

"It is known that the famous Dr. Liu Peng lives here and so we are safe so long as the gate is not opened," they told her, "but if the gate is opened, how can we be responsible for your life? Wild young people are everywhere roaming the streets, seeking those they wish to kill."

She was aghast. "But who are these whom they would kill even here in the capital?" she asked.

"Those who, they think, are rich, those who, they think, do not obey the Chairman."

She had yielded to them and had remained all day behind the locked gate, and the rain fell steadily as it continued to do now in the evening.

"Can it be possible that you would think of leaving our country?" Grace exclaimed.

"But if I can do nothing to help, if certain years must pass before we have peace, if I must live out my life alone, without grandchildren—"

Here Madame Liang broke off. A wily look crept over her face. She began again. "And you, my daughter, living as you do with this man as your lover and never your husband—oh, I understand you very well! He is a man of powerful force. Being what you are, a strong woman—no, still I cannot understand why is he not your husband!"

Grace did not reply for a moment. Then she spoke. "I will not force him. Let him be free. I can decide only for myself. I will never leave him."

"I know that," Madame Liang retorted. "I even know that you can so decide your life. Do not forget I, too, in my youth was a revolutionist. Alas, it is also my fault that my beloved country is in her present turmoil! Yet I once believed that I was serving my people, when I joined with Sun Yat-sen to overthrow our government. Ah, how right we thought we were, and how wholly wrong we were! We were never able to build the new government of which we dreamed. Fewer than five hundred of us there were, and yet we changed the lives of all the hundreds of millions of our people. Into the desolation we created, there came this—this—"

She broke off to listen. From over the walls came a long, wailing scream. There was an explosion somewhere not too far off and then the crackling of flames devouring old wood. Grace ran toward the open door, but before she could run through the curtain of rain Madame Liang caught her wrist.

"What can we do against them?" she cried.

"It is of Liu Peng I am thinking," her daughter cried back.

But Madame Liang would not release the wrist she held. She pulled her daughter into the room. "Think of yourself —think of yourself! Is he more than a man? In this disorder what will compel him to stay with you forever? Where are my grandchildren? They are in a foreign country because their parents dare not let them live here. Where are your children? I ask you, do you even dare to have a child? No, you dare not! Is this order? In the name of our ancestors, is this decency? You cannot answer me. I will go to America. I give up hope for my own people. Perhaps when I am a ghost, a wandering ghost for a thousand years, I can be born again in peace in my own country—"

She was weeping now, she who never wept. She loosed her daughter's wrist and sat down again to weep, and Grace was frightened because in all the years since she was born she had never seen her mother weep. She knelt before her mother and chafed her mother's cold hands and coaxed her with comforting words.

"M-ma, don't cry! I will be a better daughter to you— yes, I will—I will try. I will even ask Liu Peng to—to allow a ceremony—not the old one, but we will go to the marriage hall together. I'll not be proud anymore. And then we'll have children and you'll have grandchildren here, too. Will you like that, M-ma? Grandchildren on both sides of the world? M-ma, don't think I forget those years I spent in America—happy years. It's no use to talk of them, but I don't forget. I learned so much there. Someday when the turmoil is over—when we've found our way again—our people are a great people, M-ma, worth everything, even our lives. That is why I stay with Liu Peng. I can't explain —only I know I can't leave him—ever—ever—any more than I can leave our people—"

Madame Liang dried her eyes as she listened. "I can't leave, either—I was dreaming again. It is true that I helped to create this chaos and I must stay with my own people. I— I don't even know why I left my home. I must return to it. It is my home. One's home is one's home to live in it as one pleases. I must go home. I will stay there the rest of my life—quietly, the rest of my life."

"M-ma, don't—"

She would not allow her daughter to finish. She rose from her chair, pushed her daughter aside and went to pack her box. Sometime before dawn, when the city had quieted for sleep, she went to the airport, accompanied by her daughter. Liu Peng had not come home. He sent word by a messenger that he must work all night because of the many wounded. There were few passengers on the aircraft, for those who wished to escape had long ago left the city. Now it was idle to escape, for turmoil was everywhere, and here at least the people knew their hiding places.

"M-ma, come back to us," Grace said and clung to her mother's hand.

But Madame Liang shook her head.

"Forgive me," she said. "I have no right to reproach you for anything—I who helped to begin it all. Take care of yourself, my child—and forgive me, forgive me—"

She did not wait to hear her daughter's denials, her pleas. She walked resolutely up the gangway, found her seat, leaned back and closed her eyes. She was on her way home.

The city was quiet when Madame Liang reached it by the bus from the airport hours later. It was twilight and few people were on the street. She waited for a while, seeing no vehicles, but her box was heavy and she put it down and sat on it to rest and waited until a pedicab came near, drawn by a very old man. He stopped when she hailed him and when she had climbed into the pedicab he pedaled away for half an hour or so while the dusk deepened. At her gate she descended and paid him off.

"Shall I wait until someone opens the gate?" he asked, after he had put her box on the stone threshold of the gate.

"No," she said. "Someone is here."

He lingered nevertheless, yet no one came. She pushed the gate then with both hands but it would not give. Then she felt a bar across the gate which she had not felt before, and by the light on the pedicab she read rude words on the wooden bar, scrawled in red paint: "This capitalist house must be burned to ash."

She turned to the old pedicab driver, bewildered. "My home is to be burned," she faltered.

He could not read and so he did not know what the red words said, but he understood the look on her face.

"They have burned many houses," he said.

He waited because he did not know what else to do. He was alone and she was alone. He had never had a house or a home and now neither had she. Where then would they go?

Each asked the same silent question. The answer came from unknown persons. At this very instant a band of wanderers came singing down the street. They were all young, some of them almost children, and they, too, were homeless. Singing their wild song, they stopped to stare at the two old persons standing before the barred gate. Then, seeing them so old and helpless, suddenly they turned their singing to wild laughter. Madame Liang cried out to know who they were, but they only laughed the more wildly and, pointing at their red belts and still laughing, they swarmed about her. In terror she clung to the old pedicab driver and he tried to shield her with his arms. It was useless. He could not protect her. With sticks and stones they fell upon those two aged persons and beat and pounded them to death. When they were dead those young went on their way again, singing.

Of Madame Liang's three daughters, only the eldest was present at her funeral. It was the finest funeral that had taken place in recent years, and all were surprised at the numbers of people who crowded about the bier. The funeral itself was a strange mixture of old and new. Thus, Buddhist priests chanted their mournful litanies, although Madame Liang had not been a Buddhist. The minister of a small Christian church came out of hiding and made a prayer for her soul, although she had not been a Christian. Unknown persons, whom for years she had cared for and fed, gathered quietly into the main dining room of her restaurant, which now was empty except for the bier where she lay. All furniture in the spacious house had been destroyed by the violent young. Her personal rooms had been ransacked and her personal possessions robbed. These rooms were now closed. Only the main dining room had been cleaned and made ready for the unique funeral.

Among the guests was also the Minister Chao Chung. He arrived late with his entourage, and he carried a bouquet of white flowers, which he laid beside her. He stood for a moment, gazing down at her face, which even in death was unmarred and beautiful, though waxen pale. Chou Ma had dressed her in a rose red gown of brocaded satin and had combed her hair. The cruel wounds on her body were hidden so that as she lay in her coffin she looked as though she was sleeping.

What thoughts were hidden in the minister's mind none could know except that they were grieving thoughts, memories of the past, perhaps, and fear for the future. Who knew? Watching that handsome and sorrowful face, Grace could only wonder. How much of her mother's life she had never known and now could never know! Though Liu Peng was at her side, suddenly she felt alone. The love between them was intensified by this death, for Liu Peng, divining her loneliness, had been more than usually tender toward her. Yet she was aware of the tenuous quality of the bond between them, and though she had passionately defended him even in her thoughts, now she wished that the bond were not so tenuous.

When the funeral was over, when Madame Liang's body had been consigned to earth, Grace returned to the house in the *hutung* of the Three Foxes. All was the same there and yet nothing was the same. Even her love for Liu Peng was not the same. Now that her mother was gone, there was more than loneliness in her heart. She felt a responsibility, a duty toward her dead mother. Madame Liang had been sustained by faith, not in gods but in her own people. True, by her own people she had been killed, and yet in a strange sense that faith was transmitted, as Grace reflected upon her mother's life. Only now was she beginning to understand her mother. It was as though that beautiful woman, so steadfast, so silent, was communicating with her daughter in some unknown way which could not be explained. It was as though the daughter was absorbing into herself the spirit of her mother. With this spirit she felt strong, even in love, and she became so resolute that Liu Peng was aware of a change in her which he could not understand.

313

Thus days passed until one night she even declined his lovemaking, which had never happened before. He flung himself out of the bed they shared, and shouted at her.

"What—have you stopped loving me?"

She lay, looking at him, her hands clasped behind her head. "I love you more than ever," she told him honestly. "But it is true that I have changed. I am more than a woman in love."

"What nonsense is this?" he demanded, and sitting on the bed, he glared down at her, his black brows frowning.

To his surprise he saw no fear in her eyes. Instead she gazed up at him tranquilly, and her voice when she replied was calm.

"We have thought only of ourselves, you and I. I marvel that love can be so selfish. I see now that ours has been a halfway sort of love, reaching no further than two persons here in this house. Sooner or later it will die unless it grows, and it will grow only as we grow enough to sustain it. Liu Peng, I will not do what my sisters have done. I could go away and live in peace elsewhere. But I choose as my mother chose. I choose to stay—not because of you—not only because of you. . . . I choose as she chose. I have faith in our people. Liu Peng, I can't live as we have been living. I want you to marry me. I want to marry you. I want your children. I want to live in the old way—husband and wife and children—"

Liu Peng listened stubbornly, his eyes unwaveringly upon hers. "And what if I refuse?"

She looked back at him as unwavering, as stubborn.

"Then we part," she said firmly. "I have my work to do and I will do it."

"You don't love me," he muttered.

"I love you and something more," she replied. "I love—" Here she broke off smiling but with tears in her eyes.

"Will you marry me?" she asked, not demanding but so winsomely that he could not resist her.

Yet he would not yield easily. It was not his habit to yield. And while he was silent, struggling against himself, she considered him most tenderly. A powerful man, a willful, impulsive man, an angry man, a man of strong emotions, an honest man, a man with infinite capacity to grow, a man who could go astray for lack of knowledge, a man often unwise because he did not know, a man who was peasant and the son of a peasant, a man of the people—ah, that was he, a man of the people! She loved him for being what he was, and because she loved him, she shared her mother's faith in others like him.

He spoke at last, gruffly, as though he were angry. "I will marry you because I cannot live without you. You are bourgeois, but I cannot live without you. If you must have children, then have them. I cannot live without you."

She listened and laughed and pulled him down until his head was upon her breast, and she cried out in the midst of her laughter.

"Oh, how I love you!"